W9-AEO-906

Daughter of the Morning Star

By Craig Johnson

The Longmire Series

The Cold Dish

Death Without Company

Kindness Goes Unpunished

Another Man's Moccasins

The Dark Horse

Junkyard Dogs

Hell Is Empty

As the Crow Flies

A Serpent's Tooth

Any Other Name

Dry Bones

An Obvious Fact

The Western Star

Depth of Winter

Land of Wolves

Next to Last Stand

Also by Craig Johnson

Spirit of Steamboat (*a novella*)

Wait for Signs (*short stories*)

The Highwayman (*a novella*)

Stand-alone E-stories

(Also available in *Wait for Signs*)

Christmas in Absaroka County

Divorce Horse

Messenger

CRAIG JOHNSON

DAUGHTER OF THE MORNING STAR

VIKING

VIKING
An imprint of Penguin Random House LLC
penguinrandomhouse.com

LIBRARY OF CONGRESS CATALOGING-IN-PUBLICATION DATA

Names: Johnson, Craig, 1961- author.
Title: Daughter of the morning star / Craig Johnson.
Description: [New York] : Viking, [2021] | Series: Longmire
Identifiers: LCCN 2021016947 (print) | LCCN 2021016948 (ebook) |
ISBN 9780593297254 (hardcover) | ISBN 9780593297261 (ebook)
Subjects: GSAFD: Mystery fiction.
Classification: LCC PS3610.O325 D38 2021 (print) | LCC PS3610.O325
(ebook) | DDC 813/.6—dc23
LC record available at https://lccn.loc.gov/2021016947
LC ebook record available at https://lccn.loc.gov/2021016948

Printed in the United States of America
1st Printing

For Keeshawn Scalpcane,

we still see the world through your eyes.

Acknowledgments

I was doing a library event in Hardin on the Crow Reservation a few years back when I looked up and noticed a missing-persons poster on the community bulletin board. It was a simple computer copy with the face of a young woman, once bright-eyed and smiling and now gone. The words were desperate and pleading, and a reward was posted. Her face was faded, the paper wrinkled and yellowed with age—a fervent and unanswered prayer that fluttered against the bulletin board like a turning page every time the door of the library opened and closed.

I can't think of anything worse than losing a loved one—I mean having them turn up missing and then never knowing what happened to them. I've spoken with people to whom this has happened, and the thing I have heard over and over again is that the worst part is the not knowing—the lack of closure, having no idea if they are alive or dead, if they suffered or are still suffering.

The plight of missing and murdered indigenous women is so great that I had to reassure my publisher that the statistics contained in this novel are accurate. The numbers are staggering, and they speak for themselves. What if I were to tell you that the chances of a Native woman being murdered is ten times the national average, or that murder is the third leading cause of death for indigenous women? What if I told you that four out of five Native women have experienced societal violence, with half having experienced sexual violence as well. Half of Native women have been stalked in their lifetime, and they are two times as likely to experience violence and rape than their Anglo counterparts. Heartbreakingly, the majority of these Native women's murders are by non-Natives on Native-owned land.

The violence is being addressed, but there is so much more to do. Jurisdictional issues and a lack of communication among agencies make the investigative process difficult. Underreporting, racial misclassification, and underwhelming media coverage minimize the incredible damage that is being done to the Native community as a whole.

Whenever I write a particularly impactful statement, it usually is spoken by one of the Native characters, because a lot of the social issues I deal with are Native related. In this book, that weight went to one of my favorite characters, Lonnie Little Bird, when he states, "It is said that no tribe is truly defeated until the hearts of their women are on the ground—but what if there are no women at all?"

There are a number of wonderful organizations that are attempting to make a difference, the nearest to me being the National Indigenous Women's Resource Center in Lame Deer, Montana. All their information is available on their website at NIWRC.org. If you can, please consider making a donation. There are far too many of those missing-persons posters scattered across Indian Country—mothers, daughters, aunts, nieces, and wives who carry our hearts with them wherever they are in those turning pages. Let's bring them home.

I've put Walt in some pretty tough situations, but I don't think he's ever been in a bus full of teenage girl basketball players. As for me,

I haven't handled the round ball in about forty years, so I knew I needed some expert coaching. Fortunately, my buddy Marcus Red Thunder put me in touch with Tiger Scalpcane, the athletic director at Lame Deer High School, who was priceless not only in his knowledge of basketball but also high school students. A big thanks to the Lame Deer Lady Stars themselves, who probably wondered who the guy in the cowboy hat was who kept scribbling in a notepad.

Thanks to Aliana Buffalo Spirit for the wonderful Cheyenne language translations.

Thanks to my buddy Bo Benth and the Clearmont/Arvada Lady Panther basketball team, who let me tag along with them, and thanks for the sweatshirt. A huge merci to my French publisher, Oliver Gallmeister, for joining the pre-read team—you're first string. Also, a special thanks to Bill Dutcher and the entire staff of the MetraPark up in Billings for the behind-the-scenes tour and especially the view from the roof.

It wouldn't be a Walt Longmire novel without the usual staff—Coach Gail Hochman, Assistant Coach Marianne Merola, and team statisticians Eric Wechter and Francesca Drago. Thanks to star center Brian Tart, because he's the only one who's really tall enough to play the game, and point guard Margaux Weisman for actually keeping me on point. Thanks to Ben Petrone and Bel Banta for driving the team bus and to forward Mary Stone for arranging the trophy case.

And, of course, the biggest thanks of all to team mascot Judy "Twinkie" Johnson, who's always rooting me on to greater things and who slam-dunked my heart seasons ago.

She remembered who she was
and the game changed.

—Lalah Delia

1

"Play me."

Sometimes I drive to the borders of my county and look for the end of the world and sometimes I see it, or I think I do, but maybe what I see is myself, and that's enough to send me scurrying back the other way.

I like to think I used to be braver, but maybe I just didn't know any better.

When I was young, all I wanted was out. I was pretty sure that the only reason I participated in sports was to do that, to go on those endless bus rides even if it was just more of Wyoming, with maybe a little Montana and South Dakota mixed in.

Along the way, with a little size, speed, muscle, and brains, I was able to land a spot as one of the top-ten, teenage offensive linemen in the country. The University of Southern California took note and offered me a scholarship where we even won a Rose Bowl for the red and gold against Wisconsin 42–37.

I graduated, lost my deferment in doing so, and found myself wearing the khaki and olive drab for the United States Marine Corps. The Corps taught me a lot of things that college hadn't—like how to shine my shoes, say *sir* a lot, and take other people's lives. The biggest thing it did, however, was pin a star to my chest, something that's still there to this day.

I am the sheriff, the final letter of the law in Absaroka, the least populated county in Wyoming, the least populated state in America. Kind of a period, if you will, in the great sentence of justice. But right now, I was retrieving a basketball from dead, frozen grass and tossing it back to an eighteen-year-old phenom. Luckily, I didn't have to do that very often because she didn't miss very often. "Not my game." My words clouded the air as I threw the ball, and she caught it with long, nimble, artistic-looking fingers.

"Chickenshit." She turned and dribbled through her legs, then circled out to the top of the key where she half turned and flipped up a three-pointer, all net.

Or whatever net was left with the red, white, and blue nylon strands that had been faded by the sun, rain, and incessant wind of the high plains, the unraveled threads like a horse tail swishing at a fly. It was a fitting banner for the Northern Cheyenne, a people ravaged by unemployment, alcoholism, drug abuse, domestic violence, inadequate health care, and substandard housing.

I passed the ball back. "So, you got another note?"

She turned, dribbled to the baseline corner, and flipped the ball up again. I watched its arc as it slipped through the net, the ball caressing the nylon with a swirling sound—like hope—and then bouncing on the pockmarked asphalt before rolling to a stop near the ragged chain-link fence.

Flipping the dark hair from her face, she stared at me with polished-magnetite eyes.

"You don't answer my questions, I don't retrieve the ball."

Her head kicked sideways in disgust, but I was unfazed—I have a daughter.

"Yes."

I walked over to the fence to get the ball and bounced it to her. "Care to elaborate?"

She rolled it behind her back and then took a few quick dribbles before hoisting the ball skyward in a reverse layup. The momentum carried her toward me, where she stopped and looked up. She's six feet tall and doesn't like looking up at anyone in any way, but I'm taller than she is. "No."

I watched as she turned and retrieved the ball herself, dribbling toward the half-court line painted on the asphalt, reminding me of the prints on the parking lot at Parris Island back when I first became a Marine.

She shot, and it floated through, landing in my hands. "Do you think your life's in danger?"

She waited for me to give her the ball. "I am a young woman in modern America, living on the Rez—my life is always in danger."

I tossed her the ball. "Can you think of anyone specific?"

She circled the three-point line. It's where she earned the nickname Longbow, Jaya "Longbow" Long: the hands went up, the ball came down, three on the board.

"No."

The suicide rate for Native teenagers is two and a half times greater than the national average.

I tossed her the ball. "No enemies?"

She dribbled in the key just below the foul line and pivoted, tipping the ball up in one hand in a reasonable impersonation of a Kareem Abdul-Jabbar–style skyhook.

I held the ball.

An exaggerated sigh as her shoulders dropped. "I'm in high school—I've got nothing but enemies."

Native women are three and a half times more likely to be raped or sexually assaulted than the national average.

I tossed the ball. "You want to tell me about Jeanie?"

There was a brief pause, a nanosecond when I pierced the otherwise stoic reserve. Jaya began dribbling again, punishing the asphalt as she stalked toward the top of the key, then the half-court line. I waited for her to turn and shoot, but she didn't. She walked toward the double doors of the school with the ball under one arm, leaving me standing in an empty parking lot.

Native women are six times more likely to be murdered.

"That went well." Glancing over my shoulder, I saw my faithful companion sitting in the passenger seat of my unit, his dog breath fogging the glass.

I walked to the car and let the beast out, all one hundred and fifty-five pounds of him. He stretched and then picked a lamppost to water before looking up, rubbing his muzzle on my jeans. "Think you'd have more luck than me?"

There was a loud noise, and we both looked in time to see a decrepit '64 Buick Wildcat, with the license plate 2REZ4U, belching black smoke as it came around the corner of the building with Jaya Long at the wheel. Not looking at either of us, she took the drive leading down the hill from the school, her arm trailing out the open window, and then turned left toward the town of Lame Deer, Montana.

I looked down at Dog, who was sitting on my foot. "Maybe not."

I nudged him with said foot, but he refused to move.

"C'mon, I'll take you into town, and we'll have lunch at The Big Store, but I have to talk to someone first."

He stared at me.

"Ham."

He got in the truck.

There's a buffalo head in the main hall of Lame Deer Morning Stars high school, and black and turquoise banners printed with motivational sayings, and plaques with photos of assorted teams, championship pennants, and standout individuals.

There are three with Jaya "Longbow" Long hanging in the lobby, one with her sophomore year team, one with her junior year team, and a photo of just her with the ball on her hip and her head cocked sideways the way it had been out on the parking lot only a few moments ago. There is also an article from the *Billings Gazette* with a photo of her powering past a hapless Hardin player and the headline JAYA GOES LONG. She looks like her aunt, the chief of the tribal police department, in this particular photo, but it's not photos of her I'm looking for.

Working my way down the wall of time, I got to the point where the photos go from color to black and white. There is a team photo of the Montana State Champions and a familiar player, front and center, holding the ball. His smile is like an arc light, the shining eyes in the broad face conveying a confidence and good will that's undeniable. Lurking in the back row is another face I know very well, this one a bit more somber, but the intensity of the eyes is there too—the guy looks like he could crush your spleen.

Smiling, I turned and walked toward the doors of the gymnasium.

There's a silence to an empty basketball court, a churchlike quiet that stills your breath.

I stood there near the gleaming wooden floor and stared at the feathered dream catcher inlaid at its center as the sound of a ball bounced across the floor toward me. Stooping to pick it up, I glanced over at the doorway at the far end of the bleachers where I could see a tall man who looked a lot like the intimidating youth in the team photo, powerfully built, holding a leather jacket over one shoulder. "You didn't play here."

"No. I played in the old, linoleum-floor gym across town."

"The middle school."

Henry Standing Bear walked toward me. "It was a junior high school back then." He glanced around. "I do not think they have junior high schools anymore."

I palmed the ball and nodded toward the line of photos out in the lobby. "You only played your sophomore year here?"

The Bear nodded, sweeping the dark hair from his face. "Yes, before I moved down outside of Durant to live with my grandmother."

"Who was the scariest person I ever met."

"She used to embarrass me by pulling over and plucking quills from dead porcupines." He smiled. "And she used to put evaporated milk in her coffee."

I thought back. "She made killer chicken and dumplings."

"If it really was chicken." He took the ball from me, dropped his jacket, and turned toward the nearest basket about forty feet away. "Five bucks?"

"No way."

He shot, the ball bouncing from the rim to the top of the backboard and then against the wall and out of bounds. "You should have bet."

I followed him toward the locker rooms and the athletic director's office. "Hey, are you intimating that we ate porcupine and dumplings?"

Tiger Scalpcane was one of those indispensable individuals on the Rez, the man with the glue that held the volatile society together; a man who, in the empowering Cheyenne tradition, gave everything away, the one who never had any money in his pocket, having spent it on others. He was a conduit to his people, one of those unofficial chiefs, like Henry. Whenever there was a tragedy on the Rez, Tiger was there with a new pair of shoes, a casserole, or a pat on the back, always with his superpowered smile.

"How did it go?"

I stood looking at the whiteboard, attempting to make sense of the hieroglyphics of basketball plays. "She said about four things."

He sat at one of the tables, strewn with athletic supplies. "Hey, for Longbow that's not bad."

Henry sat and I, unable to make heads, tails, or jump shot, leaned against the whiteboard. "Has she always been like this?"

Tiger tucked an old pair of Buddy Holly glasses in his front shirt pocket. "Since her sister went missing, yeah, she's pretty much been at war with the world."

"Sounds like somebody else I used to know." I glanced at Henry and then back to Tiger. "What's the story on Jeanie?"

"Took a ride with some folks into Billings, and they had some car trouble on the way back near the Pryor Mountains exit. They had to stop to make some repairs and folks started wandering off even after the driver told them that as soon as he got the thing running, he was heading out, so they better not go too far. When they got the van running, they all piled in and nobody noticed that Jeanie was missing. They sent somebody back later, but they never found her—called in the Yellowstone County Sheriff, Search and Rescue, and finally the FBI."

"Nothing?"

"Nothing." He sighed. "It happens more than you might think."

"I think it happens a lot."

He frowned; the smile gone missing. "Like I said, more than you think."

"This was a year ago?"

"A little more, just as the season was getting started. Jeanie was good, not as good as Jaya, but more of a team player, you know? Even if she had a shot, she'd pass the ball to another player who needed the points—a real leader."

"Jaya, not so much?"

Tiger groaned, and I think it was unconsciously that he fished the glasses from his pocket and fingered them. "Jaya is the best player we've ever had, but she's so wrapped up in herself that . . . I just don't know how we're going to finish this year, let alone make it to the NNAI."

I glanced at Henry, and he grunted. "The National Native American Invitational is in Billings this year."

Tiger looked up at me. "I was talking to Harriet Felton, the girls' coach, and she said Jaya has missed about half her practices. Her immediate family is kind of nonexistent, so basketball is all she's got—in the off-season, she has a tendency to fade away."

I nodded but said nothing.

The smile came back. "Not your problem, right?"

"Well . . . My mission, if I decide to accept it, is to find where this threat against her is coming from and neutralize it before it becomes something more tangible."

He studied me. "You ever play ball?"

I glanced around at the basketball racks, ball returns, and assorted accoutrement. "Not this one."

"That's a shame, you got the height."

"That's about all I've got." I gestured toward Henry. "He was the basketball player, not me."

Scalpcane laughed. "Yeah, I played with him one year before he ran off to civilization."

Henry smiled. "Played good enough to get you to a state championship."

"That's because everybody was afraid you'd yank their lungs out if we didn't win."

The Cheyenne Nation shrugged and stood. "Probably right—I had not developed my wizened and sophisticated social skills by that time."

I pushed off the whiteboard. "Right."

Tiger offered a hand, and we shook. "You off to see the po-lice?"

"I guess so. Her aunt is the one who asked me to look into all this."

He walked us to the door. "Twenty-some notes threatening her life. A young woman with so much talent, and she has to deal with all this stuff her senior year when she's got more important things to concentrate on—just doesn't seem fair."

"What's the story on the glasses?"

"What glasses?"

"The ones that Tiger carries in his front pocket." We wound our way back into Lame Deer proper and pulled up in front of the Lame Deer Trading Post, or The Big Store as the locals referred to it—a supermarket, craft supply store, and restaurant in one. "He doesn't wear them, they're too small for his face, and I wondered why he carried them."

"They belonged to his son."

"Belonged?"

Opening the door, Henry Standing Bear climbed out. "His fifteen-year-old son, Keeshawn, went on to the Camp of the Dead six months ago—the glasses were his."

I followed him inside. "Oh."

All the cashiers and shoppers watched the Bear as we swept past the registers—traveling with the Cheyenne Nation on the Rez was like being in the company of either royalty or the prince of darkness.

We sat in one of the booths and glanced around at the colorful surroundings, the place looking similar to a bazaar in a third-world country. "Is there anything you can't buy here?"

"No." He picked up the two menus on the table, not offering me one.

A young woman came over in a hairnet, apron, and unwarranted attitude. "Can I help you?"

He handed her the menus. "How about two cheeseburgers with fries?"

"Considering your ages, sounds like a couple of ischemic strokes to me." She scribbled on a pad. "Drinks?"

"A couple of glasses of saturated lard or hydrogenated vegetable fat, if you would."

She turned and walked away without another word. I called after her. "I'd like a root beer, please?" I turned back to Henry as he spoke under his breath. "Dated her mother."

A striking woman entered the store and followed our path past the registers as if tracking our scent. She was wearing a uniform identifying her as the tribal police chief, waved at the waitress, sat in our booth next to me, and studiously ignored the Bear. "Well?"

Henry stretched out in his side of the booth, his long legs trailing over the edge, his tan chukka boots crossed at the ankles. "Want a cheeseburger?"

She stared at the side of my face. "Are you taking this job, or aren't you?"

I sighed. "Are you paying me?"

"No, of course not."

I turned to look at her. "Then it's more of a favor, isn't it?"

Her eyes hardened into shards. "Are you going to do me this favor?"

"I'm not so sure what it is I'm going to be able to do that you, the Yellowstone County Sheriff's Department, or the FBI weren't able to do."

"Bring focus."

"You mean the media?"

"Yes."

"It has been my experience that media attention is not always advantageous to cases."

"It draws a response."

"From whom?"

"The Yellowstone County Sheriff's Department, the Montana attorney general, the highway patrol, the FBI . . ."

"So, I'm leverage."

"Maybe you can get them to do their jobs."

I leaned back in the booth and grunted a laugh, studying the scythelike scar on the side of her face, souvenir of an IED along a nameless road in Iraq. "So, you want me to find out who's threatening Jaya, but you think this also has something to do with her missing sister?"

She shrugged. "Possibly."

"That's the first place I'd look."

Scooting out of the booth, she stood. "So, look."

I rested an arm along the back of the bench. "You don't really think I'll find anything, huh?"

"No."

"You don't really think I can solve the case."

She put a fist on her hip. "In a word, no."

The waitress arrived and slid our lunch onto the table and placed two root beers there, much to my relief. "Thanks for the vote of confidence."

She waited for the young woman to depart before speaking again. "I know why you'll do it though."

I picked up my cheeseburger, allowing it to drain a little grease back onto the wax paper-lined, red plastic basket before taking a bite. "And why is that?"

"Because it's the right thing to do."

Taking the bite, I chewed. "Contrary to popular belief, I don't always do the right thing."

She glanced at Henry, who was ignoring his food. "That's not what I hear." She drummed her maroon nails on the worn surface of the table where the faux wood grain faded to a palomino. "Let me know what the Yellowstone County investigator says."

"I haven't agreed to do this."

"You will." With those words she walked away, no one in her path daring to meet her eyes.

I took another bite and chewed, looking over at the Cheyenne Nation, who was smiling to himself. "Not eating your lunch?"

He shook his head. "Hell no, that shit will kill you."

We stood on the side of the surface road, listening to the 18-wheelers Jake-braking as they came down the big hill east of Billings. The I-94 overpass vaulted above, the sluggish creek drifted below, and the leafy cottonwoods had long ago shifted to a golden yellow, dropping leaves to the ground.

"So, that's Pryor Creek?"

"No, that is Cottonwood Creek." Henry turned and pointed south, where Dog stood a little ways away. "That is Pryor Creek."

"And the exit where we got off is Indian Creek?"

"Yes."

"That's a lot of creeks." I gazed south. "The Crow Reservation is that way?"

"Yes."

"How far?"

"A half mile."

"What was the weather like the day she was lost?"

"Night." He took a deep breath and sighed. "Bad—one of those early storms that came in at the beginning of November; not too much snow, but a lot of wind."

"And no sign of her?"

"So they say."

I glanced around at the naked hills to the west where a fire had wiped out the trees, only dead black branches remaining, like tendrils attempting to grab the cold sky. There was a power pole to my right, and I could see a faded printout of a crude, handmade poster covered in a plastic binder sleeve stapled to the wood. I walked over and looked at the sheet of paper. The words had disappeared, but the image of half the girl's face was still evident, like a negative. Dark hair parted at the middle; her mouth was closed but kicked in one direction into a lopsided grin.

"This her?"

Henry approached, looking over my shoulder. "Yes."

"I'll need to talk to the people who were in the van that night—you can arrange that?"

"One way or another."

He watched me as I walked toward the whatever creek it was, with Dog in tow, turning to look at the embankment that led to the highway where a couple of wreaths, a white cross, and garland were looped together in a shrine "So, is Jaya still being courted by those big schools: Stanford, UConn, Duke?"

"Not so much. I think the big universities can be cautious about offering scholarships to Natives, afraid that they might be wasting them on students who are not going to stick it out and get degrees—that they will just quit."

"You didn't."

He laughed, the bitterness in his voice sharp enough to grate cheese. "And yet, here I am, the prodigal son returned."

"You didn't have to." He didn't say anything more, and I turned back to the creek. "Just too much of a coincidence."

"Both girls, possibly."

"Why possibly?"

"As Tiger said, it happens here a great deal more than you would suspect."

"If."

He waited a moment and then asked. "If?"

"If Jeanie met with foul play, it's reasonable to suspect that the same person who did that is now threatening Jaya."

"If Jeanie had been threatened."

"Was she?"

"I do not know."

"Who would?"

"The mother." He turned and started back for my truck. "Unfortunately, I know where she is."

The Yellowstone County jail is conveniently located only three miles from the Yellowstone County Sheriff's Office and is a little different from my own. First off, the county seat and city it resides in is the largest in Montana, with a population of over a hundred thousand. The Magic City was given its moniker as the result of its rapid growth as a rail hub and was named for Northern Pacific magnate Frederick H. Billings.

We sat in Detective Chuck Shultz's guest chairs. "How cold is the case?"

The investigator of cold case files grunted. "Glacial." The short, heavyset man with the mustache and glasses sighed. "Between us and Big Horn County we have the highest concentration of missing and murdered Native women in the country."

I looked out the window at the graying sky. "Do you suspect foul play?"

"Of course I do, Sheriff. I'm a cop—it's my job to suspect foul play." He reached into his desk and pulled out a pile of manila folders that looked to be about a foot thick. "Over thirty women have been lost on the road from here to LD, Lame Deer, or LG, Lodge Grass—take your pick."

I glanced at the pile. "Do you have a file on Jeanie Long?"

"You mean Jeanie One Moon. Where did you get Jeanie Long?"

"She has a sister, Jaya Longbow, over in Lame Deer whose name is Long, so I guess she's adopted that from the woman she's staying with."

"Long, as in Chief Lolo Long?"

"Yep."

He stared at me. "Oh, boy."

"She's the one who, um . . . convinced me to investigate the situation concerning Jaya."

He made a face. "The basketball player; so, what's the situation with her?"

"She's been receiving threats for the last year or so."

"But she's not missing?"

"No."

"Well, thank God for small miracles." He slumped back in his chair.

"No one has reported the notes?"

"Sheriff, according to the FBI's National Crime Information Center, 5,590 indigenous women went missing last year alone. There's been a public outcry, and the Department of Justice has been coordinating task forces and cooperation between federal and local authorities, but it's like we're in a war here. Women are disappearing at such a rate that we can't keep up, so threats really aren't high on the list."

"Can I see the file on Jeanie One Moon?"

Ignoring the large pile, he picked up another, slightly smaller one from the surface of his desk and handed it to me. "You can have it—I made you a copy."

I sat back in my chair, opened the folder, and looked at the same poster that had been stapled to the power pole. You could see the family resemblance, but this face was more open than Jaya's, ready to meet the world and be a part of it.

"There's no great conspiracy here, Sheriff. No one's trying to sweep these women under the rug, but there's only so much we can do with the limited manpower and personnel that we have to work with in the kind of geography we're talking about here—I mean the area in question." He looked at the files and shook his head. "And then there's the inherent difficulties."

"Such as?"

He pointed at the file. "In this one family alone—one brother who was shot by an officer here in Billings, another sister who was hit by a car and killed, and an eleven-year-old who committed suicide—where is a kid like that supposed to go?" He looked at the ceiling. "Where's the hope?"

Henry stood, walked to the window, and stared out.

"We had officers from Wyoming and South Dakota up here helping us with thermal drones, helicopters, you name it . . . We've even got a YouTube channel." He flipped the top file onto his desk. "Barbara Heeney, fourteen years old, found two weeks later, hypothermia." He flipped another file onto the desk. "Bela Gray Wolf, mother of five found in the Pryor Mountains, hypothermia." He flipped another. "Kayla Morning Flower, found in somebody's backyard in Hardin, lying there with the firewood where some jogger discovered her. Hypothermia." He tipped the stack over, and it slid across his desk like an avalanche. "We can't keep up."

"Controlled substances?"

"Controlled, I like that . . ." He snorted. "Alcohol, methamphetamines, crack, you name it, but it's hard to find trace elements after exposure. Hell, Sheriff, you know what a body looks like after two weeks in the wild."

"Physical abuse?"

"Hell yeah, you tell me why a woman runs out into a blizzard and tries to sleep in a doghouse."

I closed the file. "And then there's Jeanie."

"And then there's Jeanie." He slumped in his chair, his hands falling to his lap. "No sign, no nothing—like she disappeared from the face of the earth. I like to think that she caught a ride with some guy, and is out there living on the coast, someplace warm like California, someplace away from all this shit—but you and I know that isn't the likely case."

"No, probably not."

He picked up the files and began restacking them like he'd done it many times, so many times that I doubt his hands or mind were even aware of what they were doing. "Seventeen years old and you let her go out partying here in the big city with a bunch of people who drop her off one night and just drive away like she's some garbage you leave on the side of the road. Who does that?"

We didn't say anything. He looked over my shoulder toward the door. "Oh, hey, boss."

A dapper-looking individual with silver hair high and a tight, matching handlebar mustache stood behind us. He was wearing a black uniform that looked as if it might've been tailored.

I stuck out my hand. "Hi, Thom."

He shook it. "The great Walt Longmire."

"I prefer the term *marginally capable.*"

"Lolo Long has you up here, involved in this?"

"For now." I gestured toward the Cheyenne Nation. "You know Henry Standing Bear?"

The Bear stood, and they shook. "No, I don't think we've met." He turned back to me. "I wouldn't be doing my job if I didn't offer you every cooperation . . ."

"Thank you."

"I also wouldn't be doing my job if I didn't warn you that it's not the Wild West up here and that we don't need any kind of dramatic situations."

"Dramatic?"

"Headline stuff—we'd just as soon avoid those kinds of complications."

"You bet."

He studied me a moment more and then glanced at Henry.

"Nice to meet you." I got one more glance before he turned and disappeared down the hallway.

Shultz handed me another piece of paper. "Here's your prisoner visitation form for the mother." He glanced at his wristwatch. "Your appointment is set for two thirty, so you better get moving."

I stood. "Will do."

We started toward the door as he called after me. "I hope you find her, Walt Longmire. At the least, be great and find the piece of shit who's been threatening her sister—I'd say that family's been through enough."

It was a long line of compartmentalized phone cubbies facing the Plexiglas, with a young corrections officer leaning against the concrete wall beside the door. He was evidently bored and talkative. "Quiet for a Saturday. We usually get a lot of family members in here on the weekend."

"It's more of a case."

"What kind?"

"Threats against a Native woman."

He stared at me. "You're kidding, right?"

"Nope."

"Wow." The kid glanced at Henry. "You involved?"

The Bear did not look at him. "In what way?"

"Family?"

"We are all family."

They ushered Theresa One Moon in on the other side of the barrier and seated her in the chair across from us. I picked up the phone from the side and gestured to the one to her right as she stared at me with eyes as dead as yesterday's cod. She wore the ubiquitous orange jumpsuit and clogs, a handwritten tag on her uniform read ONE MOON.

Henry leaned into the light so she could see him.

She paused for a moment and then picked up her phone. "Yes?"

"Ms. One Moon?"

"Says so on my shirt, so I must be her." She studied me. "You must be a detective."

I tried not to smile, but it was tough. "Um, a sheriff."

"How do you know?"

I lifted the lapel of my jacket away, revealing my badge. "It says so on mine."

She glanced at Henry. "So, what do you want?"

"I want to stop the threats that your daughter Jaya is receiving."

Her eyes came back to me, and for the first time they carried a little fire. "I wasn't talking to you."

The Bear leaned in some more and spoke under his breath. "O'háae, mónavata."

"What do you know about it, hotómoehnohtsëstse?"

Growling, he repeated the word. "O'háae."

She stared at him a long while, then her hand crept up to her neck where she sent it to her hair, straightening it. Her eyes came back to me. "She's my last one, you know?"

"That's what I've heard."

Her eyes softened the tiniest bit as she gazed at me. "You got any kids?"

"A daughter."

"How old?"

"Old enough to have my granddaughter."

"You look out for them?"

"When I can."

She sat there, considering my response. "And how are you going to protect my last little bird?"

"By finding out who's threatening her."

"So, what do you want from me? Currently"—she glanced around and slumped in her chair with comic effect—"I am detained."

"Were there any threats to Jeanie before she disappeared?"

Her eyes changed as she glanced at Henry. "They don't tell you about those little birds, you know?"

"What's that?"

Her eyes came back to me. "That it's like a nest: once one falls out, they all start falling." She cleared her throat and then leaned in. "No, no one threatened Jeanie—that would be like shaking your fist at the sun."

I glanced down at the file in my hand. "Do you mind if I ask why you allowed her to go to Billings with that group?"

Her eyes flared again, and she opened her mouth to speak. Her hand came up but then slipped away like a falling leaf as she laughed a choking sound. "What makes you think I knew?"

"You didn't?"

"No."

"Do you know of anybody who might wish your daughters harm?"

"A couple."

"Would you like to tell me their names?"

She lip-pointed to the folder in my hands. "That file on Jeanie?"

"Yep."

"You got the names of everybody who was in that van?"

I placed it on the counter and looked at her, attempting to envision the woman she had been before alcohol, methamphetamines, and—the most powerful poison of all—grief had withered her to the husk I was looking at now. "I believe it does."

"You start with them, Detective."

"Sheriff."

"Whatever." She stood and hung up the phone, but she did so gently, as if there were more to say but she'd used all the energy she had for now.

2

Henry scanned the list of passengers from the van while he sat in a camp chair in front of the smoldering fire on which we'd prepared dinner. I allowed Dog to inspect the sprigs of dried grass near the edge of the gravel lot near the White Tail cabin. It was cool, but the warmth and smell of the fire made the place feel close.

"Two whites, four Native—two Cheyenne and two Crow."

"Nice even numbers." I glanced around, enjoying the solitude of Custer National Park after season. "So, this is still pretty much a hunting cabin?"

"Yes," he mumbled.

"That would explain the bunk beds."

"Hmm."

"Thirty bucks a night; that's pretty good." I lifted my almost empty Rainier and took a final swig. "God bless the US Forest Service and keep it strong."

"Hmm."

"Firewood included." Pulling Dog over, I unclipped the leash, figuring I could trust him and that no one would complain, seeing as how there was no one else around. He immediately abandoned me to sniff the plate at the Bear's feet, which still contained an uneaten quarter of cheeseburger. Henry stuck a boot out to block Dog's path. "If you want the rest of my meal, you must ask for it politely."

Dog sat.

"Very well." He moved his foot and Dog moved in, eating the burger and threatening to devour the paper plate until Henry took it from him. He scratched Dog behind the ears. "I know it smells like food, but it is not." He tossed the remains into the fire, prompting a flare and brief sizzle.

"What's wrong?"

The Bear glanced up at me as Dog sat beside him, expecting more scratching. "Theresa One Moon."

"What about her?"

He reached down and picked up his can of Rainier, lowered to such a level of culinary repast since I was the one who had brought the supplies. "Can you imagine having a son shot, one daughter run over, another committing suicide, and then having the last go missing?"

"No, I can't." I thought about my own fragile little family. "I'd imagine it'd be enough to drive anybody over the edge." I walked around the firepit and sat in the camp chair opposite him as the sparks flew up between us like bad choices or mediocre consequence, unsure of which was worse. "What's her relationship with Jaya like?"

He grunted. "Bad."

"How bad?"

"Very bad." He resettled his can by the leg of his chair as Dog lay down beside him, head on paws, staring into the fire. "Theresa's mother, Jaya's grandmother, Big Betty, kicked her out of the house when she was a teenager." He motioned with the file in hand. "She is the one who reported Jeanie missing the night they came back from Billings."

"She was living there, with her grandmother?"

The Bear smiled. "Yes, you will see her at the games, with a lot of hair, in a purple and turquoise sweater, wearing buttons of her grandchildren's faces on her bosom."

"That's a lot of buttons."

"It is an ample bosom." He stared at the fire with Dog, his hand wandering down to scratch the ear, so the beast flopped over onto his side, displaying his light-colored belly, which the Cheyenne Nation dutifully scratched. "Theresa would go up to the bars in Billings, the tough ones on the south side of the railroad tracks on Minnesota Avenue."

"Reservation Row?"

He nodded. "She would drink with men she knew, men she did not . . ." He sighed. "I think Jeanie and Jaya are the only two from the same father."

"You know him?"

"I know of him."

"Worth talking to?"

"Everyone is worth talking to at this point in an investigation, yes?"

"Yes." I deposited my empty into the cooler and took out another ice-cold Rainier. "So, I guess we need to talk to all the family and friends and see if we can find any patterns in the notes that Jaya's been receiving."

"So, the focus of your investigation will be Jaya and the notes?"

I glanced at him. "That's what Lolo asked me to concern myself with, why?"

"It appeared that your queries might concern Jeanie."

"Only peripherally, for now."

"Good."

"Why good?"

"It seems to me that delving into the tragedies of the One Moon family might begin an unending journey."

"That doesn't sound like your usual, hopeful self."

He sighed, continuing to scratch Dog's belly. "There are a few glimmers of hope here."

"I'm going to want to go back to the Pryor Creek exit and knock on doors."

"North or south?"

"South."

He smiled, pulling his hand up from Dog to raise his beer to his mouth. He sipped and then made a face. "How can you drink this?"

I sipped my own and smiled back at him. "This is a fine macrobrew, you elitist."

He went back to watching the fire. "I was there the last time Jaya and her mother met. It was a game less than a year ago, not long after Jeanie had disappeared between LD and LG."

"That would be Lame Deer and Lodge Grass?"

"You are catching on." He sat the beer back down. "Big medicine in that the game is tribal, Cheyenne versus Crow."

"I would've thought that Hardin would be more of a rival."

"Not so much of a tribal rivalry, Hardin is half white or almost half white, so they do not count. Anyway, you cannot imagine how intense those games can be."

"I played in a Rose Bowl."

"And your point?"

I grunted a laugh. "Go on."

"The bleachers are extremely steep and in that concrete building the noise is earsplitting. Half the crowd comes from Lame Deer, but you know you are in enemy territory. The teams always enter the building from the buses in groups and no one is allowed to go anywhere on her own."

"Lodge Grass is good?"

"They have more state championships than any other tribal team, almost as many as the national champion Navajo Eagles."

"A town of three thousand versus the largest reservation in the country—impressive."

"On this Rez, you are born with a basketball in your hands." He started to lift the beer again but then sat it back down. "It was a very hard-fought game, tight, with a lot of physicality. Jaya was playing with a broken finger but refused to leave the game, just taped it over and scored thirty-two points. There was a girl on the Crow team who liked to set up in the paint and just live there like a monument. The referees allowed her to get away with it, but Jaya had had enough, finally driving in in an attempt to take her out." He looked up at me. "Have you ever seen her play; I mean, really play?"

"No." I sat up. "Even when we stopped at that three-on-three tournament in Billings a few months ago, we left before they actually played."

"She is truly phenomenal."

"So, what happened?"

"She pulled up momentarily at the top of the key, just enough to get the Crow girl moving toward her and then charged forward, walking up her like a ladder and pivoting just enough to flip the ball home. As the Crow girl fell backward, she grabbed Jaya's foot, and after the ball went in, they tumbled under the basket and then against the wall, punching and kicking at each other the whole way."

"Where does Jaya's mother enter into this?"

"At this exact point, Theresa was screaming and came out of the stands, stumbling drunk and dropping a bottle of Ten High Sour Mash, but not so drunk that she could not grab a folding chair from the home bench, run across the court, and begin beating the Crow player with it."

The Bear sat forward, picking up a stick and probing the fire. "The tribal police dragged her from the gymnasium and she ended up in rehab again."

"Again?"

"Nine times. The last time, she spent a week in a padded cell, and the doctors pretty much told her that if her liver lasted till spring it would be a miracle." He poked the fire and then tossed the stick into the rejuvenated flames. "She wrote a note to Jaya, apologizing. It was not long after that that Jaya moved in with Lolo Long."

"Why not her grandparents?"

"Jeanie had lived with them, and it is my understanding that Jaya did not wish to be reminded of her sister by sleeping in the same room as she had."

Standing in the wide Pryor Creek valley, I looked south and watched a bright yellow crop duster bank along the barren hills and fly over the alkali soil, freshly tilled for winter wheat. There was a combine running a pattern as well, that moved back and forth across the dark earth like some gigantic green and yellow beetle that couldn't decide which way it really wanted to go.

I'd been waiting for the better part of an hour for Lyndon Iron Bull to finish up and talk to me, a conversation he had no idea we were going to have.

Henry had elected to head north in my truck, away from the

Crow Reservation, but had promised to come back and pick me up when he had gotten through knocking on the three doors within walking distance to the north.

According to the official transcript under my left arm, Lyndon's wife, Ethel, had gone to the bathroom the night Jeanie went missing and had seen someone standing by their mailbox. Coming back to bed, she'd told her husband, who had gotten up, dressed, and walked out to the road where he found no one but had seen prints in the thin skiff of snow.

Ethel had been kind enough to answer my questions and even offered me a piping cup of coffee before directing me to the field where her husband was working. She said he had poached an antelope yesterday so to make sure he knew I wasn't a game warden, or he might try to run over me.

I stood at the gate, my coffee still steaming into the cool morning, frost clinging to every available surface. The combine seemed to be taking a little extra time over by the creek where a small white cross was wired to the fence. Modern combines are a wonder with closed, air-conditioned cabs, GPS steering . . . But the biggest thing about them is just that: the bigness. Almost four times larger than the machines I used to know in my youth, the new ones look like cities on wheels. As the metropolis rolled toward me on eight-foot tires, I thought about stepping into the wide opening of the gate. But without letting Iron Bull know which government agency I represented, it was possible I could become fertilizer. The big John Deere finally lurched to a stop halfway through the gate and a glass door flung open.

Carbohydrates are something the Crow tribe has particularly taken to, resulting in some truly large individuals, including my friend Brandon White Buffalo and his uncle Virgil, and I had to admit that Lyndon Iron Bull was at least in their league.

He pointed at the travel mug in my hand, with "BOSS LADY" spiraled in pink cursive across the side. "That's my wife's mug."

I nodded. "Yes, it is."

"Did you have to fight her for it?"

"No, and she filled it full of coffee for me too."

"You must've scared her, which is good because she doesn't fight fair." He studied me. "You must not be a game warden then."

"I am not."

He swung his legs out, lodging an enormous, muck-covered boot on a fender. "Then what are you?"

"Walt Longmire. I'm the sheriff down in Absaroka County."

"Wyoming?"

"Yep."

"What are you doing up here, Walt Longmire?"

"Asking some questions about Jeanie One Moon."

He nodded, looking off into the distance. "The Cheyenne girl."

"Yes, sir."

"You find her?"

I stepped closer in between the two massive wheels. "Unfortunately, no."

He nodded. "My wife says she saw her that night, out by the mailbox."

"I read that in the report and thought I'd follow up. The weather was bad that night?"

"Terrible. One of those early nor'westers that came in at about fifty miles an hour—took shingles off the roof." He sat a little forward. "Ethel, she's got a bladder the size of a pea and has to go to the ladies' room about three times a night; better than a watchdog. Anyway, she comes back to bed and gets all covered up and says there's somebody standing out near the mailbox by the fence. I ask her if it's the Wicked Witch of the West, but she slaps my shoulder and says she's not kidding, that somebody is out there, and I need to go take a look."

A tired sedan came down the gravel road and tooted its horn as Iron Bull lifted a calloused hand before looking down at me. "What's a Wyoming sheriff doing involved in all this?"

"I was asked to look into it by the tribal police over in LD."

"Where?"

Just what I get for trying to appear hip and in-the-know. "Lame Deer."

"Oh." He tipped his stained, black cowboy hat back on his wide head. "So, I get dressed and go out to the kitchen where you can flip on the back-porch light and see the mailbox, and there's nobody there. Well, not wanting to waste the trip, I pull the carton of ice cream out of the freezer and get a spoon and take a few bites before putting it back." He stopped talking and stared at the shiny fender of the combine, studying the reflection of the low-angled sun in the dark paint.

"Mr. Iron Bull?"

He looked up at me, almost as if he'd forgotten I was there.

"Are you all right?"

He took off his sunglasses and held them in one hand, twirling them by the earpiece. "I didn't tell this to them."

"I don't think the police care about the ice cream, honestly."

"No, what I'm about to tell you, I didn't tell them. Them being white men and all . . ."

I smiled. "I'm white."

"Yeah, but you've seen things." He cocked his head back and studied me. "I read about you, Mr. Sheriff Man. You see, us Iron Bulls are related to the White Buffaloes, and I read about you."

I said nothing.

"When I was putting that carton back in the freezer that night,

I saw some movement out of the corner of my eye. You know, something you're not sure if you really saw or not?"

"I know exactly what you mean."

"So, I grab my coat and hat and I go out there into this gale, looking for whoever might be out there. We get 'em sometimes, people whose cars break down out on the highway or just get loose, drunk, lookin' for someplace to hole up till the weather passes."

"Sure."

He scrubbed a hand across his face. "You gonna drink that cup of coffee?"

"No." Smiling again, I retrieved it from the post and walked over, handing it up to him.

He held it to his face, allowing the steam to soften his features, before taking a long sip.

"When I got out to the mailbox, the gate was hanging open and slapping against the fence. Now you can say the wind did it, but I think it was more than that." He took another sip. "The snow was blowing sideways, those little flakes that look and feel like beads?"

"Yep."

"Grabbing hold of the gate, I looked down, and there were prints, small ones—I mean smaller than mine, which could've been anyone." He smiled. "I remember very clearly because the little seed-bead flakes were filling up the prints."

"Boot prints?"

"No, you could see the treads—they were sneakers. You know, basketball shoes."

"You're sure of that?'

He gestured toward the folder under my arm. "It's in that report. It was wet, but the snow was hard and trying to erase the prints, that's what I remember thinking—this storm is trying to make this girl disappear."

"You knew it was a girl. How?"

"I don't know; maybe the size, but I think it was just a feeling."

"But all of that is in the deposition."

"I'm about to tell you the part that isn't." He sipped the coffee again and then threw a thumb over his shoulder toward the field. "Standing there in the wind and holdin' on to the gate and my hat, I see something out there in the pasture. A shape, almost like something is there but not something, more like the lack of something, like the snow and wind won't occupy the space that this, whatever it is, is taking up—you know what I mean?"

"I think so, yep."

"So, I'm standing there looking into the space, and all of a sudden, it waves to me—waves for me to come over and follow it, wherever it's going." He stared at the fender again. "I ain't scared of much, Mr. Sheriff Man, but I'll be damned if I was going to follow that thing, whatever it was."

"I can't say that I blame you, considering the weather conditions."

"The hell with the weather—I wouldn't have followed that thing in broad daylight."

"What did you do?"

"Went inside and went back to bed and didn't sleep a damned wink." He sipped his coffee again. "About a week later I came out to check on this same field. It was late in the afternoon, and the mist was coming off the creek down there and was filling up the bottom land the way it does. Well, I walk to the edge of the fog and everything looks good, so I turn and start heading home when I get this cold feeling running up my back, like somebody ran a finger up my spine. I mean really, like I could feel it in my skin all the way down to the bone."

I stood there, looking up at Iron Bull and noticed his big hands were shaking.

"I didn't want to turn, but I had to see what was behind me. At first, all I could see was the fog and it was coming at me like it was going to cover me up, but it didn't. I could've reached out and put my hand in it, but I didn't. I just stood there looking into it like a TV between channels, you know?"

"Static."

"That's it, like static—nothing but gray. A busy gray, though, like bees humming." He swallowed. "Like it was alive and reaching out to me, even though I wasn't reaching back." His eyes welled, and he thumbed the moisture away with a gasp. "Then I saw her, there in the fog—not her, but the absence of her. It was an outline of that girl, Jeanie One Moon, and I could hear her voice. No words, just the voice."

I glanced back at the tilled field as if she might've been there, seeing only the broken earth and the white cross on the fence.

"She was singing, and it was the saddest song I've ever heard. Neh-Ehvah sii Eh-jest, Na-Hoe-eh sidun—Cheyenne, so I didn't know the meaning of the words, but you didn't have to know the words to know what she was singing about."

"What did you do?"

"I didn't move. I just stood there listening to her and after a while the singing began to fade, and she was gone." Climbing down, he handed me the mug, and we stood there eye-to-eye. "I did some research after that, went over to the college and saw tapes of her doing interviews and playing basketball and volleyball . . ." He walked past me around the huge tire and rested a hand on the treads, then looked back at the field leading down to the creek. "I see her."

I followed him. "Excuse me?"

"The part I didn't tell them white men. Hell, I don't even tell my wife, but she knows something's up because I neglect this field." He stood there for a long while before speaking again. "I see her here."

I said nothing.

"Whenever we have a warm day followed by a cold night, in the evenings, as if the sun is trying to pull her up from the ground before the moon can catch hold of her." He glanced over his shoulder toward the rising sun. "But he never gets her all the way out, you know?" He sighed and turned to look at me. "I spoke with a Crow medicine man about it, but he didn't have no idea what I was talking about. I tried to forget about it, but every time the conditions were right, that fog would come up and I'd hear that singing."

I dangled the coffee mug on my trigger finger and stared at the dirt.

"Me and Ella, we were having dinner over at the trading post, you know, Putt's place?"

"I do."

"There was a woman I knew, Cheyenne, Esther Small Song, one of those half medicine women. You know, knows stuff, even more than other women." He smiled. "So, I start asking her questions, and she just looks at me and says, Éveohtsé-heómėse." All at once I felt that finger that ran up my spine. "The *Wandering Without*, an all-knowing being, a black spiritual hole that does nothing but devour souls. She said that girl was singing—*Bring me back, I don't belong here, and I want to go home.*" He walked out into the field, gazing in that direction. "I believe that thing has that girl and will not let her go. I also believe that if I'd reached into the fog that evening that thing would've taken me too. Everybody thinks the dead of the night is the scary time, but it's not. The time of danger for the living is the time of change, from day into night or night into day, when the world isn't sure what it is or what it wants to be."

Looking over his shoulder at the white cross I asked, "Are you a religious man, Mr. Iron Bull?"

He turned to look at me and slipped his sunglasses back on so all I saw was my reflection. "I am now."

"Éveohtsé-heómėse, huh?"

"That's what he said."

The Bear sat on the steps in front of the tribal police office, taking in the last rays of warmth before the angle of the earth changed and the high-plains winter made itself known. "You're sure that's the word Iron Bull used?"

"I am, and he got it from Esther Small Song."

"Artie Small Song's mother."

"The same." I readjusted my back, trying to find a soft spot in the concrete. "Have you heard of it?"

"Yes, but not in a long time." He turned his face to the sun and removed his sunglasses. "The *Wandering Without* is a term the old people use, and I have not heard it in a very long time; it is an entity used to frighten children."

"A boogeyman."

"Of sorts—it is also a plain of existence between the two worlds, the camps of the dead and the living."

"Limbo?"

"Something akin, but not exactly."

"How do you get away from it?"

He straightened and thought about it. "An act of extreme bravery must be performed by a family member or someone close to defy the Éveohtsé-heómése, but there is risk involved."

"What kind of risk?"

"The loved one must take the captured soul's place."

"No paying the fine and going home?"

"I am afraid not."

"Boy, you Injuns are hard-asses." I crossed my legs, glancing up to see Dog, sitting in the passenger seat. There were far too many strays wandering around the tribal headquarters, and I didn't feel as though he should be engendering another generation. "How was north of the interstate?"

"Uneventful, although there was a young ranch wife who invited me in for the afternoon, but I did not feel it was an integral part of our investigation." He turned to look at me. "Where is your undersheriff these days?"

Victoria Moretti, the Philadelphia transplant within my staff, had been dubious about my helping with an investigation on the Rez. But because she'd gotten a new vehicle only a few months ago, she'd kept those thoughts mostly to herself. "Flattening the hills and straightening the curves along the Bighorn Mountains."

"She is going to kill herself in that . . . What do you call it?"

"The Banshee."

"Right, right. How is Barrett doing?"

Rounding out the report on my staff, Barrett Long, Chief Long's younger brother, had gotten a job with me as a part-time, weekend dispatcher and to everyone's surprise had turned out to be something of an asset. Even my longtime dispatcher, Ruby, appeared to like the kid. "He's doing really well, playing chess with Lucian when I can't make it."

Henry made a face. "Tuesdays?"

"Fridays, when things are slow, Lucian brings the set over and they play on the dispatcher's counter."

"You are kidding."

"Nope." Thinking about my old boss and predecessor, I had to laugh. "He keeps accusing Barrett of cheating, but I think the kid is just good."

"Who is?"

We both looked up into the sun at the dark figure towering over us.

"Your brother."

The shadow of the dark figure turned in profile, but there was only one person it could be. "Yeah, I've been meaning to talk to the two of you about that . . ." She stepped between us, yanking open the door and continuing in, leaving us to our own devices.

"Should we follow and face the music?"

"I suppose so."

We both stood and ambled in after her as a pockmarked, heavy-set individual looked up at us from the dispatcher's panel. "Hi, Charles." The man said nothing. "Long time no see." He still said nothing, which was his pattern. "Well, it's been great catching up."

We walked down to Chief Long's office at the end of the hall, where she now sat behind her overburdened desk. She looked over the neatly arranged piles of paper at the two of us. "You poached my brother."

Sitting in one of the chairs, I looked at her. "Lolo, you were never going to hire him, and I think he was getting tired of rolling Lonnie Little Bird around like a rickshaw driver."

"He's my brother.

"Don't you want him to succeed?"

"He's an idiot, and I'm worried he'll get hurt."

"He's a part-time dispatcher—the worst thing that could happen is static shock or a paper cut."

"You should've asked me."

"He says you're his sister, not his mother, and he doesn't have to ask you."

"*You* should've asked me."

"Professional courtesy?"

"Yes."

"Well, I'm sorry."

"I am not." The Cheyenne Nation stared at her.

She ignored him and kept her eyes on me. "I'm not talking to you."

"No, you are talking *at* me."

Finally turning, she leveled her gaze on him. "When I am talking to you, you'll know it—and why is it I've got a feeling you're behind all this with my little brother."

"Okay, kids, that's enough." Glancing around, I noticed that she had placed all the offending notes to her niece in plastic bags, which were hanging on the large bulletin board behind us. Standing, I turned and studied the wall. "This is all of them?"

She also stood, coming around her desk and standing beside Henry. "Yes, except for the first few that they just threw away."

I turned to look at her. "They threw them away?"

"It's not unusual for women on the Rez to get these kinds of notes, so they didn't think it was such a big deal until they kept coming."

"How many in all?"

"Thirty-one."

I turned and looked at them, thumbtacked to the cork. There

were a few written on loose notebook paper, a few on what looked to be the backs of grocery bags, and some scrawled on paper napkins—all with the same marker lettering. All caps and scribbled over in emphasis, the same handwriting, if you could call it that, on every note. "Did you have anybody look at these?"

She nodded. "The FBI lab in Billings, but they say there's no telling features to the paper itself, which is generic, and the notepads are available everywhere. The grocery bags are from a local chain, the closest being the one in Billings on Twenty-seventh Street that we call the Crack Albertsons."

"The pen?"

"Two different markers, but the same brand, Sharpie."

"How were they delivered?"

"Different every time—one was under the windshield wiper of Jaya's car . . ."

"That would be the '64 Buick Wildcat I saw her blowing out of the high school parking lot in?"

"*Protector*, the bane of my existence." She looked down at Henry with an expression of disdain. "That thing breaks down almost as much as this one's truck."

The Bear shrugged. "One either has an affinity for classic automobiles, or one does not."

"Where did it come from?"

"Her father, Jimmy Lane."

"And where is he?"

She gestured vaguely. "Around."

"In the official sense?"

"In every sense—drugs, alcohol, theft, domestic violence, aggravated assault—you name it, he's done it. He's working for a painting outfit in Billings along with some truck driving jobs."

"So, this Jimmy Lane and Theresa One Moon are a pair?"

"You've met her?" I nodded. "Still the poster girl at the Yellowstone County jail?"

"As of late." I studied the notes along with her. "Delivery points here in Lame Deer, Billings . . ."

She used her index finger like a truncheon, tapping each note individually. "Hardin, Lodge Grass, Birney, Colstrip, Forsyth, Ashland, Garryowen, Crow Agency, Broadus, Miles City, Glendive, Rosebud . . ."

"How many of these were in towns they were playing basketball against?"

"Almost all."

"Have any of the other players received these kinds of notes?"

"No."

"Other than under her windshield wiper, where else did Jaya find them?"

"In her gym bag, in our mailbox at home . . ."

"At your house?"

"Yes."

"Wow, that takes nerve, leaving messages in the police chief's mailbox." I studied the notes. "Notwithstanding the tone of the things, I can't help but think that this looks like the work of a fellow student—they're the only ones I can think of who would have the kind of access you'd need to deliver these."

"Does that look like the language of a teenager?"

I read the hateful words. "No."

She retreated behind her desk and sat. "We interviewed all the girls on the team, and there are the usual petty jealousies, but nothing that would lead me to believe they had anything to do with this."

"When I talked to you in Billings you mentioned a group, the Brotherhood of the North?"

"A white supremacy group that has a compound in the northern part of the state up by Canada."

"And where in the world might I find one of their representatives so as to have a little conversation?"

The dark eyes came up to mine, threading through her manicured brows. "Jaya's father, Jimmy Lane, is a member."

3

Sitting on the bleachers in Lame Deer Morning Stars high school, we watched the Lady Morning Stars running practice on the gleaming floor. There was one girl, Misty Two Bears, who was even faster than Jaya, but in the entire time we watched, I never saw her shoot. Watching Jaya take a thirty-foot shot and sink it, I then observed three other team members shoot and miss, a ball caroming off the rim and bouncing toward us. The Cheyenne Nation stood and stepped down to retrieve it, tossing it to a tall, heavyset girl, Rosey Black Wolf, who caught it and turned away with a hand covering an embarrassed smile.

Henry grimaced. "Half white supremacist, half Indian."

"That must make for uncomfortable holiday gatherings."

He shrugged. "It is not as unusual as you might think. Half-Natives go into the prison in Deer Lodge and come out indoctrinated."

"Strong faction of the Northern Brotherhood in the state pen?"

"Very strong." He watched the girls play. "You become the wolf you feed."

"Where does this Jimmy Lane live?"

"The last I heard he was in South Side Billings."

I watched as another easy layup was missed by Stacey Killsday, who squinted at the basket and who played without enthusiasm. "So, this is the varsity team?"

"Yes."

I leaned in, even though it was doubtful the girls could've heard me even in full voice. "They aren't very good."

"No, but maybe they will get better—they have to. If they do not win the next three games, they will not make it into the tournament."

A tall, blond woman standing near the sideline blew a whistle, calling the girls over and speaking to them as they huddled up. "Ladies, we have a guest here, Mr. Henry Standing Bear, who was on the last state championship team the school had." She turned to him. "When, exactly, was that?"

The Bear looked a little evasive. "I . . . would rather not say."

She laughed and then shouted down to the girls as she climbed the bleachers to stand in the aisle beside us. "All right, ladies . . . As I've said, the object of our efforts here is to put the ball in the basket. Now, when we graduate to even thinking about our opponent Thursday night, the idea will be to keep them from doing the same—do I need to review?"

They stared at her, at least some of them did, while others clutched opposite elbows or examined their shoes or arranged the remuda of ponytails.

The coach blew the whistle again. "Shooting drills!"

We watched as they lined up in patterns, feeding one another the ball and attempting to make baskets, sometimes actually scoring a few. Henry said nothing, so I felt compelled to comment. "They look good."

She glanced at me, more than a little incredulous. "This your first time, seeing basketball?"

"Well, they could use a little work."

She blew the whistle. "They could use a lot of work, but we've got another game tomorrow night and they might not get it in time."

Watching them, I was curious. "Tell me about the rest of the team, other than just their names?"

"You mean that misbegotten group of misfit toys down there?" She shook her head and muttered. "I've got three seniors, one junior, a sophomore center, and a bench of two."

"The tall young woman is the sophomore center?"

She nodded toward the girl who had just lost the ball in our direction. "Rosey Black Wolf—she's got the size and the weight, but I just can't seem to get her to introduce a little aggressiveness into her game. She's always slouching, trying to convince the girls she's their size."

Henry gestured. "And the other point guard?"

"The one who couldn't hit water if she fell out of a boat? That's Stacey Killsday, the fastest in the state, and she used to be so good, but she seems to be dropping off. Last year she started the season with about fifteen baskets a game, but then ended with nothing."

Henry pointed again. "The power forward?"

"The one who keeps bouncing the ball off her foot? Misty Two Bears, she's solid, but she just won't shoot the ball. I've seen her under the basket, completely alone, and she'll pass it to another player in double coverage."

"The other forward?"

"Wanona Sweetwater, the junior who just wants to be everybody's friend, including the players who are trouncing her."

"And Jaya."

"And Jaya . . ." She watched the girl go in a full rotation, laying the ball up on the glass, left-handed. "She can do it all, ball-handling, shooting, defense—you name it, she's got it, except for being a decent teammate." She blew the whistle. "All right, let's get some leg drills done with some line work." She waited as they groaned and then ambled toward the baseline nearest us before lifting the whistle to her mouth. As the girls began running, she would blow the whistle again, setting them in the opposite direction.

As they ran, she approached.

"What's the problem?"

"Inconsistency, one minute they're the Lakers, and the next, they can't hit the open man on the give and go." She blew the whistle again.

"Distracted?"

"Mostly. That's the thing about coaching girls that's tougher than boys: they bring all the crap in their lives onto the court with them."

"It's a tough age."

"Yeah, I know—I'm still in it." She smiled and blew the whistle again and then stuck a hand out. "Tiger said you guys might be coming by. Harriet Felton."

I stood, and we shook. "Walt Longmire."

"The sheriff?"

"One of 'em."

"You're here because of Jaya?" We watched as she blew the whistle again, just before Jaya was about to pass the line. Sliding, the young woman pivoted and sprang back in the other direction like a possessed puma.

"So, she's as good as everyone says?"

The coach smiled. "Superior."

"Then what's the problem?"

The coach blew the whistle again. "She's not a leader, and she needs to be. All these girls know she's better than they are, and she could reach a hand back down the ladder and help them to become a better team—but she doesn't."

"Does it have to do with her sister going missing?"

"Jeanie was not as good as Jaya, but she was a natural-born leader and the girls just played better because she cared about them." She blew the whistle a final time, and we watched as the players slowed. "Showers, ladies!" she bellowed. Jaya moved toward the locker room in a solitary strut. Felton watched her and then shook her head. "She just doesn't give a shit."

Henry stood. "Is there anything else that might be bothering her?"

"Other than the death threats?" She sighed. "There's talk of a boy. Well, a young man . . ."

Henry stepped down the bleachers, past her, and then looked up. "Name?"

She folded her arms. "These girls trust me."

The Bear didn't move. "I can get it elsewhere."

"She's kind of dating him on and off."

"If she is dating him, on or off, he is already involved in this. It is our job to follow all of the leads until we discover something."

She turned to look at me. "That the case, Sheriff?"

"Pretty much."

She stared at her own shoes. "Harley Wainwright."

"The son of Digger Wainwright?" The Bear sounded surprised.

"Yes." Her eyes came back up. "But you didn't hear it from me." She moved down the steps past Henry, pausing to give him a look, and then crossed the floor toward the locker rooms without another word.

Stepping down to join him, I made the sideline as he reached over to palm a ball from the rack. "And who is Digger Wainwright?"

"Big rancher north of the Rez near Colstrip." Stepping forward, he bounced the ball a few times and then poised to shoot. "Five bucks?"

"Considering your last shot, sure."

He fired, and the ball made a poetic arch, nestling into the eighteen-inch hoop with just a whisper of net.

Fishing my wallet out with a sigh, I handed him a fin. "He white?"

He started toward the lobby with maybe just a touch of swagger. "Very."

"I do not think this new young man is going to work out. Um-hmm, yes, it is so."

Glancing around Lonnie Little Bird's office, I couldn't help but have a little wall envy. The Head Chief of the Great Northern Cheyenne Nation had certificates of achievement from four different presidents of the United States, an officialdom Lonnie begrudgingly recognized; documentations of great service from every part of Montana, another bureaucracy he attempted to pay no heed; and credentials of lofty success from every facet of Indian Country. "You got a Nobel Peace Prize up here somewhere, Lonnie?"

The old chief ignored me as the young man in question entered, bearing a tray overloaded with a coffee pot, cups, saucers, milk, sugar, and silver spoons, which he carefully slid onto Lonnie's mammoth oak desk.

The young man stood, his hair parted to the right, ironed shirt and polished shoes at the ready. "Will there be anything else, Chief?"

Lonnie ushered him away with a vague wave of his hand but

then joined us in watching him go, the glass-paneled door with the tribal seal and Lonnie's name in gold leaf quietly closing behind him.

Henry reached over and began pouring coffee for the three of us. "What is his name?"

"You know, I don't know." Lonnie sat back in his wheelchair and thought. "Willard, his name is Willard." He thought about it some more. "Wasn't there a movie about a rat named Willard?"

The Bear finished pouring and sat Lonnie's cup on a saucer. "I think the rat's name was Ben and the boy was named Willard."

The chief leaned over, looking through the frosted glass to see if the young man might be loitering near. "I could see Willard controlling rats."

Taking my coffee, I stood and walked over to the wall-of-fame, sure that if I looked long enough, I'd see the heads of the enemies who had underestimated the legless man. "Seems like a nice kid to me."

Lonnie waited patiently as Henry, familiar with the old chief's tastes, dropped two cubes of sugar in his coffee and then added a spoon before sliding the cup and saucer the rest of the way in front of him. "Yeah, you think that until the rats come."

I turned to look at him.

He sipped his coffee and glanced up at me. "He's too polite. I am always thinking he's up to something."

I shook my head and sipped my own coffee. "You want your old driver back?"

At the sound of Barrett Long, the old man brightened. "How is he doing?"

"Fantastic. He's dispatching on weekends and covering for Ruby whenever she wants a day off."

"Ruby, that is that good-looking woman in your office?"

Pushing eighty, I was pretty sure my dispatcher would've been pleased at being described as such. "One of 'em."

"Has he gotten his gun yet?"

"No, he'll have to go through training down in Douglas before he's armed."

"He wants a gun."

"I know, but even your police chief wouldn't give him one."

"She is a harsh woman. Um-hmm, yes, it is so."

"You're her boss, if you wanted her to you could order her to give her little brother a gun."

He shook his head and stared into his coffee. "I'm just the chief."

"Doesn't that mean that everybody has to do what you say?"

"No, hardly anyone does what I say."

I glanced at Henry, who rolled his eyes.

Lonnie sat his cup down and looked at me again. "You want to buy some of my commendations? I'll make you a deal."

I gestured with my cup. "They've all got your name on them."

"Oh, a little Wite-Out and you can put any name you want on them." He leaned back, placing his fingers on the leather blotter that spread out before him. "How 'bout this desk, would you like to buy it?"

"Lonnie, it's your desk."

"Not really, that thief who had the position before me stole it and had them bring it in here." He pulled open a drawer and then slid it closed. "I keep looking for all the money he stole, but I haven't found it yet."

"Lonnie, have you heard about the situation with Jaya Long?"

"The basketball player?"

Henry nodded. "Héehe'e."

"The threats against her life?"

I came back and sat, resting my cup on the purloined desk. "Yes."

"One Moon, that is a tragic family. The grandfather, he is a good man and his wife, they tried to keep their daughter safe, but somehow they could not keep her on the straight and narrow—that is the way, sometimes."

"Do you know of anyone who might know who has been threatening Jaya?"

"There are the usual threats whenever our players go out into the white world, but these people are only misguided and not particularly dangerous, just racially overenthusiastic." He glanced at me. "But we have a case?"

"What do you know about the sister, Jeanie?"

"The old saying among my people was that you never conquered an enemy until their women's hearts were on the ground—but what if there are no women at all?" He looked up at me. "That is why I am glad to have you here, my friend. I am hoping you can help save us from this most horrible of atrocities."

"How many Native women have gone missing here, Lonnie?"

"Close to three hundred missing person reports last year alone. We make up only 6.7 percent of the population but account for 26 percent of the missing persons, the majority of whom are women. Most of our cases are closed within a day or two—runaway teenagers, tribal police find them walking on the roads, or child custody cases that are resolved. But the statistics remain that our people make up more than a quarter of the ones who go missing in the state."

"We're going to have to go around and knock on some doors and ask some questions."

He glanced at me. "You are asking for my blessing?"

"I guess."

The Bear sipped his coffee and then lowered the cup onto the saucer. "Lonnie, have you ever heard of the Éveohtsé-heómėse?"

He started. On his face we could see that the words wrested something deep within. "I have not heard that term since I was very young."

"But you have heard it?"

"There was a girl I knew; she was strange and something of an outsider who just didn't fit in anywhere. You would see her out in places where nobody was, all alone. I remember my mother told me to not be like her—that the Éveohtsé-heómėse would come and take me if I lingered too long from the company of the people. One day in the schoolyard, I saw her standing out by the fence and I went to her. I told her that if she persisted that the Éveohtsé-heómėse would come and take her away, and all she said was that at least someone would want her . . ." He reached out and took his coffee, holding it in both hands as if attempting to stay warm. "I told my mother about this, and she said that I should befriend this girl and look out for her. The next day I went to school with great emotion, ready to tell this girl that I was her newfound friend and would protect her." He took a sip of coffee. "She was gone, and I never heard of her spoken of again."

We waited, but he was silent. "Lonnie?"

He looked up at me. "You have my blessing."

Henry's truck, Rezdawg, would only go forty-five miles an hour. It took us two hours and thirty-three minutes to get to Billings because it was as fast as Rezdawg would go. Because it was an undercover operation, he'd decided that it called for the special abilities of his sixty-year-old truck, although I couldn't think of any special attributes other than its ability to burst into flames, spring leaks, go flat, short out, or lose parts at the most inopportune times. "Have I told you lately how much I hate this truck?"

"Do you mean in the last five minutes?"

"Yep." Sitting outside the house on the south side of Billings, we did what hunters do: we waited.

"Yes, you have."

Not the nicest neighborhood in the Magic City, we were pretty well halfway between the Yellowstone County jail and the Montana women's prison on Twenty-seventh Street. The Bear had said that maybe Jimmy Lane liked to keep his options open.

It was a small, off-white clapboard house sprayed with tags from the various surrounding gangbangers, a stripped-out Impala up on blocks in the front yard. We'd been there for a few hours and hadn't seen any signs of movement in or about the house. It was getting late in the afternoon, and we wanted to get back down toward Lame Deer before the final practice, but it was looking more and more like we wouldn't make it.

I reached over and fed Dog a bit of my beef jerky. He sat on the shower curtain seat cover that was held on with bungee cords.

"Please do not feed that to Dog."

"What?"

"It is bad enough that you eat those things; please do not give that poison to your dog."

"Are you getting bored?"

He reached over and took his bottle of filtered water from one of the rust holes in the floorboard. "What?"

"You get cranky when you're bored."

"I am not bored." He unscrewed the top and took a sip. "Maybe a little."

"Why don't you go take a walk?"

"You do not think I will draw attention to myself?"

I glanced around. "They'll just think you're another local thug."

"Local thug?"

I shrugged. "Crime lord?"

He pulled the handle and threw his weight against the door, wedging his way out of the junkyard derelict that was filled to capacity with the three of us. "I am taking a walk."

"Say, I didn't hurt your feelings, did I?"

He shut the door with a little more force than was necessary.

I gave Dog another bite. "My, aren't we sensitive."

I watched as he approached the house and kept watching as he hit the sidewalk and continued around the block in a nonchalant fashion, wrapped in a black leather duster—looking like, well, a crime lord.

Eating the last of my jerky, I pulled my root beer from the dash and took a swig. I could easily head over to the Kum & Go gas station and convenience store a block away to get some more supplies, but with the Bear on the move, I figured I better stay put.

It was good I did, because no more than ten minutes later, a bruised and dented crew-cab rattled up the street with an abundance of ladders, scaffolding, and sawhorses, and ground to a stop. The thing rivaled Rezdawg in the number of colors it displayed, but a lot of them were spilled cans and overspray from the multitude of house paint that littered the bed. On the side of the doors, lettered in an uneven hand, were the words ALPINE PAINTERS.

"I wouldn't let those guys paint a doghouse." I scratched Dog's head. "No offense."

After a moment, the truck disgorged a tall, thin individual in work boots and a Carhartt rip-off jacket and ball cap.

Raising my binoculars, I read the name label on his jacket—LANE.

Lowering the glasses, I rested them in my lap. "My superior

capabilities of detection inform me that that individual may just be Jimmy Lane."

Dog stared at me.

"I know, I sometimes amaze myself."

Pulling my hat down to cover my face, I watched as he spoke with the guys in the truck and then as they pulled out, driving past me as fast as the truck would go, which was not particularly fast.

Peeking under the brim, I watched as Jimmy headed into the house, which appeared to be unlocked, and closed the door behind him.

I glanced up and down the street for the Bear, but he was still out of sight.

Pulling the vice-grips that served as a handle, I stepped out of Henry's truck. I stuffed a folder under my arm and rolled the window down a bit, watching it slide inside the doorframe, and then closed the door behind me. "Stay." The last part really was necessary, because Dog had been known to blow through windows, screen doors, and other minor impediments, so an open window was an invitation of sorts.

Walking across the street, I checked both ways but saw no traffic or anybody for that matter; it was that kind of neighborhood. As I approached the house, I paused to check my old .45-caliber Colt in the pancake holster at the small of my back and thought for a moment about what I was going to do next. Coming up with nothing much, I figured I'd just play it straight.

I continued down the cracked walkway and shattered steps, one railing lying in the dead bushes, along with a lot of beer cans and garbage.

Not finding a doorbell, I raised my knuckles and reached through the empty pane of the storm door and pounded the shedding, interior door as some music started up inside.

I pounded again.

After a moment, I heard footsteps, and the door was snatched open by the same skinny guy I'd seen enter. He no longer wore the jacket with his name on it, but I took a leap of faith. "Jimmy Lane?"

He stared at me, and I had time to study the face on his oversize head, acne scarred with a withered Fu Manchu and limp dark hair that slithered over his shoulders. Oddly, his body parts were all oversize—not only his head but also his hands and feet—almost as if he'd been assembled from parts that didn't quite match. He had the look of somebody who had taken a lot of questionable chances in life and had paid for every single one of them in spades.

I hadn't thought it was a particularly difficult question but asked again, this time mixing it up in an attempt to jog something loose. "Lane, Jimmy Lane?"

"Yeah?"

Pulling my badge wallet from my jacket pocket, I flipped it open. "Walt Longmire, Absaroka County Sheriff."

He read it, or I think he was reading it. "Where?"

"Wyoming."

"Oh."

Evidently, my reputation had not preceded me. "I'd like to ask you some questions about your daughter?"

"You find her?"

"No, I'm afraid not. I'm here to ask you some questions about your other daughter, Jaya?"

He leaned against the doorjamb and studied me. "She's not mine."

"No?"

"No, I don't know whose she is, but she ain't mine."

"You're sure of that?"

He shook his head. "Look, if you're here about child support . . ."

"I'm not, Mr. Lane. I'm here because Jaya has been getting death threats."

He swallowed. "Yeah?"

"Can I come in, Mr. Lane? I'd just as soon not discuss your personal matters out here on the stoop."

He thought about it and then swung the door open and disappeared into the gloom. I followed as he sat in a chair in front of a broken TV, where there was an old Ithaca Deerslayer 12-gauge along with a .38 service revolver lying on a weathered coffee table in front of him.

Some kind of music with more rhythm than melody played from an old boom box. I glanced around and didn't see any cartons of ammunition, but that didn't mean there weren't any in the pump-action shotgun or the pistol. "Planning on doing some deer slaying?"

He pulled the pitted shotgun onto his lap. "Maybe."

"How 'bout you leave that off until we get through talking?"

He looked at me, still holding the 12-gauge. "How 'bout you go talk to that silly bitch of a mother they've got instead of me."

"I've already spoken to Theresa One Moon."

"And what did she say about me?"

"Mr. Lane, we can either talk about weapon possession while under parole, or you can put that shotgun down."

He stared at me for a moment and then carefully placed it on the table, raising his hands in mock surrender. "Anything you say, Marshal."

"Sheriff."

He nodded, picking up a pack of cigarettes and then lighting one with a book of matches from the table, taking a deep drag and studying me. "In Wyoming."

"Yep."

"What are you doing up here?"

I sighed. "Trying to find out who is threatening Jaya."

He nodded, taking another drag and expelling the smoke toward a window partially covered with a bedsheet. "Yeah, well, I don't know about that."

"Mr. Lane, have you ever heard of a group called the Northern Brotherhood?"

He glanced at me. "Yeah."

"Are you a member?"

"Not really." He waited a moment and then added. "Look, Sheriff . . . You know I been inside, right? Well, if you ain't a member of something, then you're a member of nothing and you get chewed up and spit out. I took a look at the lay of the land and figured as half Indian and half white, it was time to be all white." He took another puff of his cigarette. "It ain't exactly Rotary, you know?"

"I'm sure." I walked toward the adjoining kitchen, every available surface stacked with dirty dishes and questionable groceries. "A lot of the threats were of a racial basis, which leads me to believe that this organization might be involved. And with the number of threats and numerous locations the notes have been delivered to, it might be someone who knows Jaya."

"You think I'm threatening my own daughter?"

I turned in the kitchen doorway. "I thought she wasn't your daughter."

He snorted a laugh. "Yeah, well, that was when I thought you were sent over here from Child Services."

"I'm not." I handed him the file. "Copies of the threats; I thought you might like to take a look at them."

He tried to hand them back but then settled for laying them on the coffee table beside the shotgun. "That's okay. I've seen this shit before."

"I thought you might be able to recognize the handwriting or the paper—something?"

He twisted a cedar-bead ghost bracelet on his wrist, a type I'd seen before. "She gave me this, you know. One time, a long time ago, I took her and Jaya down to the Dry Fork on the north end of the Bighorns, trying to teach them how to fly-fish." He laughed into his lap, placing a finger under the bracelet and studying the beads. "Jeanie was flailing away with this old Eagle Claw rod I had, and I'd just told her that she was getting too close to Jaya and me when she stuck a size-ten fly into my neck." He looked up at me. "I mean, she was eight, so she thought she'd killed me and started crying. So, I started gulping and fell down, flopping on the bank like I was a fish and she'd landed a big one—pretty soon we were all laughing, and they piled on top of me." He continued to finger the bracelet, especially the cedar beads. "About a week later Jeanie gave me this; nothing special but she must've used up all the money she had to buy it. You take it, Poppy. It'll guard you against ghosts . . ." He swallowed. "I guess she should've kept it for herself."

"I'm sorry, Mr. Lane."

He cleared his throat and looked up at me, releasing the bracelet. "So, you think somebody I know might have something to do with this?"

"Well, the whole purpose of an investigation is to discover things that you don't know."

He stared at me for a moment and then flipped open the file and leafed through the pages, slowing as he got to the end and then finally handing it back to me.

"Well?"

"Nope." He smoked the cigarette some more.

"Nothing looks familiar?"

"None of it looks familiar to me other than the shit I've had thrown at me my whole life." There was a knock at the door, and he looked at it, not moving.

"You want me to get it?"

"No." The knock sounded again, a little more persistent, and he stood, leaning toward the window to try to peer past the stained curtain. Ducking his head back, he motioned for me to be quiet, holding a finger to his mouth.

A voice called from outside. "I saw you, Jimmy. We know you're in there."

He called back. "I'm busy, go away."

"Open the door, Jimmy."

He said nothing, and I stood there waiting to see what was going to happen next, but it was pretty undramatic when somebody just turned the knob and pushed open the door.

From my perspective, I could see three guys standing on the abbreviated porch, and they could see me. "Howdy."

The biggest took a step inside so that he could now see Jimmy, still seated in the corner. "Hey, Jimmy." He glanced at me. "You've got company."

"Yeah." Jimmy stood and glanced around, still puffing on the cigarette. "An ol' buddy from down on the Rez."

The larger one stepped in, and I got a better look at him. He was tall and wide with the look of a weightlifter—he had a lot of tattoos, a shaved head, and a goatee. "How you doin'?" He extended a hand. "Pete Schiller."

I gave him mine. "Walt."

He shook just a bit too long. "Just Walt?"

"Just Walt."

"You don't look like the Rez type, Walt."

I kept my eyes on him for a bit. "And what does the Rez type look like?"

He smirked and gestured toward Jimmy Lane. "Him."

He stepped in a little farther and his two friends followed, one a squirrelly looking individual with a Carhartt jacket and work boots, carrying a baseball bat, and the other, tall, wearing a hooded sweatshirt and sunglasses even though it wasn't particularly bright outside.

Looking at the other two, I couldn't help myself. "So, are you two Hegel and Kant?"

They looked a little confused, but Schiller laughed. "That's good, I like that." He gestured for them to come the rest of the way in. "This is Lou-Dawg and Silent A."

"What are you guys, a rap group?"

"That's funny too. What do you do, Walt?"

I glanced at Lane, who looked none too comfortable. "I'm trying to buy this shotgun off Jimmy here, but he keeps raising the price."

Schiller looked at Lane, then me and then back at him. "That true, Jimmy? You never told me you were selling your shotgun."

Jimmy took another drag and then cleared his throat. "I, um . . . I need the money."

The weightlifter glanced at the folder under my arm. "Working for the Census or something?"

"Or something." I turned back to Jimmy. "Let me know if you decide to sell the shotgun. I'll be in touch."

I started to step toward the door, but Schiller stepped in front of me. "In a hurry, big man?"

I stood there, not saying anything.

He glanced down, fingering a lip and chuckling. "I guess I just find it hard to believe that the only reason somebody like you would be here visiting Jimmy would be to buy a gun." His eyes came back up to mine. "You look like the kind of man who might have plenty of guns."

I still said nothing.

"Matter of fact, I bet you've got one on you right now."

"He came here asking about my daughter." Jimmy took a step forward but didn't make eye contact with Schiller.

"The one that went missing?" The man turned back to me. "People go missing all the time, they just disappear—strange isn't it?"

I tipped my hat back and hooked a thumb in my jeans and sighed. "No, the other one whose been receiving death threats."

"She a Rez type?"

"She's Cheyenne, yep."

Schiller turned back to Jimmy. "I thought you were cutting yourself off from those prairie poodles down there."

Lane spoke with his head down, finishing the cigarette and stooping to grind it out in a small plate on the table before picking up the pistol. "He just came here to ask some questions; I didn't invite him."

Schiller squared up with me again. "Look, Jimmy here is trying to get his life together and part of that is getting away from those red lice on the government teat, you got me?"

I stared at him.

"I said, you got me?"

I could feel a coolness in my face and a stillness in my hands. "I've got you, all right."

He studied me. "You down with brown—you some kind of Indian-lover?" The chuckle again as he stepped back. "I don't get it. I mean here we've got this bunch of wagon burners that get subsidized housing, tribal support checks, government aid, and free education and still whine and cry about how they're so abused, you know what I mean?"

"You don't think this country owes them something?"

He shook his head at me as the others fanned out a bit. "Anything this country owed these fuckers was paid off a long time ago."

Slipping my hand to the small of my back, I figured I'd block the anticipated swing of the right with my left forearm and then introduce the .45 under his chin before the others could enter the fray. "I guess I disagree."

"And so do I." A very faint breeze blew through the room, the kind you get on battlefields that take souls.

I watched as the two in the back turned to see the Cheyenne Nation standing behind them. Even leaning against the doorjamb like a recalcitrant cougar with his head slung to one side and half of his face shrouded, he was about six inches taller than the two in the back and worlds more dangerous.

Schiller had turned too, and it would appear that all the clever had left his mouth.

"I was wondering what had happened to you."

He smiled, teeth showing. "I walked your dog and then got to the porch and listened to this very interesting conversation on cultural diversity—I did not want to interrupt."

"Oh, I think you should join in." I leaned a little to the side, getting Schiller's attention. "Don't you?"

His turn to say nothing.

"I think you better leave." Jimmy gestured with the revolver and took another step toward us. "I appreciate you coming by and telling me about my daughter, but we've got some things to discuss and I think you better get out of here."

Figuring at this point the only thing we were doing was making his life more difficult, I drew my hand away from my Colt and stepped past Schiller, pausing for an instant to let him look me in my scarred eye. "I'm sure we'll see each other again."

As we walked toward the truck down the block, I shook my head. "Well, that was interesting."

He went around to the other side but then folded his arms and leaned on the hood of his aged truck, looking back at the tiny, dilapidated house. "Yes."

"I'm glad there was no bloodshed."

He smiled and then breathed a laugh. "Do you want to know the difference between you and me?"

"Sure."

He turned his head toward the southwest where in the moonlight the snowcapped Beartooth Range looked so clean, so pristine, and so far away. "I do not worry about dying and someday I will die—whereas you worry about dying and someday you will die."

4

We'd been on the Wainwright ranch for about five minutes when we got to the first gate, which was locked, but there was an intercom with a button. I pushed it, and the intercom made the static noise of an old phone.

"Big ranch."

Henry looked up from the file, glancing around as if seeing the place for the first time. "Yes."

Static. "Can I help you?" The female voice from the intercom sounded harried.

"Howdy, this is Sheriff Walt Longmire."

Static. "Who?"

"Walt Longmire, I'm the sheriff down in Absaroka County."

There was a long pause, even longer than I would've anticipated.

Static. "And how can I help you?"

"I'm looking for Harley Wainwright."

Static. "My son?"

"I suppose so; is he home?"

Static. "Yes. Well, I think so."

"I'd like to speak with him."

Static. "About?"

"I'm involved in an investigation concerning a young woman

he knows, Jaya Long?" Silence. "She's been receiving some threatening notes, and I was hoping to speak with him and see if he had any ideas about who might be responsible."

Static. "I don't think he's dating her anymore."

"But he was."

Static. "Yes."

"Well, I'd still like to speak with him if I could?"

She didn't say anything else, but after a moment the electric gate rose, and we followed the one road to a large log home with a number of outbuildings and a riding arena. I pulled my truck up to the front walk near the arena, and we got out and looked around. "I'd say the Wainwrights are doing pretty well."

The Bear nodded and walked away. "He owns a number of oil firms from what I understand—hence the name Digger."

"Hmm, I thought he might be an undertaker."

There was a noise from the riding arena, and since no one appeared to be running to meet us, we drifted in that direction. We entered the large door, moved over to the arena, and watched a strikingly beautiful silver-haired woman, wearing a tan cowboy hat, putting a powerful-looking paint through the paces in a precise pattern of circles, spins, and stops before turning the horse and loping toward us.

She reined the gelding in, before patting him and blowing some of the hair from her face. "Hello."

"Howdy." I glanced around at the finished interior of the elaborate building, which even had a set of bleachers on one side. "I'm impressed you could talk on the intercom while doing all that."

She pulled a cell phone from the pocket of her vest. "The gates route through our cells so we can answer no matter where we are."

Henry looked puzzled. "You have service all the way out here?"

She nodded, riding the paint a little closer. "We have our own tower."

"Of course."

"Mrs. Wainwright?"

She smiled, turning to look at me with the blue eyes sparkling as if there were a joke and I wasn't getting it. "Yes?"

"I'm sorry to bother you, but could we speak to your son?"

She seemed almost on the verge of laughter. "I called Digger, and he's bringing him here as soon as they get Harley's four-wheeler out of the bog he stuck it in chasing some cattle out of the bottom land near the creek bed."

I studied her face. "I'm sorry, Mrs. Wainwright, but do I know you?"

She burst out laughing, startling the horse, but then she reined him in and slipped off her hat and threw it at me. "We went to a Sadie Hawkins dance together in high school—Walt Longmire, you asshole!"

I picked up the hat, dusting it off and handing it back to her. "Connie Harper."

She laughed some more. "At least until Martha got her claws into you and wouldn't let go. I heard you two got married; how is she?"

"We were married, but I'm afraid she passed away a number of years back."

Her face saddened. "I'm so sorry."

"It's okay." I glanced around at all the grandeur. "So, Connie Wainwright."

"For about twenty years, now."

I gestured toward the Cheyenne Nation. "I don't know if you remember Henry Standing Bear?"

"Only from afar. You kind of came and went between up here and down in Durant, didn't you?"

He nodded. "I did."

She smiled, and I began to remember her as the wild spirit she'd been back then, a genuine cowgirl who enjoyed out-riding and out-roping the boys in the area. She gestured toward me. "After this one broke my heart, my family moved to Houston, Texas, and I married the wrong guy in River Oaks. Then after we got divorced, I married Digger—and here I am." She patted the horse again. "Let me get this fella taken care of, and I'll meet the two of you up at the big house."

She turned and rode away toward the other end of the building where I saw a ranch hand waiting for her by a row of stables.

Henry pushed off the fence and started toward the house. "Did you really date her?"

I followed along after him. "I think I lost my virginity to her."

She poured me some iced tea and then one for the Bear. "It's not something a girl forgets. Actually, I think it was me that took advantage of him."

"That does not surprise me, he has always been a bit slow."

"That's what I liked about him." She sipped her own tea, settling back in the tufted leather sofa while kicking off her boots and stuffing her feet underneath her. "Kids?"

I drifted toward a wall of family photos, a lot of them of a handsome young man riding and roping. "One daughter who works for the attorney general down in Cheyenne and a granddaughter who toys with my heart on a regular basis."

"Oh, my."

I tapped one of the photos. "Harley your only child?"

"Yes, God help the world if I'd had twins." She turned to Henry. "What about you, tall, dark, and handsome?"

He shrugged. "Still looking for Miss Right."

"You mean Miss Right Now?"

I moved back over to the conversation island in hopes of conversing. "So, Harley's not dating Jaya anymore?"

"I don't think so, but I try not to be too interested in his private life. I mean he's eighteen years old and should have the right to date anybody he wants. There are some things a mother is better not knowing."

I sat on a tufted leather ottoman and sipped my tea. "Do you know of any threats to Jaya that Harley might've mentioned?"

"There was the predictable stuff from both sides." She glanced at Henry. "Natives angry that she was dating Harley, whites who were angry he was dating Jaya—the usual stuff."

"Other students?"

She glanced out the big picture windows that faced west. "Pretty much."

"Nothing you would consider a real threat?"

"Well, when it's your child you think it's all threatening."

"Why do you think they broke up?"

She turned back to me. "It was just too much pressure. They're both great kids, but with all the things you're dealing with at that age, I think the added burden of other people's racism was too much."

There was some noise emanating from the dining room and kitchen toward the back of the house, with some banging and cursing. Connie stood and moved in that direction and was met by an older man, diminutive in height and whippet thin.

He was in socked feet with mud-covered jeans and shirt, a once very nice silverbelly hat perched on one side of his head, sweat-stained and mud-coated. "Well, that took half the damned day."

Connie pointed at him. "Don't you dare come off that kitchen tile with all that mud on you."

"Well, what the hell am I supposed to do? Go outside and shake off like a damned dog?"

"There's a robe in the mudroom along with a pair of slippers. Where's Harley?"

The man turned and started back through the kitchen. "Down at the tack shed showering off; he's even worse than me."

She followed him. "Well, he needs to get up here; there are some people who want to talk to him."

"What people?"

"A sheriff and his friend."

"Gordo?" I could hear him coming back. "Talk about what?"

"Go change your clothes, Digger."

The conversation was closer now, probably in the kitchen, and I felt like I should turn and meet the man, but then thought I should let them finish their talk.

"The hell I will—Rosebud County?"

"No, from down in Wyoming."

"What the hell is he doing here?"

There was a pause. "He's a friend."

"Talk to Harley about what?"

"Jaya."

"Oh, horseshit."

"Digger."

There was a longer pause. "Fine, I'll be right out."

She returned and took the pitcher from a tray on the coffee table and freshened our glasses. "He's a little grumpy. He bought the four-wheeler for Harley so that he could get to the cows faster than with a horse, but so far all he's succeeded in doing is getting it stuck."

The man reappeared in a bathrobe. He was wearing his hat from which he had scraped most of the mud. "Digger Wainwright." We shook, and I noticed he glanced at the Cheyenne Nation but didn't attempt to shake his hand.

"My friend and associate, Henry Standing Bear."

He gave a wave as the Bear sat looking at him and then seated himself next to his wife. "How can I help you gentlemen?"

"I understand your son used to date Jaya Long. She's been receiving threats, and I was hoping to speak with your son about it."

He made a face. "He's not threatening that girl, and he's not dating her anymore either."

"I wasn't interested in Harley as a suspect, but rather as a source of information as to who might be threatening Jaya."

"She's a headstrong young woman. And she rubs a lot of people the wrong way."

"Yourself included?"

He leaned back in the sofa and glanced first at his wife and then me, finally snatching off his hat and tossing it beside him. "So, now I'm a suspect?"

"I don't think I'm far enough along in the investigation to have any suspects, Mr. Wainwright. I'm just trying to get an idea of why someone would go to such lengths to intimidate or upset this young woman."

"So, why hasn't the FBI or the sheriff of Rosebud, Custer, or Powder River or any other damn county in Montana come in here to ask me these questions?"

"I'm kind of under a retainer with the tribal police."

He barked a laugh. "The tribal police. You mean those yahoos who run around here with their notebooks and pencils playing cop on the Rez?"

"Mr. Wainwright . . ."

"Look, that girl's father is a convict, her mother is a drunk, and most of her damn family's been killed in some fashion or another, including a sister who simply vanished off the face of the earth. Now, how the hell is my son going to help you sort through all the shit in that girl's life?"

"I just thought Harley might—"

"I want you two out of my house. Now." He stood, tightening the sash on his robe. "I'm not kidding, I mean now. You come in here asking me and my family a bunch of questions with no particular authority . . ."

I looked up at him, pretty sure he wasn't aware of his ludicrous appearance. "We thought you might want to help."

"There isn't any helping people who won't help themselves." He glanced at Henry and then began making an exit toward the entryway of the house where a large circular stairwell led upstairs. "I want the two of you out of here now, or I call the real sheriff and have you locked up."

With that, he went up the stairs. I turned to look at Connie. "I want to thank you for your hospitality."

She gasped a laugh. "Right."

I stood, and the Bear did the same. "I guess we better get out of here."

She climbed off the sofa and walked us to the front door, where she paused before opening it. "He's a little upset and gets like that. I'll wait till he calms down and then see if we can come up with anybody we think might be a threat." She hung on to the door. "That poor girl."

I handed her one of my cards. "Thank you."

She studied it. "Wow, I've never seen one of these without an email."

"My dispatcher won't let me have a computer."

She smiled but still didn't open the door. She looked up at me. "Do you remember that scarf I had on while I was riding in the arena?"

It seemed like an odd thing to say. "Um, no."

"The red one I had on; I think I might've lost it, so it must be down there somewhere."

"I don't think you had . . ."

Henry interrupted. "I remember the scarf. Would you like us to take a look around the arena before we leave?"

She opened the door. "If you don't mind, I'd appreciate that." She glanced at the card and then took my hand and held it for a moment. "It was so good to visit with you, Walter."

As we walked toward the arena, I could see a young man straightening his shirt as he headed toward us. The Bear shook his head. "You truly can be slow at times."

"We dated for the better part of a year." He was a very nice and courteous young man who looked a lot like his mother and behaved like her too. Freshly showered, he sat there in a T-shirt, jeans, boots, and a letterman's jacket.

"What happened?"

"I'm not really sure." He smiled, resting a chin in a palm as we all sat there on the bleachers with the Bear leaning against the fence. "One day everything was fine, and then the next she broke up with me."

"She broke up with you?"

"Yeah, why?"

"Well, the way your mother described it, it was kind of a mutual thing."

He nodded. "There was a lot of stuff we were having to go

through, but I was willing to stick it out. She drove up with me to watch a game we were playing against Roundup . . ."

"Basketball?"

"Football. Basketball is her game, not mine."

Henry smiled. "Position?"

"Backup quarterback." He glanced up at the Cheyenne Nation. "You were a running back for Cal Berkeley."

"Yes."

"Not exactly a football powerhouse—why did you choose them?"

"Football was my minor; I was majoring in revolution at the time."

He glanced at me. "You were an offensive lineman for USC."

I gestured toward the Bear. "I was offensive in a lot of ways, just ask him."

"I looked you guys up." His eyes came back to mine. "You were really good—how come you didn't go pro?"

"I did, for a cup of coffee."

"You're kidding."

"Nope."

"What happened?"

"I lost interest after Vietnam."

"Oh." He laced his fingers in his lap. "Anyway, I stayed that night in Roundup, but she got a ride back with somebody and the next day we were splitsville."

"Any idea who she got a ride with?"

"No."

"Did you know Jeanie?"

"Her sister, oh yeah. I dated her before I dated Jaya."

The Cheyenne Nation chuckled. "You get around."

"Not really." He studied his boots. "We only dated a couple of times; Jeanie was too smart for me." He looked back up. "No kidding, she was a genius."

"Any ideas on what could've happened to her?"

"No, no idea. She got a ride with some people up to Billings and was on her way back when they had a breakdown and she wandered off. There was a big group of us that went out there and walked a grid for a few days—my dad even helped."

I rested my back on the edge of the seat behind me, finding that muscle to the center of my shoulder blade and giving it a little mauling. "Well, the reason we're here today is to ask if you know of anybody who might be writing death threats to Jaya?"

"Yeah, I heard about that." He shook his head. "She can be a little edgy sometimes, but after what's happened in her family, I can't imagine anybody would have it out for her." He thought about it. "It's funny, but after Jeanie went missing everybody kind of tried to surround Jaya and comfort her, but she eventually drove them all away—including me, I guess."

"Was there anybody in particular that she had trouble with?"

"Honestly, nobody comes to mind, but then I was her boyfriend, so it's not like people like that are going to confide in me." He laughed. "There was one guy who hated her."

"Who?"

"The bus driver for that big turquoise and black sports bus, the Morning Star."

"What about him."

"He just didn't like Jaya. I mean, she'd get rambunctious on the bus, and they'd get into shouting matches. You know Jaya, she wouldn't back down from a herd of wolverines on bath salts. Well, there was one time when they got into it, and it actually got physical. One of those 'don't make me pull this bus over' kind of deals. Well, Jaya wouldn't shut up, so he did, and they got into it."

"You were there?"

"No, but I heard about it. Heck, everybody did. Nobody likes that bus driver anyway."

"What's his name?"

"Melvin Rook."

"How come he has the job?"

He glanced at Henry. "Heck if I know—tribal connections, I guess."

"What are you still doing here, harassing my son?" We all turned to see Digger Wainwright standing in the opening with two men in the uniform of the Rosebud County Sheriff's Department.

Harley was the first to move, standing and walking over toward the group as they entered. He lowered himself to ground level. "It's my fault, Dad, I called them over when they were leaving. They just wanted to talk about . . ."

The smack echoed in the empty steel building like the report of a gun.

Harley stood there for a moment and then lowered his head.

Digger, freshly clean and dressed, leaned into him. "Go to the house. Now."

The young man did as he was told. Digger hopped up on the bleachers, walking toward us, each step clanging. "I'm going to go on the assumption that maybe you didn't understand me when I said for you to get off of my place." He now stood over me. "I thought maybe you needed an escort to show you the way, so I called our sheriff's department to help you."

I glanced past him at the older one of the two. "Hi, Gordo."

The silver-haired man with a nose like a ripe tomato waved back. "Hi, Walt, Henry."

"You going to cuff us?"

"No, we didn't even bring the paddy wagon."

I stood, looming over the rancher for a moment, considering how far I could pitch him into the arena with the dirt and horseshit. Figuring that would possibly get me the paddy wagon after all, I stepped past him as Henry joined me in clanging off the bleachers and confronting Gordo Hanson and his deputy.

"This mean you're going to go quietly?"

"Same as we came."

I walked past them, and we climbed into my truck. Dog licked my ear as I started the three-quarter ton and then turned in a wide loop with the Rosebud County unit following us under the watchful eye of Digger Wainwright.

A couple of miles down the road we went through the gate where we'd entered, the electric barricade rising as we pulled through and I eased my truck to the side, Gordo aligning himself next to us.

I rolled down my window as his deputy did the same. "Sorry about that."

Gordo shrugged. "Ah, he's an asshole." He gestured toward the younger deputy. "Walt, meet Terry Fraley—he's new and doesn't know a damn thing."

The recruit raised a weary hand, obviously used to being introduced in such a fashion. "Hey."

I leaned a little forward to see Gordo. "We just came over to ask his son some questions about the girl he used to date."

"Jaya One Moon?"

"Jaya Long, as of late."

"I heard she was living in Lolo's basement; could be the best thing that ever happened to her." He got out and walked around, leaning on my door and looking past me. "Think she's going to light up the brackets this year, Bear?"

"Could be."

He tipped his brown cowboy hat back. "That Wainwright, he don't like the Indians—which is pretty strange behavior for a guy who buys a ranch right in the middle of one of the largest reservation conglomerations in North America."

Henry shrugged. "Maybe he just likes the *idea* of Indians."

"I doubt it." The sheriff draped an arm over my side mirror. "He really didn't like it when Harley started dating Jaya; had us running all over the place when that kid of his didn't get home before midnight."

"Good kid?"

"Very, that boy wouldn't say shit if he had a mouthful." His head dropped. "I don't know, you see a couple of kids like that and you hope it'll work—but it didn't."

"How are you doing?"

He smiled. "Since the divorce? I'm doin' okay." He looked at Henry and me. "You know, some women marry you thinking you're a cop and have all these great stories, but then the stories aren't all that great and pretty soon they learn better and move on."

I patted his arm. "You don't sound particularly bitter, Gordo."

He waved me off and headed back to his car. "Ah, life's too short."

Boy howdy.

"So, the bus driver did it."

He glanced at me. "You have made up your mind at this initial juncture of the investigation?"

"No, I just like the sound of it—kind of like the butler did it."

He smiled the paper-thin smile, looking out the window, mumbling to himself. "Melvin Rook."

"You know him?"

"He was the team statistician and drove the bus when I played."

"Oh, shit, he must be a hundred years old."

The Cheyenne Nation pursed his lips. "Does that lower him on your suspect list?"

I drove into Lame Deer, taking the roundabout and heading past the Flower Grinder coffee shop, down Cheyenne Avenue. "Not necessarily. As an elected official I can tell you that old people like to get mad and write crazy letters."

"Present company excepted?"

"Absolutely."

"Well, you are in luck."

"Why is that?"

"I just saw Melvin Rook walk into The Big Store."

Waiting for another car to pull forward, I slipped into the spot and started to get out of the vehicle but noticed the Bear wasn't moving. "You're not coming?"

"Do you need backup?"

"Probably not—I'm hell on the octogenarian set."

"Good luck."

I glanced toward the door of the trading post. "What does he look like?"

"You will know him when you see him."

Getting the distinct feeling I was being set up, I closed the door and started in, once again glancing back at the Bear, who appeared to be covering a smile with his hand.

The Lame Deer Trading Post was humming on a weekend with lots of women and children and a few men. The lines at the cash register were long, and there was a general bustle as people worked their way up and down the aisles.

It was always interesting to me to see the difference between the Rez grocery stores and the ones back in Durant, starting with the craft section with beading supplies and leatherwork, T-shirts, blankets, and jewelry.

Moving past the end of the aisles, I spotted an elderly man in the condiments section. He was holding a bottle and reading the ingredients. He was tiny and looked to be the prescribed one hundred years old, or maybe older. He wore thick-lensed glasses and an age-worn black sweatshirt that read LAME DEER MORNING STARS.

Once again relying on my uncanny powers of deduction, I approached him. "Mr. Rook?"

He continued studying the mustard bottle.

I stepped in a little closer. "Melvin Rook?"

"I heard you, young man."

"Sorry, but you didn't respond . . ."

"Just because I didn't respond doesn't mean I didn't hear you. How is it I am to hear you when you don't speak up?"

Raising my voice, I tipped my hat back and smiled, attempting to convey an open and friendly persona. "Sorry. My name is Walt Longmire."

He finally turned to look in my general direction, raising the bifocals from his eyes to peer at me. "I know who you are."

I was a little surprised. "Well, good. I—"

"You used to hang around with that other good-for-nothing, Henry Standing Bear, as I recall."

I wasn't quite sure what to say to that. "Right, well . . ."

He turned toward me fully, still holding the mustard. "Did you ever make anything of yourself?"

"What?"

"You played football as I recall, at least well enough to continue on to college." He continued to study me. "You seem to have gained weight, and from the multitude of scars on your hands and face and that missing part of your ear, you give the appearance of having become a thug—am I correct in my assumptions?"

I tried to laugh. "Actually, I'm a sheriff."

His face remained still. "Well, there's our answer."

I took a breath and started again. "Mr. Rook, I understand you still drive the Morning Star bus for the high school?"

"What do you mean, *still*?"

I noticed people were stopping and staring at us. "Well, that you still drive the bus?"

"Are you implying, young man, that I am too old to be doing the job?"

"No, I . . ."

"For fifty years I have been bestowed the responsibility of safeguarding the children of the Great Northern Cheyenne Nation. With millions of miles traveled without incident, I have relished the opportunity to contribute in some small way to the athletic success of our people and have seen some of the greatest Native athletes pursue glorious achievements beyond our wildest dreams."

"I'm sure you have." I cleared my throat in hopes of putting a little space in the conversation. "Do you know a student by the name of Jaya Long?"

He cocked his aged head, shaking it at me. "You mean last year's girls' MVP who averaged 33.6 points, 22.3 rebounds, 18 steals, and 2.3 assists a game? That Jaya One Moon?"

"Um, yep, that would be the one."

"And what would you like to know?"

"I understand there was an altercation on the school bus?"

"Altercation?"

"An incident where you had to stop the bus, and there were words between yourself and Jaya Long, er . . . One Moon?"

He sighed. "Mr. Longmire, have you ever driven a bus full of schoolchildren?"

"Well, no."

"There are nothing but altercations of the type you describe, things I'm afraid you cannot even imagine."

"Well . . ."

"In the instance to which you are referring, the young woman was attempting to throw another student out the window. Now, this may seem like an atrocious act, but I can assure you that it is the kind of thing that happens daily. In this instance, I stopped the bus, went back and had a conversation with the young lady in question and voices were, indeed, raised, but it was nothing more than that. Now, might I ask where it is that you got the idea that this was anything more than a run-of-the-mill incident?"

There was a crowd now that had developed in the aisle, most of them laughing and whispering among themselves. "Um . . ."

"Who, may I ask, told you about it?"

"One of the students."

He carefully replaced the mustard back on the shelf, nudging it to join its brethren. "A student."

"Yes."

"I had thoughts of asking how you were coming along in your chosen profession, Mr. Longmire, but after speaking with you I've drawn my own conclusions." He dug a hand in one of his pockets, pulling out a coin and giving it to me. "I would like you to use this quarter to call the attorney general of Wyoming and tell him there is serious doubt as to whether you should continue as a sheriff."

5

"So, do you still have the quarter?"

I pushed another handful of popcorn into my mouth, figuring it was the only dinner we were going to get. "The guy is so old he still thinks there are pay phones."

Henry nodded, reaching over and stealing a handful of dinner for himself. He expertly tossed a kernel in the air and caught it in his mouth. "I am sorry the conversation did not go well."

I shrugged. "I've moved him up the suspect list."

"Because?"

"He made a laughingstock out of me in the grocery store."

Both the girls' teams were Northern Cheyenne, but you wouldn't know it from the way they were playing each other. The one from Lame Deer, the Lady Morning Stars, is the public school, the colors of the team being turquoise and black. The Ashland team—the Lady Braves—is from the private Catholic school St. Labre, thirty miles and worlds away. Its colors were purple and gold, and the team's mascot a screaming warrior in profile.

I watched the Lady Morning Stars warming up on the other end of the court, and other than Jaya, they still looked a little hapless. The shooting guard was lapping baby jumpers from all around, not missing any as the others trailed after their missed shots, sometimes running into each other. "This doesn't look good."

"No, not now."

"What's that mean?"

"Jaya has a way of rising to the competition."

"What about the others?"

"We will see."

I pulled the "Tribal Police Department" folder from under my rump and studied the list typed on Wyoming Tribal Police Department letterhead. "So, these are the six people who were in the car the night Jeanie went missing?"

He sipped a bottle of water. "Yes."

"Can you get addresses for all of them?"

"I am sure Lolo can." He looked past me to the nether reaches of the bleachers. "But I am betting a percentage of them are here tonight."

I glanced around. "Can you make them?"

"Let me see the list again."

I handed it to Henry and watched as he scanned the piece of paper with a scrutiny rarely found among the human element of nature, an acuity usually reserved for predators. "At least one of them." He lip-pointed to the far corner where a man sat behind the makeshift, two-person band comprised of Mr. Hurtick, the band teacher who played the French horn, and his wife, who played the clarinet.

"The man in the glasses against the wall, Edwin Black Kettle, was the driver."

"It's going to be hard to talk to him with the band right there."

"I will keep an eye on him and tell you if he moves."

"Anybody else?"

He glanced around some more. "Leanne Chelan, up in the last row, center."

"The one with the purple jacket."

"Yes." He tilted his head slightly. "George Three Fingers, the one at the railing, standing."

I nodded, studying the large man with short hair, who was stretching his back, obviously in pain.

"You want to go with me?"

"I will save our seats, unless it looks like you need me."

"You're not setting me up again?"

"No." He smiled. "I have a history with all these people—not all of it good."

"Right." I stood, still looking at the file and then stuffing it in my jacket. "We've got four Natives and two whites on here—we'll need to go talk to them." I figured I'd start with the closest, so I moved up to the crosswalk, trailed along the bleachers, and then went down the other aisle to sit a little away from Three Fingers, the man with the back spasms, who, as near as I could tell, had all his fingers.

"Howdy."

He turned to look at me but then turned back to look at the court where the girls on both teams were warming up, finally lowering himself onto the bench without a word.

"I'm Walt Longmire."

He looked at me again.

"I've been contracted by the Long family to look into some threats that have been made to Jaya Long-One Moon." He glanced back toward the court. "Yep, her."

He gave me a resigned expression. "What kind of threats?"

"People have been writing her notes and leaving them for her in a number of places."

He rubbed a big pawlike hand across his face, all five fingers accounted for. "And you're with the police?"

"Well, kind of on a retainer."

"How much are they paying you?"

"Nothing."

He nodded and then spoke. "You want to know about that night."

"The night that her sister, Jeanie, went missing, yep."

"You're thinking that whoever is doing this might've done that." He slowly exhaled, looking out onto the court where the game was about to tip-off. "Not much to tell."

"Still, I'd like to hear it from somebody who was there."

"We were in Black Kettle's van . . ."

"Why were all of you in Billings?"

He paused for a moment. "Um, there was a party and Jeanie wanted to go."

"But from what I've gathered, she wasn't much of a party girl."

We both turned to watch the tip-off as the tallest girl on the St. Labre team manhandled the ball with a powerful swipe, knocking it toward one of her forwards, who galloped down the court for an easy layup.

He shifted his weight toward me. "I don't know, it seemed strange to me, but she wanted to go with us. Come to think of it, I hardly saw her at the party, but she was there again when we headed back."

Watching the Lady Morning Stars inbound the ball, I saw the girl with a squint toss it in the general direction of Jaya, who scooped it up and trotted slowly down the court. "And when was that?"

"Late, I guess. I wasn't in any condition to know what time it was."

Jaya pounded the wooden surface of the court with the ball in a direct line toward the basket but then flipped sideways, rolling between two defenders and jumping, the ball released at the very top of her ascent. "I see."

The ball swept through the net.

"BK's van is a piece of crap and always breaks down, but those guys are mechanics out at the mines and can usually get it running. That night the motor was running rough, I can't remember why because I was sleeping on the way back, although it was like trying to sleep on a bucking horse."

"You made it to the Pryor Creek exit?"

"Yeah, it was mostly downhill off the ridge, but that thing wasn't going to make it all the way back to Lame Deer."

"What was the weather like?"

"Cold. There wasn't much snow at that point, but the wind was starting up and the temperature was dropping. BK and one of the other guys were out there working with the hood up—I remember because the thing blew down and hit them both in the head. They would get in the van once in a while to warm their hands up." He thought. "It was strange."

"What was?"

"Jeanie wanting to get out of the van. I mean a couple of the others did, but only to go to the bathroom and they got back in as quick as they could."

"What did she do?"

The Lady Morning Stars inbounded and tried a few passes, but one of the St. Labre forwards stole the ball and drilled a jumper with both teams in pursuit.

"She said she wanted out, that it was too warm and stunk in the van. She said she'd just walk down toward the creek and then be right back."

"Anyone go with her?"

He glanced back at the woman in the purple jacket who was in the last row. "Leanne Chelan went with her, but she was knocking on the door of the van in no time."

"And Jeanie?"

"It started snowing, and she never came back."

Wanona Sweetwater of the Morning Stars dribbled up the court, but even though there were a couple of players on the baseline who were open, she passed the ball to Jaya, who shot and missed.

"Did anyone go look for her?"

"I didn't." He took a breath. "I used to drink a lot back then, and I got hurt on the job out at the mine and got messed up on those pain pills." He sighed. "After I got clear of those I quit, cold turkey."

"Did anybody else go look for her?"

The Lady Braves brought the ball up the court, but instead of falling back into her defensive position, Jaya crowded the two other defenders in an attempt to get the ball back.

"Kettle warned everybody that if they got the van going again, they were pulling out and heading home so they should all stay pretty close, but I think that was after Jeanie had gone." He sighed again. "I honestly don't know if anybody else went out there after her, but I remember the side door opening and closing a couple of times because that wind sliced in there like a butcher knife."

Jaya lunged and missed, and the Lady Braves dumped it off to the side where a guard sank her shot in two steps with a quick post-feed kick out away from Stacey Killsday.

"The next thing I remember was waking up here in Lame Deer with somebody pushing on my shoulder and asking where

Jeanie One Moon was—and I don't even know who. There were a few who went back to look for her from what I understand, but that would've been at least two hours after she'd wandered off." He shuddered. "You don't make it too long out there in weather like that."

"Had she been drinking?"

"No. I mean, I'm not sure, but I don't think so."

"She didn't drink at the party?"

"No, like I said, I didn't even see her there."

We watched the Lady Morning Stars bring the ball in, but there was a lack of animation in their play.

I stood and handed George a card as Harriet, the coach, turned to see me. She looked away quickly and, appearing to be on the verge of a heart attack, yelled at her team. "Thanks, if you think of anything, anything at all, give me a call?"

He nodded, and I continued on toward the far end of the bleachers where an extraordinarily thin man leaned against the wall. Sitting next to him, I stuck out a hand. "Mr. Black Kettle, I'm Walt Longmire."

"Yeah?" He shifted the ball cap on his head but kept his hands to himself. "You want something?"

We watched as the members of the Lady Morning Stars continued their lackluster play just as Tribal Chief Lolo Long entered below in full uniform and jacket. She stood by the doorway and studied the action. "I'd like to talk to you about Jeanie One Moon?"

"No."

Ignoring the response, I leaned in as Lolo saw me. "I understand you were driving the van the night she went missing?"

"Look, I done told the police and everybody else everything I know."

"You haven't told me."

"And I'm not gonna."

I sat outside my lawful jurisdiction and thought about getting the tribal police chief but then came up with a better idea. "Mr. Black Kettle, do you see that man two thirds of the way over on the bleachers? The one who is watching us?"

He glanced past me. "Who?"

"That big fellow in the leather jacket with the long hair?"

"Yeah . . . I see him."

"He really wants you to answer my questions."

"An' if I don't?"

"He's likely to come over here and stomp you into a canoe."

He looked back out onto the court. "Standing Bear."

"In the flesh."

He eyeballed Henry for a second and then went back to watching the game. "He don't scare me."

"That's great, because he scares the shit out of me." I started to get up, but he put out a hand.

I sat, and he took a deep breath and then snorted it out. "What is it you want to know?"

"Just what happened that night."

He nodded and spat out the words. "The damn van broke down; piece of shit never did run right."

"Uh huh."

"We were on our way back and . . ."

"What were you doing in Billings?"

"I, um . . . I had some business I needed to get taken care of."

"What kind of business?"

"There was a girl I was seeing, and she had gotten into trouble, so I was there getting her some money."

I averted my eyes to the court where Misty Two Bears of the

Lady Morning Stars had the ball, taking a little heat off the questioning. "Was that at a party?"

"Kind of."

"Did you see Jeanie there?"

"Yeah."

"You're sure of that?"

"What do you mean?"

"I know she got a ride with you to and from the party, but did you actually see here there?"

He thought about it as the Stars moved the ball around until Jaya got it and shot from the perimeter, sinking a three-pointer. "No, now that I think about it, I don't think I did. Does that mean something?"

"Maybe. On the way back, tell me what happened?"

He clasped his hands together in his lap and leaned forward. "We made the ridge, but the thing was bucking and kicking like a vapor lock, but it's fuel-injected, you know?"

We watched the St. Labre team drive down, only to pull up short, a shooting guard extending the Lady Braves' lead to a dozen points. "What happened?"

"I got it coasted off the highway, and we stopped at the frontage road, the one that goes back under the interstate. I got out and raised the hood and tried to get it to run right . . ."

"Anybody help you?"

"Um . . . Yeah, Gabriel Popescu got out and tried to help, but we couldn't figure it." He grunted. "I swear that shitty van is haunted; it would run great one minute and then all of a sudden it would just cut out and quit."

"Anybody else help?"

"No, but people were climbing in and out of the van, wanting to know what the holdup was and how long it was going to be.

Then it got colder—the wind came up, and it started snowing." He thought about it. "I heard some people climbing out again, and I yelled at them, telling them that if I got the van started that I was jumping in there and pulling out, so they better not go far, or they were going to get left behind."

The Lady Morning Stars were fumbling the press and the Lady Braves were picking them apart with quick, steady ball movement resulting in another score. "That last time, you don't know who got out of the van?"

"Somebody said something about one of the women having to go to the bathroom, but I don't know which one."

"What happened then?"

"The wind really picked up, and we were warming our hands on the engine, you know? Anyway, we climbed back in, and I hit it just to see if it would start and it did, so I turned around and yelled to see if everybody was in there. Somebody said yeah that they were, and I put her in gear and pulled out. In five minutes, I think I was the only one awake. By the time we got back here, people were climbing out of the van, and there were some people to meet us. Someone asked about Jeanie, I don't know who . . ."

"Me."

We both turned to see that the tribal police chief, Lolo Long, had sat on the bench beside me.

"Hey."

"Hey." She nodded at Black Kettle to continue.

"Yeah, I remember now. Anyway, she wasn't in the van, so a big group went back that night to look for her."

"Not you."

He stared at her. "No, not me."

"Why not?"

He stared at his boots. "I was tired, and cold, and I didn't think it was a big deal." His eyes came back up, watching the girls play, and he added weakly, "I went out with the search and rescue guys the next day."

"And no one ever saw anything?"

"No. The snow came in that night, but there were no tracks, and then even if there were when everyone had been out there walking around, there was no way to tell which ones might've been hers."

Pulling the folder from my jacket, I asked him, "Louie Howard, Gabriel Popescu, and Lesa Hopkins—you know those three people?"

"Louie works at the mine with me, but I don't know the other two. I mean, I'd know 'em if I saw 'em, probably, but I don't know anything about 'em other than they were in the van that night."

I closed the file. "Is there anything else you can think of?"

"No." He glanced past me at Lolo. "I'm sorry."

I stuck out my hand again, and this time he took it.

"I hope you find who did this or who's doing this; that girl deserved better."

I handed him a card. "If you think of anything else, contact me."

I stood and walked toward the aisle, Chief Long following, clanging down the bleachers and exiting through the opening into the lobby outside. Walking over to the concession stand, I bought two cups of coffee and handed her one. You never had to ask a cop if they wanted a cup of coffee—they always did.

I blew into mine. "I think your team is in trouble."

"Yeah."

I sipped, studying the scythelike scar on the side of her face as she watched the game. "Your niece doesn't trust her team."

She nodded, and her eyes came back to me. "So, I heard you pissed off Digger Wainwright."

I shrugged. "It wasn't intentional."

"It hardly ever is with me either."

I turned to the game. The court seemed to tilt toward the Lady Morning Stars' basket. "His kid, Harley, seems nice."

She sipped her coffee. "I've never had any dealings with him."

"Well, that's a plus."

"Getting anywhere?"

"I'm not sure. There are some inconsistencies in what might've happened with Jeanie, so I'm going to keep asking around. Do you know . . ." I flipped open the folder. "Louie Howard, Gabriel Popescu, or Lesa Hopkins?"

She nodded. "Louie Howard works at the mine as a mechanic, Gabriel Popescu is a bouncer over at the Four Arrows Casino Bar and Lounge, and Lesa has a used bookshop over in Hardin, next door to the old Hotel Becker."

"Have you talked with any of them?"

"No, but the Yellowstone County investigator and the FBI have." I nodded, and she gestured toward the court with her cup. "What about Jaya?"

"I spoke with her mother and father, before our conversation was interrupted by some of his white-supremacist pals."

"Schiller?"

"He was one of them, yep."

"Watch that guy, he's one of the original Brothers of the North—even got his son involved with them."

"Will do.

"What if the two instances aren't connected?"

"Then I drop the investigation of Jeanie and focus on Jaya."

She watched the girls play, finally shaking her head. "I might want you to do that."

"Why?"

Chief Long's eyes lingered on the young woman desperately trying to steal the ball from the big center before turning and starting toward the outside doors. "She's alive."

I figured the Lady Morning Star locker room was no visitors allowed, so I wandered into the hallway where I'd met the athletic director, Tiger Scalpcane. Henry, listening to the screaming inside, was standing by an alcove. "Sounds instructional."

He nodded. "Trying to shake them up, maybe scare them a bit."

"You don't think they're scared enough?"

"Standing Bear!" We both turned to see a heavyset woman with an outrageous hairstyle and a black and turquoise sweater adorned with numerous photo buttons. She was entering from the court and heading straight for us. "They've got to get the ball to my granddaughter."

Henry straightened. "I do not think that is the problem, Betty." He gestured toward me. "May I introduce my good friend Sheriff Walt Longmire."

She turned her formidable bosom toward me, and I could see a button for Jaya and one for Jeanie, clattering among numerous others. "They aren't passing the ball to my granddaughter, which they should. That girl scored more points than any other player in the state last year."

"That may be true, but the St. Labre team has at least three shooters, and unless she can outshoot all of them, the Lady Morning Stars are going to lose."

She looked at me, her sculptured hair bobbing as if with a life all its own. "And you're some kind of basketball expert?"

"No, but I know when a team is dysfunctional. Jaya doesn't trust or respect her teammates, and it undermines any discipline.

The Stars are better players individually, but the Braves are a better team and one look at the scoreboard proves it."

She stared at me for a moment more and then blew between us and into the locker room.

The Bear folded his arms. "Well stated, but I do not think you made a new friend."

There was more yelling, and after a moment Big Betty was ejected from the locker room. Still screaming at the coach, she stormed down the hallway before turning and looking at me. "You are the one who is looking for Jeanie and guarding Jaya?"

"Yes, ma'am."

She snapped her fingers at me. "Dinner at our house on Tuesday night—there will be a sweat—not Crow style so bring swimming trunks, nobody wants to see your wrinkled old white ass."

She left, and I turned back to the Cheyenne Nation. "Did I just agree to something?"

The door to the locker room sprang open and Harriet stood there, red-faced. "No one comes in here, you got me?"

Henry nodded. "Yes."

Her eyes shifted to me. "Get in here."

I glanced at the Bear and then back to her. "I thought you said no one."

"Get in here."

"Yes, ma'am." I followed her through the door as Henry set up a blockade I doubted anyone would pass. The players were scattered on benches and on the floor and looked completely exhausted.

Felton carried her clipboard to the whiteboard and turned to regard them, first addressing the center. "Rosey, you've got that other center by a good two inches and I've seen you outjump her in other games, but she's moving you out of the way in the paint like you've got wheels."

I sat at the end of a bench.

"Stacey, if you miss one more shot, I'm going to chain you to the free-throw line for the next six weeks." She turned to the next girl. "And Misty, let me explain to you how this works. The idea is to score more points than the other team, but if you don't shoot, you don't score." She stepped from the board toward the other bench. "Wanona, what are you smiling about—you think this is funny?"

The young forward sank her head. "No."

"Then why are you smiling?"

"I don't know."

"Well, don't—there's nothing to smile about, trust me." Finally turning to the young woman leaning against the lockers appearing to be somewhere else, the coach focused on Jaya Long, who was staring up at the lights. "Jaya, have you heard a word I've said?"

Turning her head away, she mumbled. "This doesn't concern me."

Felton stepped in front of her. "Excuse me?"

Jaya whipped her face around. "I'm not the problem here."

"Yep, you are." Both she and the coach turned to look at me.

Harriet glanced at Jaya and then back to me. "I can't seem to get through to her." She stepped back. "You wanna give it a try?"

Jaya started to move toward the door, but I stood, effectively blocking the way. "Hold up." Almost running into me, she pulled back, and I thought for a moment she might take a swing at me, but she just stood there thrusting her chin out. "Who is the captain of this team?"

They all looked at one another, Misty Two Bears shyly lifting her hand. "I guess I am?"

I turned back to Jaya. "Do you want to play this game?"

She said nothing.

"Do you? Because right now you're not." I gestured toward the others. "Let me introduce you to your teammates—without them, you're going to lose this game, I can guarantee it."

She made a noise in her throat. "What do you know about this game?"

"I know enough about sport to win a national championship, but I didn't do it alone. You want to keep playing? Do you want to win a division, a tournament, a state championship? Well, then you better get your head on straight and start playing team ball—otherwise you're going to be the best one-on-one, playground player in Lame Deer. You think that's going to punch your ticket to a decent school, the WNBA, or a shoe contract? Think again."

She glared at me. "I've had enough of this shit."

I stepped between her and the door again. "I don't think your coach is through."

"Well, I am."

"No, you're not." I pointed toward the bench. "Sit."

She glowered at me.

"I said sit down."

She threw herself on the bench, folded her arms, and stared at the floor in a defiant sulk.

Making the ultimate sacrifice, Felton sat her two-guard at the end of the bench, making Jaya watch the rest of the lopsided game. The St. Labre Lady Braves didn't pour it on, but the team didn't exactly let up either.

I sat with Henry near the end of the bench, I'm not sure why, other than to make sure that Jaya didn't just get up and walk out. I glanced over my shoulder. "If you keep an eye on her, I'll go talk to the last person in the room who was in that van."

"As you wish."

I climbed the steps as the first half began winding down, approaching the woman in the purple jacket in the top last row. I noticed she was knitting as I sat a few seats away. "Howdy."

She turned to look at me through a thick set of glasses and smiled. "Hello."

I extended a hand. "Walt Longmire."

She shook and then went back to knitting. "The Lady Stars don't look very good, huh?"

"Not right now, no."

"Are you involved with the team?"

"Not directly, but I'm helping it out." I scooted in a little closer. "Mrs. Chelan, I understand you were a passenger in Edwin Black Kettle's van the night Jeanie One Moon went missing?"

She rested the knitting in her lap and continued smiling at me. "And who, exactly, are you, Mr. Longmire?"

"I'm a sheriff down in Wyoming, helping with the case."

She studied me, peering into my eyes in an unsettling fashion. "And which case is that?"

"Jeanie One Moon."

She sighed deeply. "You're a little late, aren't you? That young woman has been missing for going on a year."

I nodded and watched as the Lady Stars continued to be thrashed. "Yep, but there have been threats made to her sister and a thought occurred to me that we might be looking for the same person."

"The same person who what?"

"Might've done something with Jeanie."

"Well, everyone knows what happened to Jeanie."

"They do?"

"Why, of course. The angels came and got her."

"Angels."

"Yes." She scooted in closer. "I don't blame you, I used to be confused about these types of things, but then I found the Lord and now walk the Red Road, the Chanka Luta—I see angels and miracles everywhere I go."

"Ah."

"I was on a very Black Road or the Chanka Sapa that runs east and west, a path of nonspirituality and self-centered destruction. Drinking, drugs, and things far worse than anything you can imagine. I see devils too."

She started to speak again, but I interrupted. "Mrs. Chelan, I'm really interested in what happened the night in the van. I understand you got out with Jeanie?"

She folded up the knitting in her lap. "That was during the bad period when I was on the Black Road." She sighed, and her eyes came up to mine and stayed there. "It was a year ago, but I remember everything. We went to a party that night, and I was very drunk. I remember being in the van and hearing Jeanie saying she needed to get out of the van, and even as inebriated as I was, I knew she should not be out there alone. So, I remember getting up with a big scarf wrapped around me and stumbling out into the darkness." Her face turned upward as if for divine assistance, or maybe she was just trying to remember. "Jeanie had walked down the trail leading toward the creek and was just standing there, singing."

"Singing?"

"Yes, she sang a song, but the lyrics didn't make sense."

"It wasn't in Cheyenne?"

"It was, but it was a strange song to be singing."

"And what was it about?"

She sang the song, softly to herself in her native language; a pleading, sorrowful song, and then turned to look at me and translated. "Bring me back, I don't belong here, and I want to go home."

I sat unmoving.

She studied me. "You have heard this song?"

Clearing my throat, I thought back. "No, but someone else I've spoken with has."

"I walked up behind Jeanie and saw that she was shivering, so I took the strange scarf and wrapped it around her shoulders as the snow began whistling past us, making it feel as if we were moving forward when we weren't." She took a breath. "I asked her why she was singing this song, and she said that she had heard singing coming from the creek and had sung back, because it was the first song to come to her mind." The woman stared off into an unexplained distance. "I didn't know what to say, so I told her that it was becoming cold and she shouldn't stay out there too long. I turned and walked away, but after a few steps I heard more singing and turned back to look at her, and that was when something strange happened."

"What's that?"

"For a long time, I thought it was the drinking and that I couldn't trust what it was I was seeing or, more important, hearing, but now I know it is what I truly heard."

"Which was?"

"She was standing there with the wind blowing the snow around her, wrapped in that red scarf."

I said nothing.

"It was dark, but I remembered the color from inside the van when the dome light had flickered on—red, I know it was red. That much I remember." She turned to look at me. "I reached over and put a hand on Jeanie's shoulder. She stood there, and I was hoping to read her lips and sing along with her, but then she turned her face, and I could see that it was not Jeanie who was singing."

6

"The scarf she described was red."

He stared at me from over the fire in front of the White Tail cabin. "You are sure that is what she expressed?"

"Perfectly." Henry nodded, and I watched the reflection of the fire in his eyes as I moved my chair in hopes of avoiding the smoke. "No big deal, it just struck me as odd."

"My people believe that red is the only color the spirits can see. Wearing red helps to draw the missing spirits back from other realms so that they might rest."

"But Jeanie wasn't gone then."

"No, but it is possible that wearing it drew the Éveohtsé-heómėse to her." His eyes stayed on the fire. "Did you ask the Chelan woman about the Wandering Without?"

I sat my chair down and seated myself as Dog moved over to me. "It didn't seem appropriate." He grunted, and I reached into the cooler to pull out an iced tea. Popping the top, I took a swig. "And the singing, it was exactly the same wording that the Crow rancher Iron Bull used."

"Yep." I stuck a hand out to warm it. "She also said she sees angels."

"Angels?"

"Yep."

"Where?"

"Pretty much everywhere—and devils." I took another sip of my tea. "It all seemed a little strange."

"That would be because it is strange." He looked down the road that led to the cabin. "Someone is coming."

I turned to see a pair of headlights in the distance, off the main road and then bumping along on the access road toward the Forest Service cabin. Standing, I walked a little away from the fire, with Dog accompanying me, and then waited as a glossy BMW pulled up and stopped, the driver's side window sliding down with a whir.

"Is it safe to get out?"

"Not if you're a ham."

Connie Wainwright opened the door and stepped from her vehicle. "So, it's your wolf?"

I scrubbed Dog's ear as she shut the door and approached. "More like I'm his."

She kneeled, stroking his wide head as he leaned forward and licked her face. "Oh, you're a love-bug. Got an extra chair around the fire, cowboy?"

"I'm sure we can find something. C'mon over." Leading the way, I patted my leg and Dog followed as the Cheyenne Nation stood.

"Hello, again." Connie extended a hand to him and glanced at me. "You guys are a little off the beaten path."

I opened another camp chair and bade her to sit. "How did you find us?"

She sat, drawing her thermal fleece a little tighter around her. "I called the number on your card, and there was a nice young man who told me where the two of you were staying." She glanced around. "He gave me very detailed directions on how to find you. Is he from around here?"

"Barrett Long, Police Chief Lolo Long's little brother. He's working as a weekend dispatcher for me."

"In the conversation we had, he doesn't seem like her."

"You know Lolo?"

"Well, when Harley and Jaya were dating, I had a few run-ins with her . . ."

"Run-ins?" I turned to Henry. "Is that what everybody does with her?"

He nodded. "Pretty much."

Connie glanced around. "Can't say I've ever been over here."

"Would you like an iced tea?"

She rubbed her hands together. "Got anything warm?"

"Not really."

"Then I'll take the tea." The Bear opened the cooler and extracted one, handing it to her. She opened it and took a swig. "I suppose you're wondering why I'm here."

"I'm guessing it's not for the tea, but if you'd like to tell us I'm sure we'd be happy to listen."

She leaned forward, and I watched as the silver hair created a halo around her refined face and intelligent eyes. "I just wanted to apologize for my husband's actions; there was no excuse for the way he behaved."

"Oh . . ." I shrugged. "He was upset."

"Yes, but why?"

I thought about it. "Maybe you can tell us."

"There's something strange going on there."

I looked at Henry, just to make sure I wasn't the only one who wasn't following. "Where?"

Her eyes drew from the fire, and she looked at me. "We've got places in Texas, Santa Fe, Jackson, and now here."

"I'm still not following."

"Besides wanting to be near his energy concerns here and in North Dakota, Digger had this idea that he wanted to live near a reservation."

Henry smiled. "And what happened?"

She shook her head. "He met some actual Indians."

The Bear laughed. "We can sometimes be prickly."

"He was okay with the idea of giving Indians things; he just doesn't like the idea of them asking or, worse yet, demanding."

He nodded. "I see."

"It was different with Jaya. At first Harley was afraid to even tell us about her, but when he did, Digger asked if he'd bring her to dinner at the house and he did. I'll be honest with you, I was a little worried, but Digger was on his best behavior and the two of them got along famously." She glanced at Henry and then at me. "For a while."

"What happened?"

"That's just it; I don't know, and that's what worries me. I mean Digger suddenly decided that he didn't like her and that was that."

"Was this after the disappearance of Jeanie?"

"Shortly thereafter."

"But Harley dated Jeanie too?"

She waved a hand. "For a short period, so short that we never met her . . . Well, I never did, but I think Digger met her once when he went to pick up Harley at football practice and she just happened to be there."

"But your husband went and looked for her, along with the sheriff's department and search and rescue?"

"Everybody did."

The Bear stood and stepped toward the fire, warming his hands. "The changes that Jaya went through after her sister went missing appear to have resulted in her pushing everyone away. It is not surprising that she did the same thing to both your husband and son. Unfortunately, it would seem that your son took the more mature response."

She shrugged. "Digger is used to getting his way . . . I'm just trying to figure out why he behaved the way he did today."

"Does he know you and I dated?"

She glanced at me and then laughed. "Good God, no. That was a million years ago, Walt."

"Give or take a thousand. I just thought . . ."

"No, I don't think that's it."

"Then I'm at a loss." I spread my hands. "Maybe he was just angry about dragging his son's ATV out of the mud."

The Cheyenne Nation stretched and yawned. "Well, I will leave the two of you to it. I am not used to all this investigating and need my beauty sleep." He stepped to her, extending a hand. "Good night."

She shook and then watched him go. "I didn't say anything to offend him, did I?"

Dog sidled over and sat at my feet. "No, that's just one of the many wonderful things about Henry—if you piss him off, you'll be the first one to hear about it."

"I could use some more people like that in my life."

"Speaking of, how exactly is your life?"

"Lousy, how's yours?"

I laughed. "Actually, not so bad as of late."

"I assume you're seeing someone?"

"And why would you assume that?"

"You've got a regular job and all of your teeth, but I have to admit that I'm curious about that scar over your eye."

"Sounds like the bar is pretty low."

"You haven't been dating lately, have you?"

"Is that what you're doing these days, dating?"

It was silent for a moment, then she stood and walked away from the fire. "I think the problem is that I don't know what I'm doing." She turned and looked at me. "Digger and I have been married for almost thirty years."

"That's a good stretch."

"Maybe it's over."

"Well, I'd be sorry to hear that."

"Would you?" She stepped closer. "You never answered my question."

I stood. "Which one?"

"Are you seeing someone?"

"I think so."

"Think?"

"I am."

She came much closer and handed me an empty can. "That's too bad." She started to turn away but then stopped and looked back at me. "They say there's always the one that got away, the one you wish you'd kept. I never believed in that until I saw you again, and I've got to tell you that I truly wish you were free."

"Well, I'm deeply flattered—and sorry."

"Not near as much as I am."

Dog and I watched as the shining import turned around and purred into the night, pulling out onto the main road and rocketing away. I reached down and gently tugged on one of his ears as he stood and stretched. "This is a very dangerous world we live in, my friend."

He wagged in agreement and followed in my trail as we went inside, where it was safe.

Taking advantage of a down day in the Lady Morning Stars' schedule, I drove back into Wyoming and parked in my usual spot at the converted Carnegie library behind the Absaroka County Courthouse. There was only one other vehicle in the parking lot, a battered Chevy half-ton with gray primer on the rear quarter panel that gave it the appearance of a metallic Appaloosa.

Before I could get up the stairs, a familiar voice rang down from above. "It's Saturday."

I called back. "Very good."

"And I don't know where your dog is."

"With me."

"Only an hour on the job, and I'm already solving mysteries."

Making the landing, I walked the rest of the way over to the dispatcher's desk and looked at the full-time smartass and part-time dispatcher. "You the only one here?"

He pushed a bunch of the dark hair from his face. "Except for the hungover guy in the holding cell who tried to use the drive-through at the Colonel Bozeman restaurant last night."

I leaned on the counter as Dog sidled around and got a back scratch. "The Bozeman doesn't have a drive-through."

"Exactly." Barrett Long put down the Filson catalog he was studying. "How's the Home-Rez?"

"Hopping."

"You see my sister?"

Turning the logbook, I studied the entries, but things appeared to have been quiet in my absence. "A couple of times."

"She her usual, charming self?"

I turned the book back. "Yep."

"When do I get a gun?"

I stared at him. "Are you going to ask me that every time you see me?"

"Yes."

"It makes me not want to give you a gun."

"We had a deal."

"That's before I knew you were a gun nut."

"Easy for you to say, you've got one."

"The deal was that you'd finish school over in Sheridan and have a trial period as a dispatcher till spring, and then we'd discuss the possibility of you being a regular deputy. What, you don't like being a dispatcher?"

"I like being a dispatcher fine—I have a lot of reading time and my GPA has gone up two percentage points."

"Congratulations." I pushed off the desk and started for my office but then veered toward the coffeepot, which I lifted, feeling the decided lack of weight.

"But I still want a gun."

Placing the pot back down, I retreated into my office. "How 'bout you make some coffee instead?" At my desk I stared at the phone and wondered if it was too early to call the assistant attorney general of the state of Wyoming, who was probably feeding my granddaughter right then.

I picked up the phone and dialed, then two rings. "Longmire residence."

She sounded exactly like her mother, and my heart twitched as it always did. "Is this a Longmire?"

"Last I looked."

"How is the heir apparent?"

There was some jostling and a little yammering in the background. "On a hunger strike, as we speak."

"What's for breakfast?"

"Tapioca pudding."

"Pudding, for breakfast?"

There was silence. "Look, if you want to come down here and try and get her to eat . . ."

"Sorry, sorry . . ."

There was a clang of metal like the sound a spoon might make landing in a partially filled bowl. "So, what are you doing at the office on a Saturday morning?"

"How do you know I'm at the office?"

"Caller ID." I listened as she adjusted the receiver in the crook of her neck.

"I've been up on the Rez with Henry."

"The threats against the Cheyenne basketball player?"

"Yep."

"Any leads?"

"Leads?"

"Isn't that what you gumshoes call it?" I could hear her thinking. "*Gumshoes*, where does that phrase come from?"

"Soft-soled or galoshes used by police detectives in the nineteenth century, so they could be stealthy."

"So, got any leads, shamus?"

"A couple, but I'm not sure if I'm being much of a success . . ."

"These types of cases take time, or so my badge-wearing father once told me."

"No, I think one of the reasons I was asked by Lolo Long to take part in this investigation was to draw some media interest, and so far, I don't think I've had much of an effect."

"You, courting the media?"

"I know, right?"

"Maybe I can help. I know a guy down in Denver who works for the *Post*. His name is Corey Simon and I could ask him tonight. I know he's written about the plague of missing Native women cases in the West, so he might be interested."

"What's he doing in Cheyenne?"

"You caught that, huh?"

"You said ask, not call."

"He's coming up, and we're going out to dinner; no big thing."

"What are you going to do with Lola?"

"Coming with."

"I like him already."

"Don't get your hopes up, it's just a date." She paused, and I could feel her smiling. "With a two-year-old."

Breakfast at the Busy Bee Cafe was always an adventure. Sometimes the special was the usual, or the usual the special, which, as near as I could tell from years of experience, led to an unending number of permutations.

Dorothy, the owner and operator, held her pad, pencil poised.

"I'm thinking."

She glanced around at the overcrowded dining room of the little restaurant alongside Clear Creek. "You're going to get toothpicks and a glass of water here in a minute."

"You know, I don't think ordering breakfast used to be this complicated."

"Brechtian, isn't it?" I turned in time to see my undersheriff and cultural liaison seat herself on the stool beside me. She wore civilian clothes. "Why don't you just have the usual?"

Dorothy sat a cup of coffee in front of her.

"Because I'm never sure what the usual is."

"So, in a way it's kind of symptomatic for life in general—making plans and then dealing with the shit as it happens." She glanced at Dorothy. "I'll have the usual."

Writing on the pad, I got Dorothy's attention before she whisked herself away, holding up two fingers. "I'll accept my fate."

Vic Moretti rolled up the sleeves of her flannel shirt and added the ubiquitous five sugars into her buffalo china mug, lifting it in a toast. "Here's to fate."

I lifted my own mug to my lips. "So, what you're saying is that all the worry is for naught?"

"Yeah, fuck it."

I shrugged and took a sip. "If there's really nothing more to life than a good cup of coffee, might as well make the best of it since it's all we have?"

"Exactly."

Placing my mug back on the counter, I looked at her. "You wake up on the philosophical side of the bed this morning?"

"I've had a lot of time on my hands." She stared at me in the mirror on the bar back behind the counter, the tarnished gold eyes like searchlights. "How goes the case on the Rez?"

"The Lame Deer Lady Morning Stars are not exactly burning up the court."

"Nowhere to go but up?"

"That's one way of looking at it." I glanced at her. "Did you play basketball?"

She rolled her eyes. "Some."

"Why am I not surprised?"

She shrugged. "I had four brothers."

I thought about my late son-in-law, one of those brothers. "Michael play ball?"

"They all did, so I did." She smiled. "Michael coached kids' tournaments in the city. He was really good at it—I never had the patience . . ." She grew quiet for a moment and then sniffed and continued. "So, any clues on who's leaving the X-rated notes for the phenom?"

"A few."

"Bobby Knight?"

"Jaya Long had a sister, Jeanie, who disappeared a little over a year ago. Went missing on the road between Billings and the Rez."

"How old?"

"Seventeen."

"Any leads on that?"

"A couple, the most disconcerting one being the Éveohtsé-heómėse."

"Gesundheit."

I shook my head. "Cheyenne for the Wandering Without. I had a talk with a Crow rancher, who told me the story of seeing the girl the night she went missing. He thinks she might be haunting one of his fields."

She stared at me.

"Honest."

"Any others?"

"A white-supremacist father and an old girlfriend who's married to an official ass whose son dated Jaya at one time."

"Come again?"

"A white-supremacist father . . ."

"No, wait . . . The 'old girlfriend' part."

Two stacks of golden-brown blueberry pancakes arrived. They were gleaming with melted butter, a small pitcher of maple syrup on the side. I looked up at Dorothy. "This is the usual?"

"Nope, we were out of the usual, so I made the executive decision to give you both the special. Bon appétit."

I unrolled my knife and fork from my napkin. "Connie Harper Wainwright, who took me to a Sadie Hawkins dance back in high school."

"You have an old girlfriend who lives in Lame Deer?"

"Closer to Colstrip, actually."

"What, she's a miner?"

"Married to an oil millionaire."

"So, she did better than you."

I ignored the remark. "She has a son who dated Jaya."

She poured more than the legal amount of syrup on her cakes. "He on your list?"

"Actually, no; he seems like a stand-up kid."

She cut off a chunk and shoved it into her mouth, talking through food. "Chief Long happy with your progress?"

I poured on a reasonable amount of syrup and then took a bite. "Not really, but I spoke with Cady this morning, and she put me on to a reporter from down in Denver who might be able to circle the wagons on the missing women."

"So, more pressure."

"I guess." I sipped my coffee. "I figure it's got to be the same person who took Jeanie who's threatening Jaya."

"Sound logic." She chewed and then turned to look at me again. "So, does the Bear think the Wandering Whoozit did it too?"

"I think he just wants to go beat up the white supremacists."

She nodded and chewed, still in a philosophical mood. "Always tempting to go punch a Nazi."

"You didn't bring me anything?"

"Feed yourself." Vic continued up the steps, walking past our earnest, new dispatcher and toward my office.

I stopped and leaned on the counter and watched as Barrett scratched Dog's head. He looked at me. "It's still Saturday."

"Right." I smiled. "Do you want to go get something?"

He glanced toward the office. "No, I just like giving her shit."

"You live dangerously, Troop." I pushed off the counter and continued to my office. Entering, I sat behind my desk and stared at my undersheriff as she lodged her boots on the edge. "What?"

"It's no fun around here when you're not here."

"I shouldn't be too much longer up on the Rez; I don't see as how I'm accomplishing anything."

"That's how you always feel, and then all hell breaks loose."

Barrett appeared in the doorway with two Post-its in hand but was momentarily distracted when he reached for the doorknob. "Why is there no doorknob on your door?"

"I like it that way."

He glanced at the notes in his hand. "Are you here to work?"

I reached out. "If I have to."

Vic intercepted and sat back in my guest chair, flicking her fingers at him. "Git." Barrett shook his head and disappeared as Vic started to read to me, but then stopped, calling after him. "Troop, you have the worst fucking handwriting I've ever seen." He appeared in the doorway again as she handed him one of the sticky notes. "What the hell does that say?"

He looked at it, and I had to stifle a laugh when he turned it upside down. "I didn't write this."

"Then who did?"

"The old guy."

She turned to me and then back to him. "What old guy?"

"The one with only one leg."

"Lucian Connally?"

"Yeah, him."

Vic sighed. "This is just his name, what did he want?"

He gestured toward me. "He wants him to come back and play chess with him."

"I thought you were playing chess with him?"

"I was, but he said I cheated—which I don't. He plays slow, and he talks all the time. I play street chess. I learned how to at the Boys & Girls Club up in Lame Deer, fast chess, you know . . . ? Anyway, he gets frustrated because I won't talk the whole time, I just play."

"He's got a lot of stories it might not hurt you to hear."

He smiled. "I listen to him, just not while I'm playing."

I leaned back in my chair. "He's as old as Lonnie. Maybe you should take it easy on him?"

"That's disrespectful." He started to go and then stopped to look at me. "Someday we'll play against each other, and I wouldn't want you to take it easy on me."

I stared back at him. "I'll remember not to."

He smiled and left. Dog came in and settled down by my desk like a one-hundred-and-fifty-pound bag of potatoes. "I guess I've been wearing him out up on the Rez."

"Well, he's not going to get a rest." She handed me the second Post-it. "Somebody turned the sprinkler system on and warped the Colstrip Colts' floor, so they had to schedule Monday's game for tonight in Lame Deer."

I took the note and saw Tiger Scalpcane's name at the bottom and slumped back in my chair. "Tonight."

"Tough, being on the Lady Morning Stars bandwagon."

I tossed the tiny square of paper onto my desk. "I've forgotten how exhausting young women can be."

"Kind of dramatic, are they?"

"Somewhat."

"I knew this was going to be trouble." She called over her shoulder. "Hey, asshat, get in here."

A moment later Barrett appeared in the doorway. "What?"

She glanced back at me. "That thing you mentioned, maybe the kid here has heard of it?"

I looked up at the young Cheyenne. "Ever heard the term *Éveohtsé-heómėse*?"

The smile faded, and he folded his arms over his chest. "Why?"

"Was that a yes?"

"Yeah, why?" He didn't move. "My sister put you up to this?"

I glanced at Vic and then back to him. "What are you talking about?"

"The hunting camp thing."

"You've got me—I have no idea what you're talking about."

"My sister didn't tell you the story?"

"No."

He leaned against the doorjamb and stuffed his hands into his pockets. "When I was in my first year in high school, I went out to elk camp near Chimney Rock, south of Livingston in the Gallatin National Forest, with some buddies of mine. I was about sixteen. I had some free time in the evening and went out on my own with a .308 of my dad's to see if I could spot a bull." He came in and leaned against the wall, looking out the window at the gray skies. "I was following a ridge when it dropped off into this canyon, rocky with a lot of trees. It was getting late, but I saw this elk running in there, and I thought if I could follow him, I might get a shot off." He shook his head. "I dropped down through the rocks trailing that damn bull and finally reached the bottom, but by then it was really getting dark. I mean, there was a little sun that got over the cliffs at the opening of the canyon, but then the rocks got higher."

"An elk, that's a lot of packing."

"Yeah, I know."

Vic glanced at me and then back to Barrett.

"I was young and stupid . . ."

My undersheriff smirked. "So, not that long ago?"

"It was like a doorway, you know. Just a great big doorway, all dark inside, and I thought there's nowhere that elk could've gone so he had to be back in there." He gestured with his hands, lifting them as if holding a rifle. "I brought the .308 up and started forward, but it was so dark I couldn't see hardly anything. I mean, I've got really good eyes, but I couldn't see back in there at all. I figured that if I spooked that elk there wasn't anywhere he could go but back out toward me. I'd just gotten to the point where the sunshine, what there was of it, stopped. I mean it was like a line, like a shore, you know?"

Vic studied him. "And?"

"There was something strange about it, and I couldn't figure out what it was, but then it dawned on me." He turned toward us. "No sound, I mean nothing. There was no birdsong, animals, or anything . . . You've been up there at twilight. There's stuff all over the place, raising hell because it's about to get dark and things that'll eat you come out." He glanced at Vic. "The birds, they sing like crazy before dark to let the other birds know that they're all right, and they do it again in the morning to let the other birds know they made it through the night."

"Maybe they just got quiet early."

"No, this was something else; I could just feel it. I remember looking up and seeing the trees swaying, the pines shimmering . . ."

"So?"

"There was no sound. Even the wind, the trees . . . Nothing, just dead silence, and it wasn't that my ears stopped working. It was like something was in that canyon with me, eating the sound, eating everything. I mean, I couldn't even hear my own breath or my heart and let me tell you it was beating." He swallowed. "I just stood there pointing that rifle into the darkness and thinking, *It's not enough, it's not enough*. I kept hoping that elk would show up in a minute and everything would go back to normal."

Both Vic and I stared at him, saying nothing.

"It was about then that I remembered my grandmother telling us about the Éveohtsé-heómėse—about how it came at those times when the light changes and that the animals get restless. People say the animals move at that point, looking for a place to bed down or move out to look for food, but my grandmother used to say that it was the Éveohtsé-heómėse and that it was hungry too. That the animals knew this, and they are desperate to avoid this thing."

"What did you do?"

"There was a ground fog creeping from the canyon at my feet, and I could feel it freezing me where I stood. Pulling loose, I stepped back and could see that the mist was filling the canyon, so I forced my feet to step back again. The only part of me that I couldn't control was my eyes. I couldn't help but look into that darkness, and I could finally see something struggling in there, attempting to get away. I knew it was that elk, and I never wanted to help something so much in my life. Whatever it was, I knew it was baiting me, trying to get me to reach in, but I knew if I did that, it would take hold of me and I would never see the daylight again." He aimed the imaginary rifle. "So, I did the only thing I could do, I closed my eyes and fired."

It was quiet in the office.

"It's funny, you know, you can close your eyes, but you can't close your ears." He dropped the imaginary rifle. "I heard the scream of that elk, but it didn't last long, almost as if something swallowed it whole. And then I ran, I ran for my life, and I remember it being dark, fully dark, as I scrambled out of that canyon. I ran all the way back to the campfire, and when I got there the only thing burning was a few embers. One of my friends looked up as I ran toward him. He stood and stared at me, asking where the hell I'd been. I asked him what he was talking about, and he pointed behind me. I was afraid to look, but when I did, I could see the sky lighting up and that it was dawn." He looked at us. "Just being near the Éveohtsé-heómėse cost me eight hours of my life. The old ones call it the Wandering Without, the nothing, the thing that takes and never gives."

7

I took the back route into Montana and drifted by the Tongue River Reservoir to the Rosebud Battlefield, where on June 17, 1876, the American Indian Wars hit a turning point when an unarmed warrior rode into a ferocious battle to save a brother.

I had plenty of time, so I pulled the truck to a stop; I let Dog out and stood by the entrance of the makeshift battlefield, very different from the Little Bighorn just up the road. There's no visitor center at the Battle of the Rosebud, just a bulletin board with a map, a trash can, and a lockbox with envelopes to deposit your eight dollars for day use. You can camp there overnight, but I had a basketball game to go to.

Nonetheless, something had pulled the wheel of my truck and called me to go the mile and a quarter up the gravel road.

There's no gift shop or trading post, just the gentle, rolling hills of the Bighorn country and a quiet stream that at one point had run red.

But that's not how the Northern Cheyenne remember it.

After paying the eight bucks, I followed Dog past the minimal signage by the gravel road, and we made our way toward the trees at the Rosebud Creek near Van Vliet's Ridge, and I looked back, the buffalo jump a scoured white in the afternoon sunlight.

Dog wandered down to the water and took a few laps before raising his head and looking at the cliffs along with me. "You better go to the bathroom. The facilities in the parking lot of Lame Deer high school aren't going to be as inviting."

He stared at me.

"Suit yourself."

In the hit-and-run experience of the Plains Indians, the Battle of the Rosebud was a long and bloody engagement. According to Captain Anson Mills, the Lakota and Cheyenne warriors put on a display of horsemanship that revealed them to be some of the greatest cavalry soldiers on earth.

One of them was a chief called Comes In Sight, who had had his horse shot out from under him in an area that was deemed as far too dangerous to attempt a rescue. Bullets from the wasichus were slapping the ground all around the young man. He finally accepted his fate and turned to sing his "death song" to General George Crook's troops, just as a lone rider broke from the Native ranks, making a beeline toward the injured man.

The troops sighted in on the rider and increased their volley, but the warrior continued to approach Comes In Sight at full speed. The rider whirled with superhuman agility and grasped the outstretched hand of the chief, pulling him from the ground and swinging hard to the left. The chief was pulled onto the back of the horse as a deadly hail of bullets whizzed after them like an angry swarm. Blasting through the wallows and back to safety, Comes In Sight slid off and looked up to discover that it was his sister, Mutsimiuna, Buffalo Calf Road Woman, who had saved him.

The amazing feat she performed that day rallied the Cheyenne in a counterattack that defeated Crook's forces, and the Cheyenne and Lakota forever referred to the skirmish as the Battle Where the Girl Saved Her Brother. Rumor on the Rez is that Mutsimiuna then fought alongside her husband, Black Coyote, and was the one who struck Custer with a club at the Battle of the Little Bighorn, knocking him from his horse.

Dog followed me as I walked up from the creek bank and crossed to the road, which I followed west.

I'd like to think that a woman such as this had a wonderful and lengthy life, but such was not the case. After eventually surrendering to the US, she and her husband and two children were relocated to a reservation in Oklahoma. They escaped in September 1878 but were recaptured, and her husband was sentenced to be executed. While Black Coyote was in prison, Mutsimiuna died of diphtheria and upon hearing this, he hanged himself.

Sometimes all it takes is one small act of heroism to chart a new path for history.

I thought about Jeanie One Moon, and how she hadn't had the opportunity for her moment of heroism, or had she and had it cost her life? That was the mystery and the tragedy of my life's work—sometimes you found the answers and sometimes you didn't.

Dog barked, and my reverie was lost.

He stood at a pipe barricade, looking to the north and the pale cliffs of the buffalo jump, panting and wagging his tail.

I looked out across the canyon but didn't see anything. "What's up?" He ignored me and took a step forward. I was starting to get worried and moved past the beast. "What?" I walked toward the edge of the canyon where the dead grass was stiff and high and the sunlight played off the conifers, dissipating the light like an impressionist painting.

I stared at him. "What's wrong with you?'

He barked again and then darted out toward the edge of the canyon, shooting off to one direction, disappearing over the side.

"Dog!" When I got to the edge, I could see him scrambling down a narrow trail toward the bottom of the canyon where a small stream threaded its way through. "Dog!"

Continuing to ignore me, he made it to the bottom, crossed where there was a narrow area of snow, and then began clawing his way up the other side as if possessed. I cursed and began finding my way down the canyon wall on the deer trail, scuffing my hands on the rocks. As I got to the bottom, I watched as he struggled his way up the other side and disappeared into the tree line. "Damn it."

I brushed the gravel from my bleeding hands and promptly fell into the creek. The thing was only about four feet wide but was covered by a skim of snow. I pulled myself up from the freezing water and slogged in the mud to the other side and onto the bank.

I looked upward but couldn't see anything. Cupping my hands to the sides of my mouth, I yelled again. "Dog!"

I stood, looked up the escarpment, and sighed.

I saw where the beast had scrambled his way up and began the long haul. This trail was a little wider and not quite as steep, or maybe I just had the advantage of knowing where my feet were. About halfway up I had to stop to catch my breath, and I was starting to appreciate the cooling effect of soaked clothing. Raising my hands again, I called out. "Dog!"

I still couldn't see anything.

Trudging forward, I did what I always did in these situations and simply began putting one sodden boot in front of the other until I finally made the edge of the buffalo jump. I stood there. The trees were thinner, and I could see farther into them from up close, but there was still no sign of Dog. Just a little panicked, I stumbled forward and looked in all directions, still seeing nothing.

I yelled again. "Dog!"

Still nothing.

Listening to the breeze pushing through the pines, I turned and looked back at where my truck was parked about a mile away. Yelling some more, I started into the trees, looking to my left and right. There was a slight rise, but then the landscape settled into a flat with stunted juniper trees and more high grass.

At the center of the ridgeline, there was Dog, sitting obediently looking at one of the junipers.

"What the heck are you doing?"

He glanced at me but then returned his attention to the bush.

When I was almost right behind him, I followed his eyes to where a weathered piece of cardboard was lodged in the trunk and a single ribbon tied to a branch, twisting in the breeze—bright red. I reached over and took the card from the bark and scrubbed at one of Dog's ears. Looking back across the canyon, I thought about Jeanie One Moon.

About a scarf.

About the color red.

I called Henry from the pay phone at The Big Store and then went outside to sit below one of the cottonwoods, a container of chicken and two drinks at my side. Jimmy Lane came around the corner and stopped when he saw me. He looked like he was ready to make a break for it. Our meeting in Billings hadn't been an altogether pleasant one, but I had nothing against the man, other than his white-supremacist friends. "Hi, Jimmy."

He didn't seem to know what to say to that, so I reintroduced myself even though I was pretty sure he knew who I was. "Walt Longmire, the sheriff from down in Absaroka County."

"Yeah, yeah." He studied my clothes. "How'd you get so dirty?"

"I had a fall." I guess I looked worse than I thought. "What are you doing here in Lame Deer?"

He cleared his throat and then looked around. "Game."

"Your daughter's basketball game?"

"Yeah."

"I'm sure she'll be happy to see you." I wasn't actually sure that was the case, but it was something to say. "Want to have a seat?"

"No." He glanced around. "I'm supposed to meet some people."

"Your friends I met at your place in Billings?"

"Um, no. Some other people."

"Are you sure you don't want to have a seat?"

"Yeah, I'm good."

I gestured. "Why don't you have a seat."

He still stared at me.

"No one can see us, so I don't think it'll ruin your reputation."

He sat, and I shoved him Henry's iced tea—I could always buy the Bear another. "There are a lot of theories about how you can tell if somebody is lying to you, did you know that?" He didn't answer but slid the cup the rest of the way toward him and stuck the straw in his mouth. "All kinds of indicators. The only ones that are really hard to catch are pathological liars because they have trouble themselves discerning between a lie and the truth—they blur those lines so much that they can't tell the difference anymore."

He pulled the straw from his lips. "So?"

"From our brief time together, Jimmy, I can say without reservation that you are not pathological at least when it comes to lying."

He shook some strands of hair from his face. "Cool."

"The downside of that is that when confronted with a trained investigator, I can pretty much guarantee they would be able to tell when you're lying."

"Are you a . . . What was it? Trained investigator?"

"Yep."

He rested his elbows on the tabletop. "So, what have I been lying about?"

"Oh, pretty much everything you've said in this brief conversation."

"Prove it."

"I don't have to, because I don't really care. I'm just curious as to why in the world you're not wanting to assist me in finding out what happened to your one daughter and attempting to protect the remaining one. I mean, these are your children."

"You ever lose a child, vóhpenáhkohe?"

"Yes, I have."

"Well, I've lost three."

"So, you don't care anymore?"

"I care more than you'll ever know."

"Then help me."

He sipped his tea and then pulled what looked to be a card from his shirt pocket. He handed it to me. "You interested in this?"

It was an old, sepia-toned postcard with scalloped edges. The photograph on the one side was weathered but still readable. There was an archway over a white picket fence with the words FORT PRATT and INDIAN TRAINING SCHOOL. There were about thirty young boys of different ages standing in what appeared to be the yard of a large, three-story building shrouded by trees in the background. The Native boys wore uniforms and matching caps, almost military in style, as they all stood at the gate at attention.

There was one boy, smaller than the others, who looked vaguely familiar. He was in perfect focus whereas the others were slightly blurred, as if they had moved at the instant of tintype capture.

I flipped the card over where there was an outline for a stamp, which had not been affixed, and a separation line to discern between the address and message, but the only thing written there was the number thirty-one.

I flipped it back over and studied it. "This Fort Pratt, is that here in Montana?"

He was about to say more when a large hand landed gently on his shoulder. Glancing back, he looked up to see the Cheyenne Nation looking down at him. "Hello, Jimmy."

He turned back to me before slowly standing. Henry's hand slipped from his shoulder. "I got things to do."

I tried to hand him the card back, but he shook his head. "You keep it, you might need it."

He started to go, but the Cheyenne Nation stepped in his way. "One more thing?"

He lowered the drink. "Yeah?"

"Do not ever call my friend here vóhpenáhkohe again."

He stared at the Bear. "You know, I know you scare a lot of people, but they've all got something to lose. Me, I got nothing. So, I'm what they call a . . . What is it?" He glanced at me. "Free agent." His eyes went back to the Cheyenne Nation. "Don't try and scare me, Standing Bear. I got nothing behind me and nothing in front of me—nothing everywhere I look. Just a big fat zero." Lane stared at him a moment and then turned, walking back toward the front and disappearing around the corner.

Henry sat, and I gave him my iced tea. "What's *vóhpenáhkohe* mean?"

"Polar bear." He sipped, taking the postcard from me and studying it. "Kind of funny, actually."

The Lady Morning Stars were down ten points at the half, and I was pretty sure Harriet Felton was going to have an aneurysm. The team wasn't exactly jelling. Even though Jaya was hitting from just about every part of the court, she wasn't passing or assisting. It was looking more and more as if the Lady Morning Stars were headed for another defeat, which would put the team in desperate straits with its chances for the state tournaments.

"There haven't been any more notes?"

"No."

I glanced across the crowd and was surprised to see Harley Wainwright with a few young friends up in the corner near the rafters. He saw me spotting him and waved, so I nodded back. "Maybe if they keep dropping in the standings, the bad guys will lose interest."

"That is reassuring." He glanced at my clothes, not for the first time. "You have not said what happened to you."

I glanced down at my somewhat disreputable appearance. "Dog decided to take an unscheduled sojourn down at Rosebud Creek." He watched the game as I explained what had happened, finishing with the color of the ribbon that was tied to the tree.

"Red."

"Yep."

"What kind of condition was it in; did it look like it had been there long?"

"Yep. Tattered and threadbare. But still a vibrant red."

"Did you leave it on the bush?"

"The prayer flag?" I glanced at him. "You're not supposed to take those things off, right?"

"No, you are not supposed to."

"But there was something else I did take." He turned to look at me as I reached into my shirt pocket. I pulled out the cardboard square and handed it to him.

He held the Mallo Cup Play Money card in his hands, his eyes widening just a bit. "You found this there also?"

"Lodged in the bark of the tree where a branch had grown around it. I tore it a bit getting it out."

He flipped it over. "Old."

"Yep."

"Very old, but still readable."

"I know."

He handed it back to me.

"Your spiritual guardian is back on duty."

I returned the card to my shirt. The Bear's reference to Virgil White Buffalo, an individual who had appeared and reappeared in my life as of late and an entity that even I was unsure of being either alive or dead. "If you believe that, which I don't really, why do you suppose?"

"Perhaps Virgil feels the Éveohtsé-heómėse is more than you can deal with on this plain of existence." He glanced at me. "You have many enemies—some of whom you have sent over to the other side."

"So?"

"The Éveohtsé-heómėse is a collective of unsettled souls, those unable to make the crossing to the Camp of the Dead because they feel their dealings with this world are not yet done, or they do not wish them to be."

"What, you're afraid my dead enemies are getting together and forming a union to gang up on me?"

He breathed a soft laugh. "Virgil is."

I thought about it. "Then why would they gang up on, say, Jeanie?"

"To bring you here."

"You believe that? Honestly?"

"That is the difference between us—I believe in everything until proven, whereas you believe in nothing until proven."

I shrugged. "That's how I make my living."

"It is depressing."

"Yep, sometimes."

"How do you explain that the card is still readable?"

I pulled the thing back out and examined it, the blue ink faded but indeed legible. "I don't know, the tree kept the sun off it?"

"In the winter?"

"What do you want me to say, it had an otherworldly, spiritual, protective shield surrounding it?" He ignored me and continued watching the game. "I'll tell you what I'm beginning to think: that at one time, Virgil ran up and down the Bighorn Mountain Range sticking these things all over the place."

"Simple as that?"

"Simple as that." The game was winding down to its last minute, and with a four-point advantage Colstrip was playing a conservative game, eating up the clock.

Jaya made a desperate cut between two of the green and gold players, getting the ball and driving for the opposite side of the court. The girl who had gotten the ball stolen from her started after Jaya at a high rate of speed, but it was doubtful she would catch the phenom before she got a shot off.

Jaya had lifted a one-arm layup and was just coming back to earth when the Colstrip player launched into her back, sending her into the concrete blocks. The Colstrip girl was on her in an instant, pounding her back and head with clenched fists as the referees moved in that direction, perhaps not as quickly as they should have. It was about then that another combatant entered the fray, a wild-looking woman with a folding chair.

"Oh, shit." I was off the bench, but the Bear was already in the aisle and halfway down the bleachers as I stumbled after him.

Theresa One Moon brought a chair down on the back of the Colstrip player, knocking her off her daughter, and the whole gymnasium erupted. I tried to get to the court, but crowds of people were surging in the same direction. Over their heads I could see Lolo Long coming in from the baseline. She grabbed Jaya's mother and pulled her away before she could do too much damage. Henry arrived in time to separate the Colstrip player from Jaya and place her against the wall as the spectators crowded in. I could see that he had created a buffer zone, which widened as he turned toward the throng.

Now the referees were attempting to clear the area to get the game started again. Henry held the Colstrip player, and I muscled in to pick up Jaya from the floor. She was bleeding profusely, and I pulled a handkerchief from my pocket and put it over her nose. I tilted her head back as she tried to bat my hands away.

Harriet came over, trying to get a look at her player. "Is she all right?"

"I think so. I've seen a lot of broken noses before, and I think this one is okay."

Jaya attempted to pull my hands away again, but I held her firm. "Do you want to shoot the foul shots or not?"

I continued to hold her head back, but she stopped squirming and nodded.

I turned to the coach as the crowd filtered back toward the stands, and we both watched the Bear as he released the other girl to the ref, who escorted her to the opposite bench with an arm movement indicating that she was being thrown from the game.

I became aware of a weight on my arm as Jaya leaned on it. Standing still as things were swept back to normal, I glanced at her and saw that her eyes were closed. "Are you okay?"

The eyes stayed closed, but she nodded. One of the referees approached Harriet.

"Can she play?"

"Try and stop her."

The ref smiled and turned toward the officiating table signaling one and one.

"You've got to be kidding." He turned to look at me. "That was the most blatant foul I've ever seen."

"And who are you?"

"Walt Longmire, Absaroka County sheriff."

He paused.

I tilted my head at him. "Get going, she's going to make both of them anyway."

With one last look, he departed to confirm with the opposing coach, and it looked like the game was about to recommence.

I turned back to Jaya. "You all right?"

Her eyes opened, and she nodded. I lowered her head, still keeping the cloth at her nose, which continued to bleed. She took the handkerchief from my hand, held it at her nostrils, and smeared the blood on her face.

Harriet tried to give her a hand towel, but Jaya held on to the handkerchief and started toward the top of the key where the rest of her team congregated.

We moved off the court as I glanced up at the scoreboard, then the clock. The Lady Morning Stars had thirty-four seconds to win, place, or tie.

I took a seat next to the Cheyenne Nation. "Was that my imagination or did Theresa One Moon just now re-create the offense that got her four weeks in the Yellowstone County jail? What the heck is she doing out in the free world?"

"Good behavior."

I looked toward the lobby but could see neither Theresa nor Lolo. "Well, that didn't last long." Turning back toward the court, I watched as Jaya continued to hold the now saturated handkerchief to her face. The referee was studying her, but Jaya waved him away, removing the cloth as the players lined up on either side of the key.

She stuffed the sodden handkerchief in the elastic band of her shorts, took the ball from the ref, and stepped up to the foul line. She swiped at her nose with the back of her hand, causing it to bleed even more. Bouncing the ball once, she swept her arms up like a swan taking flight, the ball reverse spinning as it swished through the net. The other players moved into the lane, but she didn't budge an inch.

The ref retrieved the ball and then raised a finger, handing it back to Jaya as she spun it in her hands, blood smeared along the lower half of her face. A few of the Colstrip players smirked at her, but she took a moment to hold the ball in one hand before wiping the blood away with the palm of her other. Starting to reach for the handkerchief again, she realized the officials were likely to call a time-out, so instead she placed the bloody hand over the lower part of her face, palming her mouth. The war-paint effect was dramatic as she turned to the Colstrip players, and finally, the stands, shouting. "Kómáhe!"

The Cheyenne in the stands cheered as the Bear leaned toward me and translated. "A bit more."

I shook my head as she turned back to the basket and sank the second shot like a forgone conclusion.

The Colstrip players moved into position quickly in hopes of ending the game and getting out of there as fast as possible, aiming to retain possession or lure the Cheyenne players into fouling them. There was one Lady Star in particular who was likely to try to exact some sense of vengeance.

The ball came in, and the Colstrip player tried to ease it up the sideline.

Harriet screamed at her players as the seconds ticked by. "Don't foul them, don't do it!"

Jaya approached the half-court line, drifting in the direction of the oncoming player as the rest of the team set up a defense behind her. I listened to Henry's voice rumble in his chest "Steady."

Jaya's sole focus was on the ball as the seconds swept past, and you could see the nervousness in the Colstrip players as they grew closer together on a head-on trajectory.

"Steady."

As the Colstrip player crossed the half-court line, Jaya feinted in her direction and the ball handler panicked, palming the ball up to pass it away to another teammate who ran toward her on Jaya's right. Reading the player's move, Jaya lunged forward, slapping the ball away back toward the other basket.

The other players closed fast, but Jaya was in full stride, getting into position to win the game.

Bounding down the court with two players right on her tail, I watched as she stopped dead at the top of the key, the other two sliding past as she lifted the ball up and let it sail, the clock ticking down to two seconds as it left her hands.

About three hundred people came to their feet.

The ball arced through the air in what seemed like slow motion, and I was sure it was going to hit the backboard, but it didn't, instead striking the base of the metal hoop, which sent it skyward again, rubbing a little speed off on the glass.

It seemed to pause there, not moving for just an instant, and I watched as Jaya turned and walked toward the door at the far end of the gymnasium. It was as if she'd done her job, and there was nothing more to do.

Lunch pail.

The ball dropped through the hoop.

The gymnasium went ballistic.

Jaya Long was already gone.

Henry and I skirted the crowds celebrating at the base of the bleachers and followed Jaya's trail. The majority of the team was still out there on the floor, but Harriet was behind us as we made it to the locker room.

"That was something."

"Yes, it was." She smiled. "I'll go in and check on her to see if we need to get her over to the clinic."

I folded my arms and leaned against the wall. "Roger that." She disappeared inside, and I glanced at the Bear. "Think you could beat her?"

"Yes."

"Really?"

"Yes."

"Kind of sure of yourself."

He shrugged in a very sure way. "Yes."

The door reopened and Harriet looked at the two of us. "She's not in here."

Pushing off the wall, I sighed. "Maybe she just went home."

"She always takes a shower after a game."

I glanced at Henry, and we both turned, moving quickly toward the back door that led to the small parking lot where the coaches, staff, and Jaya Long sometimes parked.

I pushed through the doors and glanced around as a few snow flurries fell. Directly under a lamppost, haloed in the drifting flakes, was a '64 Buick Wildcat.

Henry got there first, and then confirming my fears, he glanced around.

Moving to the left, I reached to the small of my back and unholstered my .45. I looked to the glistening ramp that led toward the front of the school, and walking up it, I could see something lying in the middle of the road.

I kneeled and picked up the bloody handkerchief.

8

Theresa One Moon sat in the back of the tribal police chief's car, kicking the seat in front of her and screaming as Lolo Long looked around the parking lot.

"It's going to be okay. We've got an APB out and there's no way that anybody can get her off the Rez." Sheriff Gordo Hanson and Henry were now standing by me as Lolo dropped her hand and sighed. "We'll find her."

"Where?"

I turned to my fellow sheriff. "Gordo, do me a favor and get a look out for her father, Jimmy Lane, and another fellow by the name of Peter Schiller."

He shook his head. "Oh yeah, he's a special edition of asshole."

I nodded. "Well, he's running with Lane."

"You're kidding."

"Nope, and I saw Jimmy at The Big Store this afternoon, and he said he was meeting friends." I glanced at Henry. "Fill him in?"

He nodded and followed as Gordo moved back toward his unit. "Got it."

"Also, Henry, just for giggles call Connie Harper Wainwright and ask her where her son is this evening."

He stopped. "You think she might be with him?"

"He was at the game." Gordo smiled and shook his head as he

went about sheriffing with Henry, leaving me to deal with the tribal police chief.

"Harley was here?"

"Yep, he was up in the corner with some friends. Heck, maybe she's just out sneaking a beer with the old flame."

Lolo pushed off her car and glanced around, as if expecting Jaya to simply appear—stranger things had happened. "I hope that's the case."

I nodded toward the angry woman in the back of her cruiser. "What are you going to do with that one?"

"Send her back to Yellowstone County in probation violation."

"Let her go."

She looked at me. "Why?"

"She just got out, and she was defending her daughter."

"By beating a kid with a folding chair."

"Are the parents, coach, or student pressing charges?"

"Not that I am aware of."

"Let her go."

"Folding chair beatings are just the kind of things I'm supposed to be putting a halt to in this line of work, don't you think?"

"She's going to be dead from cirrhosis of the liver in a few months, give her some time out."

She folded her arms and studied me, finally turning and opening the door. "If you don't knock that shit off, I'm going to reach down your throat and yank out your lungs." Theresa One Moon stopped moving and didn't make a sound. "Get out."

The woman looked at Lolo, making sure it was her she was talking to.

"Yes, you. Get out of my car." As she climbed out, Lolo spun her and put her against the door and uncuffed her, taking her arm and pushing her toward me. "All yours."

I caught her, the alcohol fumes causing my eyes to water. "What am I supposed to . . . ?"

"You wanted her out—now she's out."

"Lolo."

She pushed past us and climbed in her car, hit the lights, and pulled away as we stood there. Theresa One Moon looked up at me. "So, you wanna go have a drink?"

At which point she leaned over and threw up on my boots.

Driving into Rabbit Town, I dimmed my lights and looked at the woman crouched against the passenger side door. "Do you have any idea where she might be?"

"She doesn't tell me things."

I nodded as we slowed in front of a neatly kept, pastel-colored house. "Is your mother expecting you?"

"Big Betty is always expecting me, otherwise she's forced to yell at my father, who just turns off his hearing aids." She looked out the window but made no effort to get out. "How 'bout I just sleep here?"

"Well, I'm probably going to be out looking for your daughter."

She settled in. "I'm cool with that."

"I'll probably need that seat for Henry."

"Oh." She struggled up to a seated position and looked into the back where Dog sat. "Well, I don't want to get in the way of the mighty Bear."

"He's doing a lot of work on your daughter's behalf."

Chuckling to herself, she reached back and stroked Dog's head. "Oh, I'm sure there's something in it for him."

"Why do you say that?"

She retrieved the hand and covered a yawn. "Because people don't do anything unless there's something in it for them."

"Like me?"

She turned her head and even though the eyes were a little wobbly, I think she finally made me out. "Yeah, like you."

"What am I getting out of it, other than vomit on my boots?"

She shrugged and looked coy, glancing out the windshield. "That police chief of ours, she's kind of hot, don't you think?"

I stared at her to let the conversation harden just a bit. "I suppose."

"You suppose, that's all?"

"If you're saying what I think you're saying, she's half my age."

She flipped her feet up on my seat, making herself more comfortable. "Yeah, well, that hasn't ever stopped any man I ever met."

I glanced at the posture. "Look, I know you think you've got the original franchise on grief, but there's a lot of it flying around these days and most of us just suck it up and do what we can to help each other, you know?"

"Is that what you're doing, helping out the lowly red man?"

"I'm trying to assist your daughter in getting through a rough time, which is in no way being helped by you. You've lost three children, maybe you need to focus on keeping the one you've got left alive?"

She stared at me for a very long time and then, surprisingly, smiled. "I think I'll go inside and get yelled at by Big Betty. As wholesale, free shipping of guilt-to-go, she's got you beat by a landslide."

I watched as she turned to open the door, just as somebody yanked it open from outside.

Big Betty One Moon, looking like Cerberus the Hound of Hades. She stood on the driveway, and even Dog backed away in the rear seat, realizing he was out of his weight class.

"Go somewhere else. You're not welcome here."

Theresa lifted a hand in introduction. "My loving family."

The large woman leaned forward, addressing me. "Take her somewhere else."

"I don't have anywhere else to take her, so I need you to take her so I can go look for your granddaughter."

Big Betty looked at her daughter. "I heard you made an ass out of yourself at the game tonight."

"I was protecting her, which is more than you ever did for me."

"Get her out of here."

Theresa spat in her mother's face. "Fuck you."

Big Betty grabbed Theresa by the hair and yanked her from the truck, both of them falling onto the driveway.

"Oh, boy." Throwing the door open, I came around the front in time to see Theresa plant a roundhouse punch into the side of Big Betty's head, only to be rewarded with a knee to the gut that caused her to fall on top of her mother.

I tried to pull them apart, but they were like two bobcats in a burlap bag. Theresa was now on top of Big Betty, and I grabbed her from behind just as she kicked off and threw her head back, catching me in the lip.

I was reaching up to assess the damage to my face as something hit me in the back and knocked me down on the partially snow-covered ground.

Big Betty was crawling on top of me in an attempt to get at her daughter, who was kicking at the both of us. I finally caught one of her legs in self-defense. Dog had leapt from the truck and clamped his teeth on Theresa's hoodie in an attempt to drag her away from me.

I was doing a pretty good job of containing the lower part of Theresa, but it was only a question of time before my face was going to be crushed into the stiff grass by the weight of Big Betty, which caused me to list sideways before falling like a tree. Theresa took advantage and jumped on Big Betty as Dog tried to pull her away by her sweatshirt, and I was starting to think that it was a lost cause when a jet of freezing water raced across all of us. Dog yelped and the women screamed, rolling toward opposite corners of the yard.

I looked up and could see a large man, backlit by the halogen light in the driveway, holding a limp hose dribbling water. "Sorry. When they get like that, it's the only thing that can keep them apart."

"Well, at least my boots are clean."

Leonard One Moon handed me a cup of coffee. "To warm you up." I stood underneath a basketball hoop that was affixed to the house. Dog was sniffing the edge of the concrete where the Battle of Rabbit Town had taken place. "Yeah, you gotta watch her when she's been drinking. I've lost a lot of shoes that way."

I sipped my coffee, trying to avoid the side of my lip that was swelling. "Are they going to be all right?"

"Oh, yeah. I've got a shower out there in my shop and a foldout mattress that Theresa can use . . . Besides, she'll be gone in the morning."

"Where?"

"Who knows, wherever she can find a drink." He caught my glance. "We've tried everything, but nothing works. The doctors up at the clinic in Billings say she'll be dead by spring, but short of locking her up in the basement, there just doesn't seem like there's anything we can do."

I nodded. "Any idea where your granddaughter might be?"

"Not really, but like I told you, if she left her car there at the school, then she's all right. She'd never leave that car alone."

"You're sure of that?"

"Yep."

"You give it to her?"

"My cousin Buddy got it from a friend of his, Philbert, who gave it to Jimmy, who handed it down to Jeanie." He leaned against the garage door. "When Jeanie went missing, we gave it to Jaya."

I glanced around at the house. "Nice place."

"Thanks, this was one of the first HUD ones on the Rez back in the seventies."

"Most don't look this good."

"I made a lot of improvements, including a bedroom for the girls on the back."

"Jaya shared a room with Jeanie?"

"Yeah."

"Do you mind if I take a look?"

He studied me. "Why?"

I thought about why I'd made the request. "I feel like I know Jaya a little bit, but I'm still trying to get a read on Jeanie."

"Don't you want to go out and look for Jaya?"

"Not really. I mean I'd like to, but I'm pretty sure there are a lot of other people who are more conversant with the area than I am, and besides, you seem to think she's fine."

"Harley Wainwright?"

I looked at him. "You know about that?"

He nodded. "I saw him at the game tonight."

"You were there?

"Yeah, Betty had a church meeting, so I went over like I always do. When I saw him in the stands, I started putting two and two together . . ."

"You think they're still dating?"

He shrugged. "Who knows?" As he turned and walked toward the house he glanced up at the hoop. "You know, I'm the one who put that thing up there for them, but sometimes I think I should've just put up a noose." He turned and started toward the door. "C'mon, I'll show you their room."

The house was spotless but overdecorated with a lot of country-crafty tchotchkes, the touches of Big Betty I was pretty sure; Leonard not striking me as a doily kind of guy.

The room was on the back side of the house and was larger than I would've thought. "Did you add this on?"

"I did. After we started getting an idea of what was going on with Theresa, I thought the girls should have a safe place to be."

I glanced around at the bright-yellow walls and laced curtains in a room a grandfather built for his granddaughters and wondered what kind of room my granddaughter would want. There were posters of basketball players on the walls. "You play?"

"I did, for Montana State Billings."

I raised a fist. "Go Yellowjackets."

"You?"

"No, football." I glanced around at the tidy room. "You haven't changed it much?"

"Not at all, just in case she comes back, or her sister decides to live here again—I want them to feel welcome, always."

"You mind if I look around?"

"No, the FBI and others went through the room a couple of times, but you're welcome." He threw a thumb over his shoulder. "I'm going to check on the bantam weights."

"I'll be here." As he went, I pulled out a chair from the only desk. Not really sure what I was looking for, I opened the top drawer; there was nothing there but a few loose sheets of paper and a couple of pencils. Pulling the paper out, I held it up to the light, which revealed nothing.

I replaced it and closed the drawer. I stood and walked over to the bookshelf, studying the titles, most of them about basketball, with a few scattered literary titles and books about Native issues. There was a double set of Peter J. Powell's *Sweet Medicine,* published by the University of Oklahoma Press, a set of books I had myself.

I slipped the first volume from the two-book slipcase and palmed the binding, opening to a random page. Gently closing the book, I attempted to put it back into the slipcase, but it was too tight. Pulling the second volume, I noticed there was something there inside, a small moleskin notebook along with some more pieces of paper.

I leafed through the sheets, finding exactly what I thought I would, the same threatening notes in the same slashing handwriting and same black Sharpie marker.

I looked at the notebook. It was worn with a ribbon wrapped around it, a red ribbon. The name on the cover was Jeanie One Moon. It's at this point in an investigation that you start making choices. Now, the correct choice would have been to go get Leonard and show the thing to him, allowing the family to decide whether or not to share the contents with the authorities. Then there was the fast track, where I untied the ribbon and took a look at the contents, for they would help me decide what to do.

Jaya Long walked down the hill beside a utility building with a power pole next to it. She looked around before drawing the keys from her pocket, at which point she opened the front driver's side door, slipped in, and put the key into the ignition.

"You should lock your car."

I thought for a moment that she was going to shoot through the roof of the rusty sedan. The shriek died in her throat as she turned to find me sitting in the back seat. "You fucker!"

"Language."

She collapsed against the door, pulling her hair from her face. "Fuck you."

"Do you know the entire state, county, and Rez are on the lookout for you right now?"

She swallowed, attempting to get her heart rate back to normal. "I'm allowed at least some privacy."

"Not when people are making death threats to you."

"Do I look worried?"

"You did a moment ago—I thought you were going to stick to the headliner."

"You scared me. Congratulations. Now get out of my car."

I leaned forward, resting my forearms on the seat. "Do you have any idea what you're putting the people who care about you through right now?"

She said nothing.

"Okay, you don't want to talk about that . . ." I flipped the small notebook onto the seat beside her. "You want to talk about this?"

She glanced at it but made no move to pick it up. "What's that?"

"Your sister's diary."

"Jeanie?"

"Yep."

She stared at it. "I don't know anything about that."

"Aren't you curious?"

"No."

"I was."

She turned in the seat, picked it up, and looked at me. "Where did you find this?"

"In your room at your grandparents' place."

"And you took it?"

"I asked your grandfather, Leonard, if it'd be okay."

"Did he look at it?"

"After I explained, he said he'd rather not."

She turned the moleskin notebook over, examining it. "If this is what I think it is, then I don't want anything to do with it."

"I can understand that, but in an official capacity concerning a missing person case, I need to ask you some specific questions about the information it contains."

"No."

"I can just hand it over to the FBI, or your aunt . . ."

"*Especially* no."

"Then talk to me."

She looked at the small notepad. "This has nothing to do with me."

"Nothing?"

Running her fingers over the black moleskin, she stared at the notebook.

"Did you know what was going on?"

"Of course I did."

"And you didn't think to come forward with this information when Jeanie disappeared?"

Her eyes grew fierce, and even in the dim light of the beaten sedan, I could feel the heat of them. "Have you ever made a promise? A real promise, one that you couldn't break, ever? One that you made to someone you loved more than anything? A promise you made to carry to your grave, long past theirs?"

I slumped back in the seat and felt more than a few springs collapse. "A few."

"Then you should understand."

She began to cry, and I handed her the only thing I had, the handkerchief, stiff with her own blood.

"Jeanie One Moon was having an affair?" I had waited until the right moment to give him the information, just before he was getting ready to make the five-dollar shot. "With Digger Wainwright?"

"It's all in the notebook."

He turned to look at me and started to say something, but didn't, his concentration completely blown.

"I've rarely seen you at a loss for words."

"I am currently at an utter loss."

"You gonna shoot that ball?" After all, I was in it for a half-sawbuck.

He shot, missing the rim—actually missing the rim and the backboard in its entirety.

Walking off the court, he pulled his wallet from his jeans as I waved him off. "Put it on account."

He sat on the bleachers beside me. "Digger Wainwright."

"I know." I turned to him. "And there's more."

"Why should there not be?"

"He paid for an abortion at a clinic in Billings."

"You checked this out?"

"I did."

"Now what?"

"I was hoping you would have some ideas."

He shook his head. "Who, pray tell, have you informed about this?" I said nothing, and he shook his head some more. "An exclusive group then?"

"For now."

"Are you going to tell Lolo Long?"

"That was the one person I was trying to think how I could *not* tell."

"It is your investigation."

"We're on a slippery slope here."

"Agreed." I stood and walked out onto the court to retrieve the wayward basketball that looked lonely out there. "So, what do I do with this privileged information, tell the tribal police chief so she can go out there with garbage bags, packing tape, and a shovel?"

"That would be the most likely result. Her, or his wife."

"There's an idea."

"There will be numerous individuals who will want to dig a grave for Digger." His head rose as I picked up the basketball and walked back toward him, spinning it in my hands. "Confront him?"

"Seems like the logical scenario—letting him have his say before the information becomes public record."

"He doesn't seem to enjoy our company."

"I do not care."

"Somehow, I knew that was going to be your response." I studied the ball. "We could kidnap him."

"Yes."

"I was kidding."

His eyes met mine. "I am not."

Leonard knew somebody who knew somebody who knew somebody who worked for Wainwright Industries and that is how things get done on the Moccasin Telegraph. The guy who was known to the guy who knew the guy who worked for Clarence said that Digger often frequented the Jimtown Bar, north of the reservation, on Sunday nights. We parked Rezdawg in the lot at the corner of the bar in which the stools were bolted to the concrete floor to dissuade patrons from beating one another to death with them and where I hoped the damned truck would start if need be.

No more than three minutes later, a one-ton turbo diesel dually that probably tipped the scale at over a hundred thousand bucks pulled into the parking lot, nudging up to the building as if it might move it. Digger Wainwright literally glowed in his pressed, white dress shirt and silverbelly hat, ducking his head for no apparent reason as he pulled open the heavy front door and went in.

"I guess we aren't going to do it before."

"He moves fast for a little guy." We sat there in the silence for a while. "So, where is Jaya?"

"Locked in her aunt's basement, awaiting transport to either a penal colony in Western Australia or military school in the Deep South."

"She was with Harley Wainwright?"

"Not confirmed but assumed."

"These Wainwright guys do a lot of teepee creeping." He unbuckled his seatbelt and cracked the passenger side door. "Let us go."

I watched as Henry slipped out. He closed the door and looked at me through the window that had fallen into the door. "What, you're bored?"

"I was out all last night, and I do not intend to be out all tonight."

"We're getting older." I reached back and petted Dog one last time and then climbed out the scaly door of the beat-to-shit truck. "The lengths I'm willing to go for our undercover efforts."

We walked toward the front entrance. "If you said nice things to her, she would run better."

"I'm not sweet-talking your crappy truck." I pulled the door open, a blue cigarette haze following the swing. "You think this is the only bar in Montana that still allows smoking?"

He said nothing, and I followed him in.

I was pleasantly surprised that the Jimtown Bar had undergone a makeover and now had such luxuries as stools that moved, gambling machines, a television, a pool table, and what was referred to as the *bitchin-kitchen*. "Things are looking up."

"It was that or burn it down."

There were only five patrons. The bartender smiled broadly at the Cheyenne Nation. He put a hand on the Bear's shoulder. "Henry Standing Bear. Man, what brings you all the way out here?"

"I heard this was the toughest bar in Montana."

He gestured around him. "Not anymore, man. We got civilized."

"A casino, huh?"

"Gotta make money." He glanced at me. "You the sheriff guy?"

"Off duty, so I guess I'm just a guy." We shook. "Walt Longmire."

"Gary Pine. I engage in adult supervision when the owner's not here."

Henry leaned in. "Now that you mention it, we are looking for a guy, Digger Wainwright?"

"Oh shit, man." He glanced around. "He's here, probably hassling Barbara in the back."

"Barbara?"

"The cook." He lip-pointed through the pick-up window toward what I assumed was the kitchen. "When he can't find a target out here, he heads back there."

"Mind if we talk to him?"

"Only if you promise to get him out of there; I'm waiting on two cheeseburgers and a tray of mini burritos." He gestured once again toward the end of the bar where a set of swinging doors braced a doorway.

Henry led the way as we made for the opening and peered over the slatted doors where Digger had the cook backed up against a counter, both her hands full with orders. His hands were on her waist and every time she moved, he moved with her, in what I'm sure he thought was an amusing rhumba move.

The Bear turned to me, speaking in a more than loud enough voice. "Do you suppose this is why we are not getting our cheeseburgers?"

Wainwright turned to see us, dropping his head and stepping away from the relieved woman, who took advantage of the situation to escape between us and into the bar at large.

"Mr. Wainwright, we'd like to speak with you."

He hitched his thumbs into his creased jeans, turning toward us but still not making eye contact. "I think me and my family have spoken to you about as much as we intend to."

"Well, some new information has come to light, and I think it might be best if we had a little chat."

He walked toward us. "I need to make a quick visit to the boys' room, if you two don't mind?"

"Certainly." We all walked back toward the main room, where he went in the bathroom, and I gestured toward a booth in the corner, away from everyone else. "You want to set up camp?"

"No, I would rather go stand by his truck to make sure he does not take to the air."

"I was planning on doing that."

He grumbled as he made his way toward the booth. "You always get to have the fun."

Turning, I went outside and leaned against the five-thousand-dollar grille guard. After a requisite three minutes, he appeared through the door at a fly, the locks disengaging with a chirp behind me as he hit the button on his key fob.

"Howdy."

He froze, looking first at me and then for another avenue of escape.

"Forget about us?"

"Um, no. I've got some medication in the truck I need to get."

"Okay." I followed him to the door and stood in the way of him closing it as he made a show of looking around in the center console where a shiny 10mm handgun lay among the detritus. His hand paused over it.

"I wouldn't do that, if I were you."

He turned to look at me as he pulled his cell phone from his pocket. "I've already called Gordo Hanson, and he's got a deputy on his way over here."

"Good, they can join in the conversation."

He blew out a considerable amount of air and looked at me skeptically. "Concerning?"

"Jeanie One Moon."

"It's not what you think."

Henry spun his gin and tonic on the surface of the table. "And what do we think?"

"That I took advantage of her."

I glanced at the Bear. "Sixty-three-year-old captain of industry and a sixteen-year-old girl from the Rez. I have to admit that's what I was thinking—is that what you were thinking?"

"It crossed my mind."

We both looked at him. "Are you aware of the laws concerning statutory rape in the state of Montana?"

The Cheyenne Nation interrupted. "Is that the course we are going to take? I thought we would just get two shovels and tell his wife."

"As I recall she's got a temper."

"Now, hold on here, fellas." He slumped back in the booth. "What is it you want?"

"The truth."

"Money would be easier." I stared at him, and his eyes dropped to the table. "She was a lonely girl, and I was just trying to help . . ."

"By impregnating her?"

Digger looked at Henry with his mouth hanging open and then looked at me. "Good God, is there anything you don't know?"

"Yep, why?"

He started to speak but then stopped and started again. "It was just one of those things that happened."

"Like the cook back there?"

He folded his arms and said nothing for a few moments. "I know what you think of me."

Henry smiled. "No, I do not think you do."

"Was she dating your son at the time?"

"That's how it all started." His eyes, pleading. "She and Harley had a fight at one of those damn ballgames, and I drove her home. I didn't mean for anything to happen, but it did . . ."

"Like with the cook?"

"Damn it, will you two lay off with Barbara? I was just foolin' around with her. Heck, she wouldn't know what to do if I didn't come on to her." He sighed. "Jeanie was like a daughter to me. I mean after the thing happened."

Henry leaned against the wall, placing an elbow on the table and propping his chin up with a very large fist. "You mean after you had sex with her."

The air went out of Digger. "Um, yeah. She was having a rough time with a lot of things and afterward we'd just talk on the phone. That's all, just talk."

"What was she having trouble with?"

He glanced at me but said nothing.

"You realize this puts an entirely different role for you in Jeanie's disappearance?"

"Now, wait just a minute."

"As near as I can tell from the information I got from Billings and from Jeanie's diary . . ."

He leaned forward. "Diary?" he hissed. "A diary, for Christ's sake?"

"A little black book actually."

He yanked his expensive hat off and threw it on the seat beside him. "What, are they going to publish it in the *U.S. News & World Report*?"

"If you don't start telling us everything you know, and I mean everything, then you're going to be talking to somebody else in a more official capacity. I want you to take a moment and think about how the timbre of this conversation might change if Tribal Police Chief Lolo Long were here questioning you."

His eyes widened a bit and he cleared his throat.

"What, or more important, who was Jeanie having trouble with?"

"Her father and mother were a constant source of problems, especially her father, who had these friends of his from prison . . ."

"Pete Schiller one of them?"

"Yeah, big, scary-looking fucker."

"He's on our radar. Who else?"

"A fellow by the name of Artie Small Song." Henry and I looked at each other. "You've heard of him?"

"We have, but what does he have to do with Jeanie?"

"Spooky sonofabitch. He was peddling some kind of wilderness religion, and she went to a meeting and started getting together with him every once in a while—she got kind of strange after that."

"Strange in what way?"

"Just talking about how there wasn't any reason for anything and that nothing meant anything."

"Funny, Artie never struck me as the religious type."

The Bear leaned in. "This religion, what was it called?"

"I don't remember, it was in Cheyenne."

"The Éveohtsé-heómėse?"

"Say, yeah, that's it." Wainwright rubbed his face with his hands and collapsed into the red-pleather seat. "Look, are you sure I can't just pay you two off?"

9

The Cheyenne Nation eased back in his camp chair and put a hand out to warm it, his spread fingers looking as if he might be holding an imaginary basketball, or somebody's skull. "That is the problem with people who have too much money, they forget that there are some things and people that are not for sale."

I looked across the fire at him. "You think he's telling the truth?"

"No, at least not all of it, but the part about the Éveohtsé-heómėse religion is very interesting."

I sipped my beer and trailed a hand down to pet Dog, who lay on his side, his huge ribcage slowly rising and falling like a furry bellows. "Our Lady of the Wandering Without?"

"A nihilist movement that preys upon reservation youth." He sighed. "That concerns me."

"Artie Small Song worries me. Every time something unsavory happens here, he turns up like a bad penny. I don't like him—and I've only met the guy once."

"His mother is still around."

"She's the only one that worries me more than he does.

"So, I guess the next step is to go talk to her in lieu of Artie?" Henry nodded, staring into the fire with a little more intensity than I liked. "What?"

"The Mallo Cup coupons—they also worry me."

"In what way?"

"Somehow, Virgil White Buffalo is enmeshed with this, and I am not sure that is good."

"Who for?"

His eyes rose to mine through the curtain of dark hair, the few silver strands looking electrified. "For Virgil."

I laughed as Dog stood and walked away from us toward the outer light of the fire. "Virgil is seven feet tall and, according to you, traverses planes of existence like walking from room to room."

"That does not mean that he is indestructible. The Éveohtsé-heómėse is a collective of unsettled souls and carries the weight of the many, like your Biblical Legion, gathering strength through each consciousness it devours, like trophies." He turned to me. "In any sport, say chess—how many moves do you think ahead?"

"As many as I can."

"As any warrior would."

"Meaning?"

"The Éveohtsé-heómėse takes Jeanie One Moon to get you and then takes you to get to the ultimate unsettled soul . . ."

Virgil.

I thought about the giant Crow medicine man as I stood and walked out to where Dog seemed preoccupied with something, looking into the darkness of the forest between the two cabins. "How many souls do you think we're talking about?"

"We are perhaps, even with our limited numbers, speaking of millions of disturbed, damaged, and wicked souls, and in that is their power, the strength of many—chaos." His eyes went back to the fire.

I stood there, listening to myself breathe. "Okay, let's pretend there's any sense to this; what the hell can I do to protect Virgil?"

"Walk away."

"The one thing I can't do." I took a few steps back toward him. "This stuff really has you worried."

"The Éveohtsé-heómèse should not be underestimated. Imagine playing chess against a collective of millions of intelligences."

I shrugged. "If they are what you say they are, we have an advantage."

"Which is?"

"We're consumed by neither rage nor sorrow." I looked up at those self-same stars. "Henry, I don't think God took Jeanie One Moon, any more than I think the Devil or boogeyman is trying to take Jaya, or Virgil White Buffalo."

I watched him frown.

"I'm sorry, but I don't believe in the things you believe in, Henry."

He nodded. "I know that, but I respect your belief in humanity, if for only one reason."

"What's that?"

"It makes you very resolute."

"Is that a compliment?"

"Sometimes." He stood and stretched. "So, what do we do about Digger Wainwright?"

"Civil, not criminal."

"Statutory rape."

"Of a girl who's been missing for more than a year. We find her, and I'll be glad to give everything I know over to the local authorities."

"So, what happens with Jeanie One Moon stays buried with Jeanie One Moon?"

"You want to make a public announcement about it? What good is that going to do, Henry?"

"It is not a question of good, it is a question of truth."

"One case at a time." I sipped the last of my beer.

He shook his head, studying me and finally smiling the paper-cut smile. "You are using him as bait."

I shrugged. "He doesn't do us much good up in Deer Lodge."

"It might scare him a bit."

"I think he's pretty scared right now."

He nodded. "I want to speak with Artie Small Song and you want to speak with . . . ?"

I thought about it, watching my breath cloud out from my mouth. "The other three people who were in the van that night." I finished my beer and crushed the can in my hand, reaching down with the other to pet Dog.

There was nothing there.

"Dog!" Walking along the path behind the cabins, I followed the beam of my Maglite as Henry took the smaller path to our right, both of us calling after the beast.

The ground rose ahead. I saw no prints giving an indication as to where the monster could've gone. I knew the Bear was to my right, but he'd chosen to not take a flashlight, even though I'd watched his hand slip to the small of his back and the glint of his bowie knife sparked in the moonlight as he'd disappeared.

Stumbling, I'd caught my balance with a hand on a lodgepole pine. I stood there in the darkness, moving the beam in a sweeping motion. Unlike the Cheyenne Nation, stealth was not my strong suit. Dog had probably been distracted by a Western cottontail or a chipmunk and was out there now trying to find his way back.

Then I thought about his actions earlier in the day down at the

Rosebud Battlefield and how he'd seemed almost possessed. Maybe the Crow medicine man was out there, somewhere in the darkness, giving Dog a good pet before sending him back to me.

Funny how your attitude about spirituality could change when the chips were down.

Pushing off, I started up the trail again, but now I found my hand on the holster at my side, thumbing off the leather strip that secured the large-frame Colt and drawing the 1911 from my holster.

There was some noise up ahead where the trail opened a little before coming to the edge of what looked like a canyon, dropping off into the darkness. I thought about the story my new dispatcher had told in my office, of chasing the elk before having it disappear into nothingness. I got to the edge of the drop-off and stood there, passing the beam over the canyon as far as it would reach. "Dog!"

I listened, but there was no response, not a sound.

Looking to my right, I saw where the canyon narrowed and got darker where the sides of the rock cliffs wouldn't allow the moonlight access, remembering every aspect of the story Barrett Long had told back in my office about what had happened to him. It was going to be a steep climb, and I wondered why I was contemplating it in that there were no signs that it was the direction where Dog had gone. It was just a feeling.

Reholstering my sidearm, I stooped and placed a hand against the canyon wall and began my descent, slipping more than stepping. The scree of rocks fell, bouncing off the sides and skittering into the void below, and I was glad the canyon opening was more slanted than it was farther up, the drop only about twenty feet. Still, if I was able to land just right, I could kill myself.

If I found that dog at the base of a tree looking up at a squirrel, I was going to strangle him.

It was about then that my feet slipped from under me and I fell backward, bouncing off the rocks and flipping forward into an outcropping before tumbling sideways and finally sliding to a stop in the rubble at the bottom. I lay there for a moment to catch my breath and then pushed up onto all fours, shaking my head. I stretched my jaw and felt it pop before reaching up and feeling the wet at the back of my head.

I looked around and found the flashlight that I'd dropped, luckily still operating. I flashed the beam on my hand and was surprised by the amount of blood. I started to stand but the effort caused me to fall backward again, and I felt as if I might black out, so I just sat there for a moment getting my bearings.

My hat was nearby, so I stretched out an arm to pick it up and gingerly placed it onto my head. Every time I thought I was all right, though, I would find myself listing and would try to straighten up, only to feel like I was going to black out again.

Finally giving up, I panned the flashlight to get an idea of my surroundings before carefully standing. There were a few stunted pines about chest height, obviously affected by the lack of sunlight in the canyon, but it was still strange being there among them like a giant in some magical, if undersized, forest.

I scanned the base of the canyon walls, making sure Dog hadn't fallen too, but he was nowhere to be seen.

Thinking I might've heard something from above, I aimed the flashlight, but there was nothing except the canyon edge. I hadn't moved for a moment and then my left thumb did something I didn't tell it to do—switched off the light.

In the darkness, the canyon transformed, and I could see more than I would've thought possible. The moon must have moved in a perfect trajectory to an oblique angle, lighting a path up the canyon that would only last a short while.

Slipping the Maglite into the loop at my belt, I heard a breath of wind rustle the cottonwoods above the rim, the bare branches pulsing like veins as I quietly moved forward, aware that I was backlit in the canyon and making a pretty good target for anything else that was in there with me.

There was something breathing in the darkness of the ravine, at least it sounded like breathing, the air gently pulling inward and then blowing back, almost as if the canyon itself was inhaling and exhaling.

My head hurt, but I pulled my .45 from my holster and stood there.

In retrospect, most of my life has been involved with hunting, whether it was being taught by my unforgiving grandfather on Buffalo Creek, my first forays into the bars and saloons of northern Wyoming as a teenager, intercepting defensive backs at USC, the jungles of Vietnam, or simply being a sheriff. That was what I was doing now, in hopes that whatever was out here would find me and had not found Dog.

Something was definitely moving, stealthily and under the cover, moving as I would have if I'd needed to. I didn't even swallow for fear that it might make a sound, although I needn't to have worried—I doubted I could work up enough spit to bother swallowing.

There was that bit of movement again, but this time I had the advantage, its color not providing it with much camouflage. It was a young one, but pretty good size, and it's possible it had followed a relative of the elk Barrett had chased in his canyon. The big cat had come up empty-handed, however, and was now working his way out, or it was possible he smelled blood and that I was his late-night room service.

I waited a moment more till he was only about forty feet away, before straightening and letting him get a good look at who and what I was. I've had numerous encounters with mountain lions in the wild, and even though I could never be sure what they'd do, I had a pretty good idea, which made it all that more puzzling when it turned its head and looked at me with those huge eyes and headed directly toward me.

I blinked.

Raising the Colt, I thought about firing off a shot into the air, but then figured I'd scare Dog and worry Henry—of course it was possible that I was looking at the creature who might've killed my dog, but this youngster would not have had the experience and was injury and blood free.

He wasn't stalking me but kept moving in my direction, and I wondered if he'd seen me after all. I lifted the gun a little higher, not thinking he'd know what it was, but animals can read confidence in a fellow hunter and there's nothing more unnerving than moving in for the kill on something that shows no fear.

Then it did something I was surprised by—it looked over its shoulder, back into the murk of the canyon.

Something was following it, pushing it, perhaps even hunting it.

What the heck hunted cougars?

He was about twenty feet away when he turned back to me and picked up his pace, almost as if he were relieved to be in my company. He didn't head right at me but swerved a little and I thought he might be sidling up to hit me from behind. Instead, he just circled a little and pulled up about ten yards away before backtracking and looking from where he'd come.

I'd never seen a wild animal act the way this one did, standing there ignoring me and looking into the black squeeze of the canyon. Clasping the stag grips on my .45, I stared into the gloom.

Nothing. When I looked at the cougar again, he was backing away, his attention having returned to the canyon.

The shadow of the moon crawled across the rock sides of the cliffs like a living thing, seemingly moving twice as fast as it actually was, like a time lapse. I glanced back at the sky and tried to get a read on this phenomenon but then figured it had to be something to do with my head wound.

I turned back to the darkness and, as I did, felt something in my chest, almost like there was a tide pulling me forward. and when I moved to my right to catch my balance, the tiny trees around me danced, and the mountain lion continued to back away until he disappeared.

I tried to turn, but now my feet wouldn't move, so I raised my sidearm for what good that would do. I was almost to the point of pulling the trigger when, in the dead silence, I heard something that was barely audible, a sad song that seemed to be echoing inside my head.

I turned just a bit to listen. It was in Cheyenne, but I had heard this song before and understood.

"Neh-Ehvah sii Eh-jest, Na-Hoe-eh sidun . . ."

I watched the trees sway to the rhythm. They gained an energy that enabled them to swirl in patterns that created tendrils of gloom, which struck their way across the rocks like cracks in glass reflecting an endless night, each time transforming from white to pink.

"Bring me back, I don't belong here, and I want to go home . . ."

It was a bundle of something in the heart of the darkness, almost like swaddling cloth, that seemed to unfold like a flower that bloomed until the pink gave way to a crimson red and the flower became a hand that extended toward me.

I stretched my fingers and felt the small hand grab them. There was a shock that ran through me and ended in my other hand, causing my fingers to involuntarily shudder and spasm and contract. The .45 in my hand went off like a lightning strike.

Flies, at least I thought they were flies.

That was the first thing I became aware of, late-season flies, buzzing around my head and my hat that partially covered my face.

I lay in the warmth of the sun, just happy to be breathing.

"Boy howdy, do I feel like shit."

I pulled the hat from my face but immediately regretted the decision, the sunlight blinding me, so I pulled both arms up to cover my eyes like an involuntary vampire. Hitting myself in the teeth with the hammer of my Colt, I moved it to the side and then lay there trying hard not to concentrate on the taste in my mouth.

Leveraging up on one elbow, I looked around at the day and the position of the sun. "What the hell time is it?"

Reaching into my jeans to retrieve my pocket watch, I pulled it out by the horsehead fob and dangled it in front of my face, where it read 8:17. The crystal protecting the face of the watch was broken. I stared at it, figuring I must've damaged the thing in my fall. Tucking it back into the pocket, I scanned the canyon that in the light of day looked relatively benign. I guess I was lucky that the cougar hadn't come around for a second course.

I sat up a bit more and was able to grab a limb of one of the small trees nearby and was startled to see it was over forty feet.

After looking around at the tiny canyon, I realized that all the trees were at least that height. Laughing, I stood and felt the back of my head where the blood had crusted in my hair. Figuring I must've hit harder than I thought, I glanced around some more and then noticed something even stranger—I wasn't on the side of the canyon floor where I'd been last night.

Instead, I was just below where I'd fallen, the blood marking the spot where I'd slid to a stop, more blood than there would've been if I'd immediately gotten up, which I thought I had.

It was morning, and Henry and who knew who else would be worried about me.

I wondered if the Cheyenne Nation had found Dog.

Slow and steady, I climbed the rocks, and paused at the cornice where there was a little blood and hair stuck to it about halfway up—I was lucky I hadn't bashed my brains in. Staggering over the rim, I sat there catching my breath before being surprised by major league sniffing to the side of my head that threatened to send my hat cascading back down into the canyon. I caught it and turned to my partner in crime.

Dog was wagging and smiling at me, but when I reached out to him, he backed away and whined. I laughed, first at his reaction to me and then because I could count on one hand how many times I'd heard him make that noise. Maybe it was just the blood. I reached out for him again, but he ducked his big head and backed away another step. "What, I'm gone for a few hours and you forget who I am?"

A smaller whine escaped him, but he kept wagging the tail as I shambled to a standing position, feeling like my head might pop off and fall into the canyon on its own. The way Dog was acting, I wasn't sure he'd fetch it for me.

"All right then." I started off toward the cabins, but he stayed a couple of steps ahead of me, constantly checking to see if I was still following.

I laughed. "What is wrong with you?'

It was getting warmer as we escaped the denser part of the

forest and the trees broadened, allowing more sunlight in. I was feeling pretty good after finding Dog, or having Dog find me, the only worry being the constant ache at the back of my head.

As we got closer to the cabins, I could see there were a number of vehicles crowding the area, cruisers from the Rosebud County Sheriff's Department, Lolo Long's Yukon, sedans that I recognized as FBI, and for some strange reason, Rosebud County Search & Rescue.

I was beginning to think that something had happened when I saw the collected law enforcement of eastern Montana standing near the Cheyenne Nation, who appeared to be addressing the group by standing on the tailgate of my truck.

Sidling up into the crowd, I raised my voice. "What, we're having a cop convention?"

They all turned to look, about twenty of them.

The Bear stared at me, a strange expression on his face.

"What?"

One or two of the federal agents on the periphery shook their heads and walked away as Lolo Long knifed through the crowd. "Where the hell have you been?"

Some of the others drifted away when it started dawning on me that all of this might be on my account. "What, you guys thought I was lost?"

Her face grew even closer. "I repeat, where the hell have you been?"

I glanced at Gordo Hansen who had come over and then up at Henry. "C'mon Henry, I was gone for what, five hours—you could've held off on the manhunt of the century."

Long shook her head at me, finally spitting out the words. "In case you haven't noticed, we've got better things to do than be out traipsing the woods looking for you." She turned on her heels, leaving me standing there, stunned.

Gordo leaned in beside me. "I think you just got fired."

Watching her go, I shook my head. "I never got hired." And moved toward the tailgate where the Cheyenne Nation crouched on the edge. "Henry, what's going on?"

He cocked his head, studying me not unlike Dog had. "Are you all right?"

"Yep, I'm fine." I felt the back of my head and gestured toward the Grendel, who still stood a little away. "I slipped and fell, busting my head." I glanced around at some of the departing vehicles. "You think you might've jumped the gun?"

"Where were you?"

I threw a thumb over my shoulder between the cabins. "To the north here and a little west, there's a canyon that . . ."

"Willow Creek Canyon."

"I don't know. I guess."

"It is the only canyon in that direction, granite walls about a quarter mile in length with a thin tributary and trees along the bottom that reach to the canyon edge."

I nodded. "That's it, about forty feet deep. That's where I slipped and fell and must've knocked myself out . . ."

The Bear glanced at the others who had stayed. "We were there no more than twelve hours ago." His eyes came back to mine. "We combed that entire area yesterday."

"What are you talking about? I was there, I had to be. Where else could I have been?" They all continued to stare at me. "What did you say about yesterday?"

He looked at me in a way he never had before. "What day is it, Walt?"

I glanced at the other two, hoping they might let me in on the joke. "What?"

Henry lowered himself and sat on the tailgate. "What day is it today?"

"Monday," I said, confidently.

He glanced at Gordo and his deputy before returning his eyes to me. "It is Tuesday."

I breathed a laugh. "That's not possible, we went out looking for Dog last night . . ."

"Sunday night—it is now Tuesday morning." He leaned in and spoke quietly. "You have been missing for thirty-one hours."

"My dog won't come near me."

He drove, also not trusting me. "He senses something about you that he does not like." He reached back and petted the beast. "How do you feel?"

"Embarrassed, that's how I feel." I looked out the window. "Other than my head, just a little off, I guess." I turned back to him. "You're sure you checked the right canyon?"

"It is the only canyon there, and yes, we covered it thoroughly." He glanced at me again. "Tell me what happened."

"No, you tell me what happened with you."

He considered it. "Sunday night, we went out looking for Dog, and it was sometime between two and three in the morning. You took the path on the left and I took the one on the right, and after about twenty minutes I discovered him as I was coming back toward the cabins."

"Was he weird, like he is now?"

"No. I think he was concerned about you, especially when we got back to camp, and you were not there."

"Then what?"

We waited at the fire for a while, but he kept whining, so we went out looking for you and that was the first time we went to Willow Creek Canyon."

"And you didn't see me?"

"No."

"And that was how long after we parted company looking for Dog?"

"Maybe an hour."

Pulling my sidearm, I dropped the magazine and counted the rounds, plus the one in the pipe—seven. I sniffed the barrel. "Did you hear a shot fired about that time?"

"No."

I reinserted the mag and replaced the Colt back into my holster. "I fired off a round, and I'm missing one."

"At what were you shooting?"

"I . . . I'm not sure." He took a left into Rabbit Town and began the long trek toward Artie Small Song's mother's house, which was at the very end of the road. We were driving past Leonard One Moon's that I'd visited it seemed like a hundred years ago. "What's going on with Jaya?"

"As you predicted, she is in lockdown until the game this weekend that will decide if they get into the NAIA Tournament."

"That's a long shot."

"Yes, they would have to beat Lodge Grass, and there is little chance of that." We stopped at the bottom of the hill where derelict vehicles led the way up to the small cabin nestled in the trees. "She asked about you."

"Who, Artie's mother?"

"Jaya." He opened the door and stepped out. "I do not think she could stand it if another person in her life were to disappear."

He parked the truck, and we sat there.

"I'm not so sure I'm up for this."

"What?"

"Artie's mom."

He studied me. "Who is?"

"How about I just wait here, and you can go talk to her?"

"She will know you are here."

"That's exactly why I don't feel up to seeing her right now."

He climbed out and shut the door of my unit, and then looked at me through the open window. "Then perhaps you need to see her now." He started off, winding his way up the long haul of the hill, and I sat there watching him go, finally pulling the handle of the truck and slipping out, but having only enough energy to stand there.

The old woman was like a spiritual hound, and I knew she was going to sense something terribly wrong on me. I looked through the window at Dog, who sat there. Hell, everybody could smell it.

I wasn't surprised when a voice called out from above. "That you, Ahsante?"

The old woman knew me as the sheriff of the White Mountains, or in Cheyenne, Ahsante. It was her idea of a joke, kind of like polar bear. I pushed the door closed behind me and shouted up to her. "Howdy, Mrs. Small Song."

"I had a vision about you."

"You did, huh?"

"I dreamed you were lost and couldn't find your way home."

"That wouldn't be too far from the truth." I pushed off and started up, the ache in the back of my head throbbing like a warning claxon.

Henry was already talking with her when I got there. They were speaking in Cheyenne, but I caught a few words along with

Artie's name. Leaning against the hulk of an old Studebaker carcass, I caught my breath and studied the old girl, who must've been near a hundred and always looked as if she'd fallen off the gypsy wagon in an old Universal horror movie.

Her gray hair was tied back with a bandanna holding it in place, and she wore a shawl and full skirt along with men's work boots, the steel of the toes winking through the leather. As she talked with the Bear, I studied her eyes, so clouded by cataracts that I wasn't sure she could see at all.

Then she turned, and I was pretty sure she was looking right through me. Her pupils looked like the clouds overhead. "There is something wrong with you, Ahsante?"

All I could think was, *That was quick*.

I slipped my hat off and gently touched the back of my head. "Oh, I got roughed up a little—took a fall in a canyon."

"Come here."

I stooped so she could look at my head and she probed the wound with her fingers. "That is the dream I had, only in my dream you fell and kept falling and falling." She stood on tiptoes, peering at my head. "Then many people caught you, many people acting as one." She took a step back but then stopped, reaching out to me. "Give me your hand."

I glanced at Henry but then did as she commanded.

She slapped it away. "The other one." I tried again, and she took it in both of hers and stared up into my eyes, the rheumy, opaque pupils knocking back and forth as if she were picking up an electric charge from my body into hers. The old medicine woman stood like that for the better part of a minute and then let go of my hand. "Why do you seek the living in a place of the dead?"

"Excuse me?"

She sighed deeply. "You need my help."

I glanced at Henry again and then back to her. "Well, yep, we're looking for your son . . ."

"You need my help with more than that." She turned and hobbled toward the house. "Ahsante, come up and I will stitch you back together."

I glanced at the Bear. "Really?"

We found ourselves in the close kitchen of the Small Song matriarch. Soon we were sitting at a tiny table with two green-colored jelly jars in front of us, a third filled with a clear liquid. I glanced up at the cabinets on the walls advertising car parts, refugees from assorted gas stations, and sniffed my glass. "What's in this?"

"Medicine." She sipped hers and smiled, pulling a copious amount of chewing tobacco from a beaded, leather pouch and stuffing it into her mouth.

I sniffed the clear liquid some more. "It smells antiseptic. How about I just dab it on the back of my head?"

She chewed. "Drink."

Knowing full well that the last time I'd had dealings with her she'd sent me around the moon with peyote, I did as she said. Researchers from the National Institutes of Health have mapped more than a thousand gut bacterial species that live in harmony with their human hosts, and right now I was pretty sure I'd just poisoned ninety percent of mine.

She nodded and smiled through the tobacco. "Good, huh?"

I smiled back, pretty sure there was no longer any enamel on my teeth. "Am I going to go blind?"

She laughed. "Hasn't hurt me."

"Uh huh."

She stood and began going through one of her kitchen drawers, pulling out an old spool of embroidery thread and a needle with which you could harpoon whales. "You know, Ahsante, every time I see you, you're looking for my son."

"Your son is always involved in things that concern me."

"Maybe you need to find some other concerns." She spit a pinpoint stream into a dented spittoon beside the door, expertly wiping the remainder from her lower lip with a forefinger and then began threading the needle. "Take your hat off."

"Do I have to?" She ignored me, and I did as she requested. "We understand Artie's gotten religion?"

She shrugged, finally capturing the thread with the eye of the needle and then, straddling my knee, leaned over me to examine the playing field. "He is attempting to find parts of himself that are missing. Some people do that by looking within and some from looking without."

"Which one is Artie?"

She stabbed the needle into my hide, and it felt like she was scalping me. "Ow!"

"Hold still." She looked out the back window toward an old firepit in which she cooked the illegal game her son sometimes brought her. "He lives out in those woods, and there are things there in the darkness that speak to him." Her eyes came back to mine. "As they have spoken to you."

I said nothing as she pierced my skin again, and I felt the wound drawing closed.

"Something has happened to you out there between worlds?"

"I got lost and hit my head."

"More than that, I think." She looped a few more stitches as Henry sat there covering a smile. "Does it hurt?"

"Yep."

"Good, only the living feel pain—it is the price we pay." She leaned back, examining her handiwork, and then lowered her face to mine, very close, with a gravity that was more than a little unsettling. "Are you afraid, Ahsante?"

"Of you and that needle, yep."

She bent back over my head, biting the thread in two and then sat on my knee. She continued to look at me. "If I were you, I would be."

I was so desperate for something to do, I took another swig from my small glass, finding nothing there. "Why is that?"

"It has tasted you, and you are now marked."

"Marked as what?"

"To be taken by the Éveohtsé-heómėse."

10

"I can't believe this truck made it to Hardin."

He sputtered to a stop in front of the Hotel Becker and killed Rezdawg's engine, or maybe it just committed suicide. "It is only fifty-four miles."

"Like I said, I can't believe we made it."

He cracked open the door and climbed out, then he gently closed it and ran a hand over its mottled surface in an affectionate way. "If you were to say nice things to her, she would run better."

"Okay." I patted the dash in a perfunctory manner. "Nice truck. Nice shitty truck."

We met on the sidewalk, and he glanced at me. "Why did you not tell me what had happened?"

"Because I didn't want you and the entirety of eastern Montana law enforcement to think I was two bricks shy of a load."

"Too late." We walked past the Big Horn County News building and the Fort Custer General Store to an attached, redbrick structure. "I understand it is no longer a bed and breakfast."

"Too bad. It's a beautiful old building." We stopped in front of the last business on the abbreviated block, next to a fenced alleyway with outside seating, evidently shut down for the winter season.

Above a large, plate-glass window was a cream-colored rectangle with a familiar painting of a buffalo skull and a group of Plains warriors moving over a ridge along with a mountain man, and in large print the name of the bookstore: PAPER TALK. I stood in front of the door and read the gilt lettering.

The west is dead my friend but writers hold the seed,

and what they saw will live and grow again to those who read.

I pushed open the glass door to the tinkling of small bells. "I think I'm going to like this part of the investigation."

Inside, old orchard boxes were stacked along the walls, filled to capacity with books, pushing against the pressed-tin ceiling, brown paper bags hanging from pegs for patrons to gather their purchases. There was a paint-skinned counter to my right with an outdated, brass cash register and more books piled in precarious stacks.

Behind the counter was a black pit bull mix lying on his bed, snoring.

There are a number of smells I've loved in my lifetime, but few can compare with the smell of a bookstore. Stopping next to the counter, I picked up a book from one of the heaps, palming the fragile spine and allowing the pages to fall open like autumn leaves. "*We Pointed Them North* by Teddy Blue."

The Bear glanced around, aware of my weakness when confronted with the printed word. "This is going to take you an awfully long time, is it not?"

"Yep."

"I will go a block away to the Four Arrows Casino and speak with Gabriel Popescu."

"You'll know where to find me," I called after him as he swung back through the door and disappeared.

I turned back to my idea of heaven and walked down the

nearest aisle, barely fitting. About halfway down the building there was an old potbellied stove that had a bumper rail and some mismatched wooden chairs nearby, where readers could sit and peruse their potential purchases.

Taking Teddy Blue with me, I stripped off my jacket and sat in one of the chairs and then reached out to enjoy the warmth. The heat in the hundred-year-old contraption was dimming, so I picked up a piece of firewood from yet another orchard box, used it to swing open the front grate, and then tossed it into the stove before licking a finger and pushing the door closed. The crackling and popping was comforting. I thought about spending the rest of the early winter right there.

Leaning back in the creaking chair, I opened the quintessential, working-cowboy book and started reading from a random page just as somebody darted between the stacks to my left.

I waited a moment and then stood, looking for whoever it was.

Just as I was about to speak, a blonde woman came around the corner, nearly colliding with me.

"Oh, my God." She closed her eyes and took a step back, placing a hand on her chest. "You scared the life out of me."

"I'm sorry, no one was here when I came in, so I waited."

She smiled a sturdy grin. "You mean you really want to buy a book?"

"Is that strange?" I glanced around. "I was under the impression that this was a bookstore."

The pit bull sidled up beside her and yawned. "It is, we just don't sell many books."

"I'm sorry to hear that."

"Me too. Lesa Hopkins." She extended a hand, petting the dog. "And this is Pluto."

I gestured around us. "You own Paper Talk?"

"I do, the phrase comes from . . ."

"Charlie Russell, for the illustrated cards and letters he used to send out to his cowpunching pals."

"Very good." She studied me. "And you are?"

"Walt . . ."

"Longmire, the Absaroka County sheriff."

"Now, I'm taken aback."

"Stay here." She went behind the stacks and reappeared with a copy of *High Country News*—with me on the cover. "Something about your adventures in Mexico?"

"Yep, I was kind of out of my jurisdiction."

She turned the magazine back toward her, leafing through. "That's pretty much the conclusion they came to also." She pointed to the item in my hand. "You want to buy that book, nobody else has purchased anything today."

"How much?"

"1939, first edition in very good condition? Seventy-five bucks."

"Sold. If you don't mind me asking, how long have you been here?"

"About a year. I inherited the building from a distant relative. I had another bookstore back in Myrtle Beach and Montana sounded romantic—mountains and grizzly bears . . ."

"Neither of which are anywhere near Hardin."

She crossed her arms. "As they say, I was misinformed."

"Hard times for booksellers. We lost our bookstore, Crazy Woman Books, just last year."

"Where?"

"Durant, down in Wyoming."

"Are there mountains and grizzly bears there?"

"Yep. And maybe." I reached into my pocket, pulled out my wallet, peeled off eighty bucks, and handed it to her. "Consider the extra five a donation for the firewood."

She smiled and took the money. "Thanks."

"I have to admit that I'm not just here shopping for books." I sat, in hopes that she'd join me. "I understand you were in the Black Kettle van the night that Jeanie One Moon went missing?"

She immediately sat. "Oh, thank God—are you taking on the investigation?"

"In a way."

"That poor girl."

"So, you were there that night?"

"With George Three Fingers, he's one of my regular customers, and he invited me to that party up in Billings. It sounded like a good time, so I went."

"Did you know Jeanie very well?"

"Not at all, but she seemed like a sad girl."

"Sad?"

"Well, I didn't know her, but that night she seemed sad."

"Do you remember anything particular about that night, anything that might've happened, anything about your fellow passengers?"

"There was one guy who kept hitting on Jeanie."

"Which one?"

"I didn't catch his name, some guy who works in the mines."

"Black Kettle?"

"No, not the driver, another guy."

"Louie Howard?"

"Yes, him."

"You seem sure."

She nodded. "He kept singing that song, 'Louie-Louie,' about eighty-seven times to Jeanie until George threatened to beat the snot out of him."

"'Louie-Louie' in large doses can have that effect." I placed the book in my lap. "Did you get a chance to talk with her at all?"

She nodded. "Before we got in the van. We were waiting outside, a couple of us, and she wandered up."

"You didn't see her at the party?"

"No, is that important?"

"I'm not sure, but no one seems to have actually seen her there. What did you talk about?"

"Her coat was open, and I told her that it was getting cold and she should zip it up, and she just looked at me and asked, '*Why?*'" Lesa took a deep breath and settled in the chair. "I zipped her coat up for her. I mean, she was a teenager, but she seemed so much like a child at that point. She smiled after I did it and gave me a hug, and then she said something strange."

"What?"

"That nothing really mattered, but that was okay because it would all be gone very soon. I asked her what she meant, and she said that there was a hunger that was eating away at the small things in the world and that eventually it was going to be gone, but she didn't care."

"Did she ever mention an individual by the name of Artie Small Song?"

"No, but like I said, we didn't talk that long."

"Just out of curiosity, did she mention the Éveohtsé-heómėse?"

Her response was almost as if I'd struck her. "The Wandering Without." Saying nothing more, she stood and disappeared, only to return with a grocery bag of books that she sat at my feet. "You're the second person to ask about that."

"Was the other one a rancher by the name of Iron Bull?"

"Lyndon, yes. I was going to tell you about him. Have the two of you spoken?"

I nodded. "Down at his ranch. He seems to think he saw Jeanie the night she went missing and possibly since then."

Lesa gestured toward the bag of books on the floor. "That's every single reference I can find on the Éveohtsé-heómėse. A collective of lost souls that hunger for the living. The outcasts banished from the tribes over the centuries—the murderers, the mad, the deranged who were driven off to die in the wilderness." She reached into the bag to pull out a thin, brown-paper-wrapped volume tied with twine and handed it to me. "This is the most detailed description I've come across. It's entirely in Cheyenne, but I've had some friends translate a few passages—they're on the loose sheets inside."

The covers were made of a tan-colored, thin-backed board with a simple typeset print of a lone symbol of a circle with an uneven strike through it and nothing else.

She leaned forward. "There's a trademark at the bottom with another location with which I'm not familiar."

It was as she described, once again, the circle with the uneven slash through it and two words: Fort Pratt. Beneath that were some other markings, IIBS, which I assume stood for the Industrial Indian Boarding School. I looked up at her. "And the number thirty-one—possibly the number of books printed?"

I pulled out the postcard that Jimmy Lane had given me outside The Big Store in Lame Deer. "Fort Shaw I've heard of up that way, but never Fort Pratt. Blackfeet and Assiniboine in that area, no Cheyenne—at least not to my knowledge. This also has the number thirty-one on it."

I flipped open the first page of the book and looked at the

familiar yet undecipherable language. The loose page, which was the one printed in a blocked, penciled hand, read "It is a dreadful need from those who are long gone that can never be satisfied and like all carnivores it culls the herd, preying on the sad and lonely, those living in its hunting ground on the outskirts of humanity." I flipped a few more pages and then stopped. There was a cardboard rectangle obviously meant to be a bookmark—a Mallo Cup Play Money card. Lifting the coin card up into the light, I studied it, both sides. "Where did you get this?"

"The book?"

"Yep."

"I don't remember buying it or anybody ever giving it to me." She gestured down one of the rows. "I've got a Native Spirituality section in the back, and I remember when I was looking for books for Mr. Iron Bull, I discovered it back there, all wrapped up in the paper and twine."

"And the bookmark?"

"It was in there too . . . Looks old, doesn't it?" She leaned forward, looking at the mark on the cover. "I thought maybe somebody might've left it here, but it was all the way up on the top shelf, so they would've had to have reached up almost ten feet in the air to place it there."

I stuck the card back into the book, closed it, and stared at the wide planks of the hardwood floor. "Yep, they would have."

"It is written in an antediluvian form of the language and difficult to translate. I can get the general meaning, but I am afraid a great deal of the tone and feeling would be lost." He held the little book like the treasure it was. "Fortunately, I know someone."

I sipped my overpriced beer at the bar of the Four Arrows Casino, where we were waiting for Gabriel Popescu to show up for work. "Please don't tell me we're going back to talk to Artie Small Song's mother."

"Actually, I was thinking of Lonnie."

"I like that idea better." I stared at him. "What was the word you just used, *antediluvian*?"

"It is a common word."

"For the Don of Oxford, maybe."

He shrugged and continued to look at the writing. "I can tell you that it is not simply a historical reference; it is more personal than that."

"What do you mean?"

"This is an excommunication of sorts, an anathematization or cabala—as near as I can tell, an incantation of some length."

I turned on my stool and looked out at the all but empty casino. "Am I right about the press, Fort Pratt Industrial Indian Boarding School?"

"Yes." He nodded.

"Fort Pratt, it's the same one as the postcard Jimmy gave me. Ever heard of it?"

"No, but there are stories . . ."

"Such as?"

"That some of the boarding schools were so tragedy-ridden they were removed from the history books."

"Up near Helena or Fort Shaw, there couldn't have been many Cheyenne in that boarding school all the way up there."

"Starr School possibly, or maybe Sacred Heart Mission, but who can say?"

"It's just so strange, an . . . antediluvian book in Cheyenne published by a boarding school press. Since when did Indian boarding schools publish books?"

"Industrial Boarding School, who knows what it was involved with." He closed the book. "Typeset, so it was hand-printed with a press."

"In 1931?"

He shook his head. "No, I would say before that."

"Then what's with the thirty-one?"

"I do not know."

"Any idea what the image on the cover is?"

"The end of the world."

"Yeah? In what language?"

"Many tribes use the symbol; it is very common."

I watched as a beefy individual came in the front doors and made his way directly for the chip cage and down a hallway toward the inner workings of the casino's employee area. "Gabriel Popescu?"

Henry nodded. "He looks like a bouncer, does he not?"

"Predictably." I picked up my beer and took another sip. "You spoke with the manager?"

"I did. He said he would send him over to us before he started his shift." He carefully rewrapped the booklet, retying the twine and handing it back to me. "Did you buy this book?"

"I borrowed it, but I think it's become mine. She called Lyndon Iron Bull, and he said to give it to me if I thought it might help with the investigation."

"And do you?"

I carefully placed the book in the inside pocket of my coat. "Do I what?"

"Think that it will help with the investigation?"

"No, but you think it will."

"I hear you're looking for me?"

We both turned to see who we both assumed was Gabriel Popescu, with his large hands spread on the bar.

He was in his thirties, had dyed blond hair, and several tattoos. I offered my hand, which he ignored. "Walt Longmire." He glanced at Henry, and I studied the scars on his face. "Sheriff."

His eyes came back to mine. "What do you want?"

"I want to talk to you about the night Jeanie One Moon went missing?"

He stood up straight and folded his weight-lifting arms that stretched his black T-shirt, which read SECURITY. "I already told the cops about that a long time ago."

"Yep, well we're following up on it, since there have been a number of threats to her sister, Jaya."

He glowered at us. "I don't know anything about that."

"We just want to go over what happened that night in the Black Kettle van."

"No."

I stared at him. "Excuse me?"

"I'm done talking about that, and unless you've got some kind of warrant or something . . ."

"How about we arm wrestle for it."

We both turned to look at the Cheyenne Nation.

"If I win, you tell us everything you know."

The younger man smiled. "And if I win?"

"You will not."

The bouncer shook his head and grinned. "I win, you two grandpas get to buy me a drink and then get the fuck out of here."

The Bear shrugged, propping an elbow up on the bar and opening his hand. "Deal."

I'd never seen Henry Standing Bear lose at arm wrestling but had seen him dislocate bones numerous times. I hoped he'd go easy on the kid and leave him relatively intact—after all, he had a night's work to do.

Popescu reached across and propped up an arm, the bicep bulging. Henry slipped off his leather jacket, sliding it under himself on the stool, and unbuttoned his chambray shirt, rolling up the sleeve as the muscles in his own arm writhed like eels.

Propping his elbow, I watched as he placed the point of it perhaps just an inch closer to the fulcrum, a move the bouncer didn't notice. Henry Standing Bear had been in the game far too long to not take every advantage he could.

"Want me to start you two off?"

They both nodded, and I stood and placed my hands over theirs, pulling them back toward center where Popescu had already attempted to take his advantage. I glanced at the Cheyenne Nation. "You want to move your elbow back an inch?"

He looked at me.

"Just trying to have a fair contest here."

He did as I asked. "All right, on three. One, two, three." I removed my hands as the combatants both flexed, the bar creaking, the intertwined fists first moving in Popescu's favor and then straightening back again.

"You mind if I ask the questions while this is going on?"

He grunted. "Only if I lose."

"Oh, you've already lost—you put everything into that first push, and you're not getting any stronger. The veins on the side of your head look like you're going to have a blowout any second." I nodded toward the Bear. "And he hasn't even tried yet."

The bouncer glanced at me.

"Did you know Jeanie, at all?"

He grunted again. "She tried to get in here one time with some older guy."

"Shorter, silver hair, and a big hat?"

"Yeah." He grunted again, pulling Henry's hand back about two inches before the Bear straightened him out.

"Talk to her that night?"

His face was reddening. "Some. C'mon man, let me concentrate here."

"No." I moved over into his line of sight. "What did you talk about?"

"Relationships and shit; what else do girls always want to talk about?"

Two waitresses were now standing behind Henry, and a bartender and croupier stood at the end of the bar. "About the older guy?"

"No, somebody else, I think. I mean, it didn't sound like him."

"Ever heard of a guy by the name of Artie Small Song?"

"Everybody knows Artie, man, and if you're after him you don't need any trouble from anybody else."

"You know where we can find him?"

"No."

The Bear put some pressure on, slowly pushing Popescu's arm backward as the attending audience smiled and cheered, giving me the idea that the bouncer was not everybody's favorite coworker.

"I don't think he likes your answer."

He strained the words out. "Yeah, well I don't care. He can kiss my ass."

Henry pressed him for another inch.

"You'll care when he dislocates your shoulder." I leaned back. "Try again?"

"It's Artie, man, he lives in the woods—the trees don't have numbers."

"How about a general vicinity?"

"The Rez, man, USA."

Henry glanced at me, and I nodded, watching as he slowly began powering the bouncer's arm backward and Popescu started looking more than worried. "Okay, okay, okay, man . . . Yager Butte. He sometimes winters up at the fire tower there."

"The old Diamond Butte fire tower, they moved that back in the fifties?"

"No!" He grunted some more, pushing with all he had, but not quite enough to move the combined fists. "The pad is still there and somebody—I don't know, maybe Artie—rebuilt it."

"You think he's there?"

"Hell, I don't know."

The Bear glanced at me, and I nodded as he brought it all, bending the bouncer's arm back until it was about three inches from the surface of the bar. "You wouldn't lie to me, would you?"

"No, man, no!"

"Because if you did, my friend here might feel compelled to return and bend your head back over your spine."

"I swear, that's all I know!"

"How about a guy by the name of Louie Howard, you know him?"

"Yeah, yeah," he spat, catching his breath. "I know Louie. He comes in every once in a while."

"Was he making a play for Jeanie that night?"

"How the hell should I know?"

Another inch.

"Yeah, he was. She was cute, so yeah."

"Did you get out of the van that night and see where she might've gone?"

"It was freezing. I stayed in the van."

"Black Kettle says you got out to help with the engine?"

Another inch.

"Hell yeah, I got out and looked at the engine. I'm a guy and that's what you're supposed to do, right?"

Bam—the back of his hand slammed against the bar and the Cheyenne Nation held him there until I thought the guy might cry. The Bear finally let him go, and we watched as he scooped his hand from the bar like a dead bird.

"Are you all right?"

He glared at the two of us in turn and then held the hand to his puffed-out chest. "Yeah, I'm fine." He glanced at the tiny crowd that was now skittering back to their workplaces. "You guys need to get out of here."

"And why is that?"

"I don't want you here anymore."

I turned to look at Henry, who was already pulling on his coat. "I think Gabriel here might be a sore loser."

He turned to the bouncer. "Best two out of three?"

Rezdawg wouldn't start.

"I don't think that was the smartest thing to do."

Henry turned the switch, and we listened to the starter grind. "He tried to hit me; I thought it was only appropriate that I hit him in return."

"With this as our getaway vehicle?"

He turned the switch back, and we sat there in the silence. "Perhaps if you were to say . . ."

"I'm not sweet-talking your shitty truck." Glancing over my

shoulder, I watched as a Big Horn County Sheriff's Department cruiser made the intersection with lights and siren blazing. "Uh oh."

We watched as Wesley Burrell Best Bales slid to a stop beside us, opening the door and lifting his three-hundred-pound bulk from the seat. He came around the front of his vehicle and paused to pet Dog before stopping at my window. "Hey, you guys seen a cowboy and an Indian who look like the kind of lowlifes who might beat someone up?"

I made my best attempt at innocence. "Um, no?"

He nodded, zipping up his barn coat. "Well, if you do, you might tell them that sitting in front of the establishment where that kind of violent assault took place might not be the best idea."

"His crappy truck won't start."

The Bear leaned forward, smiling at my fellow sheriff. "He has said rude things to her, and now she is sulking."

Bales turned to me. "Maybe if you said something nice . . ."

"I'm not conversing with this shitty truck."

He nodded and pushed off the door with a sigh. "I've got to go in here and take a statement from this grade-A shithead Gabriel Popescu about almost getting his arm broken, and I'd appreciate it if you two would get the hell out of here by the time I come back."

"I'll walk, if I have to." He nodded and turned, pushing the glass door of the casino open and entering. "Now, what?"

"Say something nice to my truck."

"No."

"Then we are going to jail."

I sat there looking at him and then at the dash of the vehicle I despised more than any other. "I would rather go to jail than relate even the barest kindness to this piece of shit."

"Then we will not be able to go find Louie Howard or pursue Artie Small Song."

I stared at him. "I am very sorry, you shitty truck."

"First of all, you must address Rezdawg, and second of all I do not believe that was particularly heartfelt."

Looking through the windshield, I could see Bales talking with an animated Gabriel Popescu, or as animated as you can be with toilet paper stuffed in your nostrils and only one arm with which to point at us. "I'm walking."

"Say you are sorry to my truck."

I reached back through the window and petted Dog. "No."

"Then we will go to jail."

I watched as the sheriff inside took down the statement in the slowest dictation I'd ever witnessed. Clearing my throat, I looked down at the scabby dash with the blue and yellow flag of the Northern Cheyenne Nation peeling from it. "Rezdawg, I know that you and I have had a rocky relationship, but I know in my heart of hearts that you don't want us to be arrested and you to be hauled away to the impoundment lot where you might be mistaken for scrap and put in a junkyard crusher."

Henry nodded and compressed his lips. "That is as good as it is going to get?"

"Yep."

"Then we will give it a try." He adjusted the choke and turned the key, and I was stunned as the old V-8 sputtered to life. "It would appear that Rezdawg has accepted your apology."

I could see Sheriff Bales approaching the door as the Bear yanked the shifter into reverse and began backing out.

"Don't stall it."

He spun the wheel, shifted into first, and puttered down the block in an all but clean getaway.

The Diamond Eye Mine just north of the Northern Cheyenne Reservation had a conspicuous past, purchased by one international conglomerate after another until it was getting hard to know who owned the place anymore, the Australians, the Russians, the Chinese, or the Duchy of Saxony.

The man at the front gate, though, was Cheyenne and knew of Henry and gave us a free pass to the administration building at the bottom of the hill, which was surrounded by the towering walls of the strip mine and the serrated layers of dark, subbituminous coal—sixteen miles' worth, producing 43 percent of the country's reserves.

We'd changed trucks in Lame Deer, and I pulled my three-quarter ton to a stop. "You guys looking for Louie Howard?"

I took my wallet out to show him my star, as if the two-foot ones on the doors of my truck wouldn't do the trick. "Yep."

"He in trouble?"

"No, we just need to ask him some questions."

He looked past us toward a very large steel building at the other side of the complex. "He's over there in the garage." We started to walk, but he called out after us. "You might want to drive. There are a lot of really big machines rolling around here and they might miss something as small as two guys on foot." He started to go back into the building. "Ask for Nick, he's the supervisor over there and can tell you where Louie might be."

We drove over and parked by a set of the open doors, as big as a house. We left Dog in the cab and stopped at a makeshift office, where two desks faced each other on a concrete floor in a landscape of gigantic machines in varying states of disassembly.

A skinny guy with a pronounced Adam's apple looked up. "Can I help you?"

"Are you Nick?"

"No, he's at lunch."

"Well then, maybe you can help us. We're looking for a guy by the name of Louie Howard."

"He's one of our mechanics."

"I'm glad to hear that, can we talk to him?" He didn't seem to know how to respond, so I pulled out my wallet and badged him too.

He looked over his shoulder at the line of behemoth equipment. "He should be working on the dump at the very end of the row."

"You want to escort us over, or can we just go on our own?"

"You can go, just stay on this side of the yellow paint lines so you don't get run over."

"Right."

We trailed along between the walls of tools near the mechanics actually doing the work, making our way to the final bay where an individual was up in the engine compartment, the only thing visible, his booted feet, sticking out from beside the firewall of the massive dump truck.

"Louie Howard?"

A voice called out from the bowels of the engine bay. "Who wants to know?"

"Ed McMahon—I'm here from Publishers Clearing House."

Henry leaned in. "He actually never worked for them."

"What?"

The voice from the truck called out again. "Ed, who?"

"Uh, we'd like to talk with you."

"He worked for American Family Publishers and was a Marine Corp aviator." The Bear continued. "And he is dead."

"Thanks for the input."

The mechanic was struggling to get out of the innards of the big truck. He finally sat on the frame and turned to us wearing a hooded sweatshirt, the exact same hooded sweatshirt he'd worn at Jimmy Lane's house when he and Pete Schiller and his other white-supremacist buddy had shown up.

He didn't look happy to see us. "Oh, shit."

I smiled up at him. "Yep, you didn't win."

11

"I didn't know who she was."

We sat in a locker-lined break room that smelled like a combination of spoiled food, vending machine coffee, vintage sweat, and cleaning products. "I find it hard to believe that you didn't know she was Jimmy Lane's daughter."

He sat there with his hands in his sweatshirt. "No. I just thought she was, you know, cute."

I ignored the lie, for the moment. "You did time with Jimmy up in Deer Lodge?"

"Yeah."

"Mind if I ask for what?"

He grinned. "Yeah, I mind."

The Bear leaned in closer. "Frankly, I do not mind if you mind."

I gave him a second to think about it and then leaned in and whispered, "Unless it was bare-knuckle boxing, maybe you should answer."

The grin faded. "Grand theft, illegal possession of a deadly weapon, parole violation . . ."

"So, it's safe to say that was not your first time inside?"

"No. I got three hits, so I need to stay clean this time or else."

"And you think being pals with Pete Schiller will do that, huh?"

He shrugged and leaned back in the plastic chair under the fluorescent lights. "Pete's an okay guy."

"Uh huh, if you keep hanging around with him, you're going to be spending more quality time up in Deer Lodge—but that's your business. What I want to know is what happened the night Jeanie One Moon disappeared."

"She just vanished. I don't know what happened to her."

Another lie, but I was satisfied with just letting them mount up. "Were you at that party in Billings?"

"What party?"

Pausing to allow the stupid to settle, I waited a moment and started again. "Louie, it might be best for you to not play smart—it's not something you're particularly good at." I placed both elbows on the table and leaned in. "Were Schiller and the other guy at the party with you?"

"No way. That was an Indian party, and they wouldn't be caught dead there."

"You were on your own?"

"Um—yeah."

"Um—yeah?"

"Yeah."

"Louie, do you know what '*um—yeah*' means to me? It means no."

He pulled his hood back and stared at the surface of the table between us, and I was surprised he was mostly bald. "Jimmy Lane was there."

"Jeanie's father?"

"Yeah."

"What was he doing there?"

"It was a house party, everybody was there."

"Did you get a ride in Black Kettle's van up to Billings?"

"No, I just met them at the party and hitched a ride back to see if I could hook up with Jeanie." His look brightened. "I was singing 'Louie, Louie' to her and stuff. I'm a really good singer, and I think she was enjoying it."

"Um—yeah." I stood and walked over to the door with the glass pane facing down the hallway toward the shop bays. "Did you get out of the van near Pryor Creek?"

"Had to, somebody had to get the van going or we would've all frozen to death."

"Did you see Jeanie get out?"

"Yeah, her and that crazy bitch that does nothing but talk about angels and shit."

"Leanne Chelan?"

"Yeah, I think that's her."

"You saw the two of them get out, but only Leanne got back in?"

"I guess, I wasn't paying a lot of attention at that point 'cause they needed help with the van, and those guys couldn't repair Legos. Once we got it running, believe me, everybody wanted to get in it and get going. Leanne Chelan." He shook his head. "One minute she'd be talking about the Bible and shit, and the next thing she'd be talking about this friend of hers and the end of the world."

I lowered my head to make sure I was in his line of sight. "What did you just say?"

"About what?"

"The end of the world."

"That Chelan woman, she would be talking all sweetness and light and then all of a sudden she was talking about the end of the world and how there was a thing out there that was going to eat us all—crazy shit."

Henry glanced at me and then back at him. "Did she mention the Éveohtsé-heómèse?"

"The what?"

"The Wandering Without."

He looked at me. "I don't know, she talked so much crap that I just tuned it out. I don't speak the language, except for dirty words."

"Did she mention anything about a guy by the name of Artie Small Song?"

"Yeah. She said he knew shit about the end of the world and when it was going to happen and all." He looked back at Henry. "She's certifiable."

"Do you have any idea who might've been writing threatening notes to Jeanie?"

"I thought it was Jaya that was getting the notes."

I started getting curious about what Louie knew and what he pretended to not know. "You know Jaya?"

"Shit, everybody knows Jaya; she's gonna be in the NBA."

"Right. Well, Jeanie was getting notes too."

"Really?"

"You seem surprised by that." I studied him. "You're sure you don't know anything about these notes?"

"Um—yeah . . . No, I don't know nothing."

I looked at Henry as he shook his head. "Louie, you just lied to me for the . . . Well, more times than I care to count."

"Well, I mean, I know some stuff."

I walked to the table and stood over him. "Define *stuff*."

"It's not what you think."

"Good. I'm listening."

"I don't know how much I can tell you."

Swifter than a red-tailed hawk, Henry reached over with one hand and plucked the hooded man from his seat, lifting him from the ground and spinning him into the lockers, where he made a substantial dent. The Bear then lifted the clasp of a locker beside him, opened it, and slid the stunned man inside, pushing in his limbs and closing the metal door. Looking completely emotionless, the Cheyenne Nation folded his arms and leaned against the locker to afford no escape.

It was at that point that the skinny guy with the pronounced Adam's apple whom we'd met at the front desk popped his head in. "Everything all right?"

I turned and smiled. "Hunky."

"I thought I heard a noise?"

"Louie had to go to the bathroom."

"Oh, okay."

He disappeared, and I stood, walking over and rapping a few knuckles on the locker door. "Louie, how are you doing in there?"

The voice was muffled but audible. "I'm okay. It's a little cramped."

"I bet." I glanced at the Bear. "Louie, I've got a feeling that if you don't tell us everything you know, my buddy here is going to go get an acetylene unit and weld you in there till doomsday. So, how about you start answering my questions?"

"Jimmy hired us to protect Jaya."

I stared at Henry who, for the first time, registered a look of mild surprise. "You've got to be kidding."

The voice continued. "That's what we did up in Deer Lodge, run protection rackets."

"You're doing a heck of a job."

"Whaddaya mean?"

"One sister is missing, and the other is mortally imperiled."

"Well, you know, we're just getting started."

"You weren't hired when Jeanie went missing?"

"That's when we started the job." There was some movement inside. "Hey, can you guys let me out of here?"

The Bear shook his head no.

"I don't think so, Louie. So, it was just coincidence that you met Jeanie that night?"

"No, I knew she was going to be at that party, Jimmy told me. Hey, it's kind of stuffy in here . . ."

"I bet. So, what have you guys discovered?"

"About what?"

I glanced at Henry. "This may take awhile."

He nodded as Louie called out, the metal causing his voice to echo a bit. "What?"

"About the threats to the girls, what have you and the rest of the impromptu task force found out?"

"Not much."

"You're going to have to do better than that if you ever want to get out of the locker, Louie."

"She was seeing somebody."

"Who are we talking about, Jeanie or Jaya?"

"Both."

"Okay, who were they seeing?"

I noticed the Bear's head had turned, and I followed his view to where another mechanic stood in the doorway, holding the knob. "Are you guys talking to the lockers?"

"We're just talking, and the lockers happen to be here."

There was a banging as I assume Louie was kicking the door. "Hey, help! Can you get me out of here?!"

Thc man didn't move, looking at us.

"I don't suppose you'd like to pretend you didn't hear that?"

He glanced at the Cheyenne Nation. "Sure."

"We'll be out of here in no time."

"Okay." He shut the door behind him.

"Louie, we're running out of time."

"Some old, rich white guy."

"Jeanie is, but Jaya is seeing the son of the old, rich white guy."

The voice from inside the locker grew louder. "No, same guy."

"The same guy was dating both girls? Digger Wainwright?"

"Yeah, him." A moment passed, and he laughed. "Wow, we knew something you didn't, huh?"

I sighed. "Shut up, Louie, or we'll leave you in there."

"His son's girlfriend?"

"Both of them."

I drove 212 or "the Strait," as the locals called it for the number of tribe members who had died on its asphalt surface used by truckers to avoid the weigh stations at the state borders. "I guess we've got to go dig up Digger again, but first, I thought we'd try to have a meet and greet with Artie Small Song up at the old fire lookout."

Henry glanced at his wrist and the vintage Seiko that had been there since the sixties. "We only have time for one or the other; there is a game tonight in Lodge Grass."

"Jaya gets parole?"

"To play, and that is all."

"Is this the first game of the Big Sky Tournament?"

"Against archrival Lodge Grass. Yes."

"I guess we should be there just to carry bodies." I took the 484 cutoff after we got through Ashland. "I guess we'll just tell Artie he's going to have to postpone the end of the world."

I don't know why the Forest Service decided to move the lookout at Yager Butte ten miles back in 1954. I suppose it might've had to do with visibility, which wasn't exactly abundant in the more northern site of the Tongue River Breaks Hiding and Riding Area;

I got the riding part of the title but wasn't sure about the whole hiding thing.

We took a left at Ten Mile Road, the name of which made a lot more sense, and then another left at Lemonade Spring Road, which I assumed ended at the Big Rock Candy Mountain. It didn't, and I was disappointed when it just led to yet another gravel road that was in pretty rough shape. It ended with a Forest Service blockade with boulders as big as my truck.

"I guess when the rangers abandon a site, they abandon it with a vengeance." I parked, and we got out, Dog leading the way as I studied the path that led upward. "How far?"

He straddled the brown-painted log beam like a horse, his gaze lifting. "As I recall, about a half mile."

"Up." I looked at the gray skies and pulled my jacket from the truck.

Slipping on his black leather jacket, he smiled. "Yes, that is the general direction."

Picking up the trail as he and Dog moved ahead, I started thinking about Digger Wainwright and the obvious reasons he might've kept it secret that he'd been involved with both girls. I was also wondering exactly which Wainwright Jaya had been with the night she'd gone missing. The more I got to know Digger, the more I thought maybe he should be in a cage somewhere.

I tromped along but felt my hand shift to the middle of my back where the pancake holster held my large-frame Colt 1911. I knew Artie Small Song, and knew he was trouble and was generally well armed, and those two along with a religious zeal didn't exactly inspire confidence.

At the zig of an endless zag, I found Henry and Dog standing in the middle of the path looking up at what could only be described as a fort.

"What the hell?"

"It would appear that Artie has rebuilt the lookout to suit his own purposes."

The bottom portion of the remodeled lookout was entirely encased in native stone with only one solid, heavy door. The upper portion still resembled a fire lookout but with the interlocking timbers more like an old frontier fort with no windows, only small slots where a rifle might poke through.

The Bear and Dog continued on as I pulled my .45. When we made it to the base of the structure, I spotted a few corroded brass shells and picked one up. "A .308. Personally, I'm glad he's not home."

Henry examined the portal. "As far as we know."

"Why does that single door worry me?"

He nodded. "Because Artie is just the type to prepare a rude welcome for uninvited guests." He continued around the building as Dog and I followed. On the back side, there was some dead sage, tumbleweeds, and a few branches. The Bear stooped and pushed the debris away, brushing his hand across the dry dirt, revealing the wood grain of a hidden cellar door.

"You Injuns are tricky." He grunted and found the recessed handle, turned it, and started to pull. "But what if he figured whoever was breaking in would come around here instead?" He turned to look at me as I petted Dog. "You know, with a hand grenade or something? Just asking."

"Why must you make everything complicated?" He pulled the door open, and needless to say, it didn't explode. "Do you have your flashlight?"

Reaching into my pocket, I pulled out my mini Maglite and handed it to him and watched as he shone the beam into the narrow tunnel that led under the building. "Certainly not a full basement." I crouched beside him. "After you."

He shook his head and started down the rock steps that led through a channel way.

I turned to Dog and issued a command. "Sit." He did and then looked at me questioningly. "Stay." He studied me. "I mean it—stay."

I followed after the Bear and watched as he lifted the beam to another trapdoor, pushing on it, and climbed down a four-rung ladder into a large room at the base. I followed Henry's beam and took in the crates of ammunition. "Hoo-boy."

Henry shone the light toward the door where a lethal-looking tactical shotgun was wedged into a chair, a length of twine tied to the trigger and running through eyelets, making for an explosive welcome for whoever opened the door.

"Artie, you bad boy."

The Bear went over, disconnected the twine, and lifted the shotgun. "Mossberg; I do not think Artie would mind if I appropriated it."

I moved over, threw the latch, and pushed open the door. "Dog!"

He entered, tongue lolling and tail wagging.

With the light from the open door, you could see there was enough ammo to start a small war. "Well, it doesn't look as if Artie's hobbies have changed."

Henry looked around. "He must have built this entire structure back by himself."

I followed as the Cheyenne Nation moved toward the steps at the corner, which ended with another trapdoor, which he pushed open very slowly. Assured that it wasn't booby-trapped, he eased it the rest of the way open and poked his head up, looking around.

"Nobody here but us chickens?"

He didn't answer but continued up the steps, taking the shotgun from his shoulder, and I wondered what could be up there that would leave Henry Standing Bear, the Cheyenne Nation, speechless.

Dog preceded me as we went. It was dark there too, but Henry reached up and undid the clasp of a skylight, lowering the wooden cover and allowing a stark, rectangular ray to strike the rough-cut, wooden-planked floor.

It was one room with a counter that held reloading equipment, a sink that ran into a five-gallon bucket, a large cooler, and a single cot. There were no other amenities, and the only decoration was a large symbol on the wall, same as on the cover of the strange little book I'd picked up in Hardin. I stared at the design of a circle with a line through it.

End of the world.

Stepping closer, I could see the brown paint that had been used was flaking from the wood. "Is that paint?"

The Bear examined the wall. "No."

Leaning in, I could see that it was blood that covered something that had been embedded in the wood, which made the entire design the size of a garbage can lid, ivory with flashes of silver blinking in the light. "Henry, are those teeth, driven in by the roots?"

The Cheyenne Nation took a breath and then slowly let it out, whispering, "Human."

"So, have you seen Artie Small Song since we met him on Lonnie's porch that time when you put a knife to his throat?"

"No."

Sitting in the cramped, almost vertical bleachers of the Lodge Grass gymnasium, I had to lean into the Bear's ear just to be heard. "As I recall we put him in the tribal and then the Yellowstone

County jail years ago, but for the life of me I can't remember seeing a photograph of him."

"Possibly not—he was a traditionalist and felt that any photograph might steal part of his soul."

"And what soul is that?"

The game hadn't started, but the packed school was already reaching a fevered pitch. I occupied myself by looking through the throng for either Harley or his father, Digger, neither of whom it looked like had decided to attend.

We'd gotten here only moments ago, but already the place was abuzz over an altercation that had taken place when the Northern Cheyenne players had gotten off the bus. Someone had thrown one of those massive soft drink cups at one of the Lady Morning Stars, who had retaliated by kicking and punching her way in the general direction of where the thing had been launched. It didn't take much imagination to figure out which player it had been.

The Cheyenne Nation leaned back in his seat and studied the raucous crowd. "The natives are restless."

"Uh huh."

He checked his cell phone. "The Rosebud Sheriff's Department has finished clearing out Artie's fortification."

"Except for the shotgun you took."

"I arrogated it as tribute to my not getting cut in half by opening the door."

"Arrogated?"

"It is a common term."

I watched as the somewhat overwhelmed Lady Morning Stars took the court to a chorus of boos. The team's bench was in front of us, a spot we'd arrogated in hopes of providing the team with a small buffer from the Lodge Grass crowd.

The players looked out of sorts. Rosey Black Wolf was her

usual meandering self. Stacey Killsday squinted in the lights, missing more than she hit as Misty Two Bears dribbled off her foot. Wanona Sweetwater wasted her time flashing smiles at the stands, and Jaya ignored them all as she always did, lithely making layups and turnaround jumpers that would've put the fear of the Great Father having to guard her in me.

There was a thunderous report as the entire place stood and cheered as the home team Indians, yes Indians, took the court. Bedecked in orange and black, they looked to be not so big but tough. They jostled and bumped against one another during practice, their faces set in grim determination.

"How has their season been?"

Henry sighed. "They barely made it into this playoff game, but for them beating Lame Deer would be like winning the Super Bowl."

"So, highly motivated?"

"To say the least."

"And the Lady Stars are out, if they lose?"

"Yes."

"I don't like this."

The referee and two umpires came out, calling the captains to the center court where a particularly stern-looking Indian chief in full headdress glared up, embedded into the gleaming floor. After a quick meeting they cleared the court and went over to the timekeeper's table, checking the foul cards like they were going to get a workout tonight.

They blew their whistles for the tip-off as a young man with a Lodge Grass letterman's jacket approached the steps, focusing on me. "You Walt Longmire?"

"Yes."

He pushed a piece of paper toward me. "Somebody said to give this to you."

"Who?"

"Some guy outside. Said it was important."

"And who are you?"

He looked anxious to get going. "Trey."

"Trey, what?"

"Hey man, a guy handed me this and gave me five bucks to hand it to you, all right?"

I waved him off, and he continued up the steps of the bleachers, finally settling in with some other students along the railing that separated the general population from the student body.

"Something?"

"Fan mail from some flounder." Turning from the Bear, I unfolded the piece of paper and stared at the words, not unlike the threatening notes the girls had received—MEET ME OUTSIDE, NOW.

He grunted. "We should go."

"No, somebody's got to stay here and keep an eye on Jaya."

He glanced around. "There are a thousand people who are going to keep an eye on Jaya."

"I'll be fine—save my seat."

With her height advantage, Rosey Black Wolf easily outreached the opposing center, but when she tipped the ball, she thrust it in the hands of a Lodge Grass player and the Indians quickly made a three-pass push, resulting in the first basket.

Hustling to get out of the way, I dodged into the opening and started down the hall toward the exit. Pushing open the door, I looked around at the parking lot, packed with vehicles. I felt the bite of the cold, nudged my hat down on my head, and flipped up the collar on my Carhartt. I stood there for a moment, then decided that either the kid was playing a trick on me, or that whoever had given Trey the note had changed his mind.

I started back for the doors when I heard a whistle.

I turned. At the corner of the building was a collection of dumpsters and a few regular trashcans squeezed against the brick along with a rusted International Scout, a snowplow affixed to it.

I waited a moment and then heard the whistle again.

I walked in that direction until I got to the front of the Scout and looked around, but there was no one there.

I started to turn back when a voice spoke from behind me. "Don't move."

"Okay."

The voice was male, low, and probably Native. "You armed?"

"Always, you?"

"With more than you, I'm willing to bet."

"Then you won't mind if I turn around."

"Don't."

"Okay." I waited a moment. "Are you the one who wrote the note?"

"I am."

"Looks familiar." I pulled the bottom of my coat up and stuffed a hand into my pocket, getting it slightly closer to my Colt. "You write the others?"

"No."

"Then why did you write this one?"

"I thought it might get your attention."

"It did. Look, if you're who I think you are, I'd like to turn around and talk to you."

There was a pause. "And who do you think I am?"

"Artie Small Song—long time no see."

There was a longer pause "You need to leave my mother alone."

"I wasn't aware that I was bothering her—she's the one who

stitched up my head after I took a fall over near the White Tail cabins."

"I heard something took a bite out of you and you lost more than a day of your life."

"Maybe." I blew my breath out in a quickly disappearing cloud. "This is getting tiresome, how about I turn around and we look each other in the face?"

"You can turn around."

I did, and there was no one there. I looked over the dumpster and around the corner but couldn't find him.

"Up here."

I could see a large individual crouched on the edge of the flat roof about twelve feet up, overlooking the alcove where I stood. By design, he was perfectly backlit by the streetlight behind him and no matter how hard I looked I could only see his outline. He was wearing what looked like a black BDU, with the bill of a ball cap sticking out from a hood, and held the barrel of some kind of tactical shotgun that was trained on me.

"What are you, Batman?"

"I'm better, I'm real."

"Yep, well you're going to have to be real with a lot less ammunition—we found one of your caches."

"I got plenty more where all that came from."

"Why? Why are you stockpiling all this stuff, Artie?"

"The end of the world is coming, Lawman."

"So you say. You've got an interesting sense of interior design—where did you get the teeth that are driven into the wall?"

He glanced toward the distance, his breath trailing in front of his face, hiding it even more. "They were given to me."

"By whom?"

"I don't suppose you noticed that all those teeth have fillings. It doesn't like metal—can't take it with it." He shifted his weight, but the muzzle of the 12-gauge stayed on me. "I didn't write those notes to either of those girls."

"Then you have nothing to fear."

"You're right about that. I knew that girl, Jeanie. She came to me asking questions and stuff, but I had nothing to do with her disappearance."

"Come in and make a statement."

He barked out a cold laugh. "I don't think so."

"Any idea who might be writing the notes?"

"I've got a couple of ideas." He leaned out a little. "Hey, Lawman, not to change the subject or anything but have you ever heard of a place called Fort Pratt?"

"Not until recently."

He nodded, studying me. "I got a feeling you're gonna end up going there before long."

"Where is it, exactly?"

He lip-pointed over his shoulder. "North of here."

"Near Fort Shaw?"

"In that direction, but it's not really near anything."

I pulled my hand out of my pocket, trailing it back. "And why would I be going there?"

"Because a teensy part of you is already there, about a day's worth of your life—and if you want to retrieve it, you're gonna have to go get it—all the way to hell and back."

I took a step forward, pressing against the edge of the dumpster, wondering if I could scramble onto the thing and get up on the roof after him; that is if he didn't shoot me in the process. "I've got one for you, have you ever heard of the Éveohtsé-heómėse?"

He was silent for a moment. "Don't say that name out loud or too often, Lawman. You say it one time too many, and you won't have to make that trip to Fort Pratt to find it—it'll come find you."

"What is it?"

"Whatever you've made it to be, whatever you've fed it . . . And I've got a feeling, Lawman, I've got a feeling that over the years you've fed it a lot. The more you feed it, the hungrier it gets."

I worked up a smile and cast it his way. "Artie, if you know anything about me, you'd know that I don't scare easy."

"Oh, don't worry. It doesn't want to scare you . . ."

"How about the number thirty-one, does that mean anything to you?"

"No, should it?"

I slipped a hand into my coat and froze as I heard the action of the tactical shotgun charge. "Easy there, Artie." I carefully pulled the booklet from my pocket and held it up for him to see. "I found this book about the Wandering Without, or it was left for me by a friend."

"What friend?"

Moving the book up higher, I used it to cover my other hand sliding the safety strap from my .45. "Virgil White Buffalo, ever heard of him?"

"I've heard the name."

I dropped my head in a mock chuckle. "Well, if you run into this Éveohtsé-heómése or whatever it is while you're out there prowling around in the dark, you be sure to tell it I'm looking for it, would you?" Snatching the semiautomatic from the holster, I brought it up to find . . .

Nothing.

12

"How could you lose him?"

"It was easy, seeing as how I fell off the last roof I ran around on—I took my time getting up there." The Lady Morning Stars were down eight points at the half, and we sat in our spot and sipped lukewarm sodas. "I was just glad that there were footprints and that he wasn't a figment of my imagination."

The Bear nodded. "What took you so long?"

"I had to get off the roof."

"Do you believe him?"

I thought about it as the girls returned to the court and began warming up. "Strangely enough, yep, I do. I think he's concerned for his mother, which is commendable, but he also wants the wandering-whatever-it-is to have me for lunch." I took another sip of my soda, forgetting how horrible it was. "He also mentioned Fort Pratt."

"Which does not exist."

"As far as we know."

"Maybe it's just the Industrial Indian Boarding School."

"Perhaps, but that no longer exists either."

I patted the booklet in my breast pocket. "But it did."

He shrugged. "I will begin researching with my usual resources."

"You mean go ask Lonnie?"

"I was actually thinking of asking Father Kim over at St. Labre—he has made a study of the Indian boarding schools, and it is possible that he may have some information on this Fort Pratt."

The whistle sounded, and the players retired to their separate benches, the starters returning to center court. "So, we drop Artie for now?"

"Yes, I trust your judgment if not your mountaineering skills."

"Thanks." The tip-off went to the Indians, but Jaya Long had evidently had enough and sliced through the opposing players. Stealing the ball, she loped toward the opposite side to sink an easy layup off the glass. The Lodge Grass players turned and set off downcourt, but Jaya stayed with the two players who attempted to inbound the ball. "I think he's probably guilty of dozens of other things, but I'm not so sure he has anything directly to do with the harassment of Jeanie or Jaya."

"He knew what the notes look like."

I shrugged. "That's only one step above common knowledge."

"And the teeth?"

"I'll let the Rosebud County Sheriff's Department worry about that." He shrugged as we watched Jaya snatch the ball away. She turned, and sinking another, drew the Lady Morning Stars within two baskets. "I figure one case at a time."

Jaya backed off as the Indians inbounded the ball. The team cautiously moved up the court, passing the ball back and forth to stay clear of her. She was mad, and you could tell. If she kept this up, she would surely foul out.

Almost on cue, Jaya slapped the arm of an opponent and was charged for her third foul. The nearest umpire called it, and when she screamed at him, he made it a technical.

The Bear sighed. "One to go."

"She'll never make it."

"I doubt she makes it through the next possession."

"So, you want to drive out and see Digger Wainwright after the game?"

"It will be late."

"I don't care."

"Actually, I did not think you would."

The Lodge Grass player sank the one foul shot and then the next. Despite her coach's yelling, Jaya squared off at the top of the key, ready to make her move as soon as the other athletes put the ball in play.

The pass came, and Jaya went in for the kill, but before she could get there, the player who had the ball looped it over her head to her teammate, who moved quickly across the center-court line. Playing catch-up, Jaya chased the ballhandling forward, but then lost it when the Lodge Grass player tipped the ball toward the basket in an assist, the center slamming it home.

The crowd, predictably, went ballistic as Jaya screamed at Rosey Black Wolf for just standing there under the basket, not even making an attempt to block the other center. "What is wrong with you?!"

Coach Felton signaled a timeout and gestured for her team to come to the sideline, but Jaya stayed out there on the court. Harriet gestured emphatically, and Jaya started toward the sideline.

The crowd was still going crazy as Rosey, crying from the dressing-down, took a towel from one of the players on the bench and wiped her face. Meanwhile, a heated exchange was taking place between coach and player, Felton's finger held inches from Jaya's face. This went on for almost thirty seconds when Jaya reached up and smacked her coach's hand away.

Harriet stood there, her face growing redder by the instant. She looked up at me and then gestured that I should come down to the bench.

I glanced at Henry and then did as she'd requested, the Bear following after me.

When we got there you could hardly hear anything, but I heard Felton as she yelled in my ear from only three inches away. "Take her home."

"What?"

"I want her out of here, and I've got a game to coach, and I don't even want her on my bench—take her home."

"I'll take her out to the bus and stay with her."

"Fine."

She turned back to her team as I reached for Jaya's arm, which she predictably yanked away. I reached again, but this time I grabbed hold and she glared at me. A few pieces of trash were thrown at us as we marched her down the sidelines.

We made our escape and quickly shot through the hallway out the doorway and to the right where the Lame Deer Lady Morning Stars bus sat idling.

When we got to it, I could see my arch nemesis Melvin Rook sitting in the driver's seat for all appearances asleep. I pounded on the door, getting his attention, as he reached over and pulled the lever, opening the folding door and looking at us questioningly. "She just got kicked out of the game."

He pulled a pair of buds from his ears and took a small transistor radio, the likes of which I hadn't seen since the PX in Saigon, from his breast pocket, adjusting the volume and then turning it off. "The young lady only had four fouls."

Following her up the steps, I sat in the seat across the aisle from where she piled herself against the window. "Her coach gave her the boot." He stared at her, shaking his ancient head, the silver crew cut standing at attention like a cock's crown as Henry passed by us and sat in the seat behind her. "Melvin, why don't you take advantage of the opportunity and go in and actually watch the game, huh?"

He studied me for a moment and then glanced at the Bear. "I can trust the two of you with my bus?"

I crossed my heart. "Hope to die."

He nodded and moved toward the door. "Close this after me and don't move this bus. In my experience with this particular contest of wills, we will need to make a hurried retreat and I have us aimed at the exit."

"Roger that." After he stepped out, he motioned for me to close the door, which I did, returning to my seat and looking at the sulking athlete. "Discipline."

She glanced at me and yawned. "What?"

"It's not a bad word, or a bad thing, really."

"What are you talking about?"

"I'm talking about something that can stand between you and the chaos in your life."

"I've been disciplined plenty, thanks."

I sat forward, unable to help myself. "I said discipline, not disciplined. Not punishment. I'm talking about timing and strength. Do you want to go through your life handing your leash to every person you meet to see if they'd like to yank you around?"

Her eyes grew fierce there in the darkness of the idling bus. "Like you?"

I had to smile. "No, I haven't completely perfected it just yet." I threw a thumb at the man behind me. "But he has."

She snorted. "The Sphinx?"

It was quiet in the bus for a moment, and then the Cheyenne

Nation stood and walked forward, opening the door. "I will take a stroll and leave you two to talk."

I waited a moment, closed the door behind him, and returned to my seat. "You could take a pointer or two."

She folded up her jacket, put it against the window as a makeshift pillow, and placed her head there, closing her eyes. "I think I've learned about all I need from you guys."

"What have you been learning from Digger Wainwright?"

Her eyes stayed closed. "What's that supposed to mean?"

"He was in a relationship with your sister when she disappeared after she had an abortion to get rid of what I assume was his child—you don't think it would've been helpful for us to have that information?"

"Helpful to who?"

"And what about your relationship with him?"

"My what?"

Her response seemed sincere, and I was starting to seriously doubt my line of questioning but decided to go on anyway. "Are you having a relationship with Digger Wainwright?"

She raised her head and stared at me. "Gross. You're kidding, right?"

"One of our sources . . ."

She now sat up fully. "Who?"

"Louie Howard . . ."

"Is a moron." She shook her head. "Who I'm seeing is my business and my business alone."

"Do you know Pete Schiller?"

"Another moron, him and his son, the one who is rebuilding that creepy hotel. That's quite a list of informants you've got here, Sheriff."

"Do you know your dad hired them to protect you?"

"The Reichstag—you're kidding."

"I'm afraid not." She slumped back in the seat, and I actually felt for the kid. "At least that's what Louie told us."

She lodged her fingers in her thick hair and then massaged her temples. "I haven't seen him in a year."

"Your dad?"

"Yeah, but at least he's not showing up at my games drunk and hitting people over the head with chairs." She pushed her hair back, turning her face and breathing on the window, then looking at the cloud of condensation. "How is my mom?"

"Last I saw her, I dropped her off at your grandparents' place." I neglected to mention the wrestling match in the yard and waited a moment before adding, "They seem like good people."

She glanced at me. "Big Betty . . ."

"I'll admit she's a character, but she and your grandfather seem nice."

She shrugged, half listening as she glanced through the fogged window toward the gymnasium, where her heart was. "You think I should go in there and apologize."

"Oh, I think you're past that."

"She can't kick me off this team."

"You watch her."

She slammed a shoulder against the seat. "Then they're going nowhere."

"I think they'd rather go nowhere than have to put up with your shenanigans."

Her eyes came back up, flashing ferocity. "None of them care about this team like I do."

"You don't care about this team at all—you care about yourself, winning and looking good, but you don't give a shit about the other players or your coach."

"They aren't good enough to care about."

I scooted forward, leaning in to study her back. "Then help them be better—it's in your power to do that." She studied on that one. "Look, I know it's a lot of pressure when people have their hopes pinned on you, but you're going to have to decide what's important, formulate a plan, and get going. Personally, I don't care if you ever pick up a basketball again, but you've got a life ahead of you and it could be a great one if you can just figure out what you want."

She stared at me some more. "You've got a daughter, huh?"

"Yep."

"You give her this speech?"

"Once or twice."

She turned, laying her forearms on the seat in front on her and resting her forehead there. "It work?"

"She's the mother of my granddaughter and the assistant attorney general of the state of Wyoming." She said nothing as I watched her. "I sometimes tell her that it would also be nice if she were happy."

There was a very long pause, and then the saddest voice I'd ever heard whispered, "What's that like . . . Happy?"

She sobbed, and I had no choice but to move across the aisle and sit there on the seat beside her, cautiously placing my hand on her back. She stayed like that for a few minutes and then turned, burying her face into my shoulder and sobbing some more.

I didn't move. "It's okay, you've got plenty of people who love and care about you."

"They cared about Jeanie too."

We sat there for what seemed like a very long time. There was a light knocking on the bus door, so I stood and moved to the front, where I could see the Cheyenne Nation standing on the other side of the glass.

I opened the door, and he put a foot up on the first step. He spoke quietly. "You are not going to believe this—the Lady Morning Stars are winning."

"You're kidding."

"No. They are not winning by much, but the defense has stepped up and they are maintaining a four-point lead."

"That's great."

"Perhaps not for her." He glanced at Jaya, who leaned against the window, looking out. "Coach Felton does not want her on the bus when the players come out, no matter what the outcome."

I sighed. "So, she wants me to take her home?"

"I am thinking yes." He glanced back at the gym. "I think she is taking advantage of the opportunity that you are here and have a vehicle."

"All right. What do we do about the bus?"

"I will stay here. They may need some assistance in escaping if they do pull off an upset."

"You bet." I moved back down the aisle. "Hey, kiddo, it looks like you get to go home early. C'mon, I'll give you a ride."

Without saying anything, she pulled herself together and tugged her jacket tighter, thumbing the sling of her gym bag up on her shoulder and stepping down in front of Henry. I followed her, calling back to him. "I'll drop her off at Lolo's and see you at the cabin."

He called back to me as he climbed aboard the bus. "Deal."

Jaya slowed, and I stepped beside her, leading her to my truck, which was a couple hundred yards away. Her breath fogged the air in front of her as she trod forward, her head down. "I haven't ever been kicked off a team in my entire life."

I withheld the comment about it being a relatively short life so far and just nodded.

"I'm not going to apologize."

"That's your prerogative, but I think your window to play high school ball is rapidly closing. Then what?"

"I'll just transfer."

"To where this late in the season?"

"Somebody will want me."

"Name one. You've got a reputation, and it's not a good one."

"Then I just quit."

"Also your prerogative." We approached my truck, and I hit the fob, unlocking the doors. "Then what, the drive-through at the Dairy Queen?"

She surprised me and snorted a laugh. "Hey, I like Dairy Queen."

"I do too, just not as a lifelong career choice." I opened the door for her, and she climbed in, tossing her bag on the floor mat. I closed the door behind her and heard a squeal. I figured my sidekick must've introduced himself.

Pulling open the driver's side door, I climbed in and fastened my seatbelt, then watched her scratch his broad muzzle as he licked her cheek. "He came from up here on the Rez—you two should get along."

She buried her face in his thick neck. "What's his name?"

"Um, Dog."

She looked at me. "You're kidding."

"No. When I got him, I didn't have a lot of enthusiasm for naming, so I just called him Dog, and it stuck."

She studied me. "But your daughter and granddaughter have real names, right?"

"Yep, they do." I started the big V-10 and pulled out of the full parking lot, a little concerned but figuring that if anybody could take on the entire Crow municipality of Lodge Grass, it would be Henry Standing Bear.

We drove down the hill toward the interstate, and I took a left, heading north. Jaya continued to pet Dog who finally hunkered there on the center console, where he buried his muzzle in her hair. Before long, they were both snoring.

There was no other way to get to Lame Deer than to drive past the Little Bighorn Battlefield and then to make a right onto 212 toward the Northern Cheyenne Reservation, the diagonal state route that stretched from the South Dakota border to where I now turned off at one reservation and headed for another.

As I drove, I thought about what Detective Chuck Shultz, the investigator for the Yellowstone County Sheriff's Department, had said about the lonely strip of highway that straddled the two reservations and the number of women who had disappeared here.

What could account for so many?

Given, we were talking about a geographic area approaching the size of Connecticut with weather conditions that would make a Mongolian herdsman rush for cover.

Still.

I became aware of two vehicles behind me, maybe about a hundred yards back. Nothing unordinary, but when I first saw them gaining on me, I slowed. They'd gotten within a couple of car lengths but then had dropped back to follow at a more sensible distance, which is not an unusual response when drivers see the lights and stars on the doors.

I continued at the speed limit as some more snowflakes darted across the beams of my headlights. Driving across the rolling hills of eastern Montana, I kept peering back at the lights behind me, keeping their distance, but still there. After they hadn't turned toward Kirby or Busby, I figured they must've been going to Lame Deer as well.

As we started climbing the high ridge outside of town, the closest vehicle pulled out into the opposing lane and passed me, a rattletrap of a white club cab Dodge that had writing on the sides I'd seen before—Alpine Painters.

The other truck pulled in tight behind me just as the one in front slowed.

For a moment I thought about just running into the Dodge, but then figured why damage my truck—instead, I slowed as they slowed, pulling into a turnoff almost at the top of the ridge.

It was a wooded area and a pretty good spot for a highwayman to ply his trade, maybe even a couple of them.

Gliding to a stop, I put the truck in park and flipped on my high beams along with my emergency lights, the blue and red tracers spinning color onto the pine trees that surrounded us along with the truck in front and the one behind.

Might as well give them the idea that the stop was at least partially mine.

Pete Schiller stepped from the Dodge and turned to look at me, pulling back his jacket to display a semiautomatic pistol in his belt and shouting, "Turn it off."

I rolled my window down, leaning out. "No."

"What do you mean 'no.' I said turn it off."

"And I repeat . . . No."

He gestured toward the gun in his jeans. "I'll shoot your radiator."

"And I'll run over you—it'll make it that far."

Because this line of conversation wasn't working, he attempted another. "Give us the girl."

"I don't hardly think so."

"We're supposed to be protecting her."

"Yep, I heard." Pulling the handle, I glanced at Jaya, who looked more than a little worried. "Stay in here, no matter what happens." Sliding out, I pulled the mic from my dash and handed it to her. "If things go badly, key that button and say, '10-78 halfway between Muddy and Lame Deer.'"

"10-78 halfway between Muddy and Lame Deer."

I rolled the window up and grazed a hand across the button, locking the cab.

Looking back at another aged Power Wagon, I could see Louie coming up on the side of my truck—he was carrying a handgun.

I went ahead and pulled mine; what the heck, the more the merrier.

Moving forward and stepping toward the road, I squared off with Schiller but left the .45 dangling in my hand as Louie continued walking up from behind to the front of my truck. "Can I help you, Mr. Schiller?"

"I told you, give us the girl."

"And why would I do that?"

"Because it's our job."

"You keep saying, but I haven't seen you up until now."

He stepped forward, gesturing with the 9mm. "You saw Louie here long enough to shut him in a locker. You think that's funny?"

"It was kind of funny, yep."

"I don't think it was funny."

"Maybe you had to be there."

"You think you could put me in a locker?"

"Probably."

"You don't scare easy, huh?"

I glanced back at the cab of my truck where Jaya held the mic to her face. "Is this going to take long? I've got to get her home, and besides, it's cold out here."

"What if I just shoot you and take her?"

"You can try. I've been shot before, how about you?" I glanced at Louie and then back at him. "I'm not talking about in the leg with a .22, climbing through a fence on a hunting trip when you were a kid. I'm talking about in the chest, lying there listening to your internal organs gurgle and watching the pool of blood fill up in the puddle in your chest and spill over the sides and hoping somebody gets there before you bleed out."

He stared at me but said nothing.

"You might get me, but I'll definitely get you and the other Stooge here—well, he'll be so shaken up, the only thing he'll think about doing is running off."

"You think so?"

"I know so." I was about to speak again when a tremendous blast blew out the back window of Schiller's truck, scattering pieces of safety glass in all directions. Ducking, just in case somebody decided to throw another round, I stepped to the side and then swung my Colt on Louie, only to find him hightailing it to his truck, where he scrambled in and fired the thing up, backing away and swinging around to roar off.

Looking in the cab, I could see Dog going ballistic and then Jaya slowly rising from the floorboards with the mic in her hand. She looked around, wide-eyed, and then gestured with the mic toward me.

I smiled, shook my head, and turned back to Schiller, who had his pistol trained on the hills above us. He looked like he might soil himself. "That wasn't you?"

"Nope. Unless I miss my guess, that was a shotgun."

"Then who . . . ?"

"You must have some enemies." I holstered my weapon. "And pretty close by—not much more than thirty yards, I'd say."

He licked his lips, his eyes and gun casting across the black hillside. "You're not gonna shoot back?"

I shrugged. "They're not shooting at me."

He licked his lips some more and then looked at the missing back window of his truck. "Shit."

"If I were you, I'd get the hell out of here."

He glanced my way before carefully creeping toward the still-open driver's side door of his truck in a cinematic crouch he must've learned from watching too many episodes of *T. J. Hooker.* "Yeah, well, you're gonna see me again."

I smiled, but in the flickering emergency lights, I doubted he saw it. "Looking forward to it and really soon."

He dove in, then slammed the door and ground the thing to life before racing the motor and spinning the wheel and bootlegging onto the pavement, where he almost lost control. Then he hit the gas and rocketed east, leaving a trail of little squares of glass reflecting blue and red off the macadam.

Watching him go, I walked over to my truck as Jaya lowered the window. "Are you okay?"

I nodded and rested my hand on the sill. Dog licked it, knowing better than to trust my self-analysis on such things.

Stretching an arm, I looked into the bed of my truck, the distance to where Schiller's vehicle had sat, and then to the murky hillside, dark as ink. Raising my voice, I called out. "Now, that moron wasn't able to pinpoint where the shot came from, but from the blast and the range, I'd say you shot from the bed of my truck."

There was no response.

"You could at least thank me for the ride from Lodge Grass."

Off in the distance, close to the top of the ridge, a voice called back over the clacking of the emergency lights. "Neaese."

I smiled and opened my door. Jaya stared at me. "Who the hell was that?"

Pulling on my seatbelt, I slipped the three-quarter ton into gear, looking behind me and pulling onto the road to climb the final hill between us and the Cheyenne Reservation capitol. "Unless I miss my guess, Artie Small Song."

Lolo Long was standing on her porch when we got there, and I was beginning to think the tribal police chief never slept. I knew how she felt. At least she was out of uniform and wearing a heavy bathrobe, her fluffy slippers at the edge of the stoop, her arms wrapped around herself as I parked and opened the door for Jaya, who showed no great enthusiasm for getting out.

I stood there holding the door as she reluctantly pulled her bag from the floor and gave Dog one last pet before sliding her sneakered feet to the sidewalk and then marching toward the small house like it was the bridge on the river Kwai and her aunt was Colonel Saito.

I followed, stopping at the steps, as Jaya blew by the chief, who turned to look after her as she yanked open the storm door and went inside. "You win?"

Jaya called back from over her shoulder, "10-78."

The dark-haired woman turned to me, fingering a strand from her face and looking at me through her eyebrows. "What's that supposed to mean?"

"I believe she's been kicked off the team."

"You believe?"

"I strongly believe."

Her phone, which I hadn't noticed in her hand, made a noise and she pulled it from under her arm. "They won by four."

"Henry stayed to provide a rear guard."

"The team might need that in Lodge Grass." Her face came up. "Well, I guess that's that."

"What are you going to do?"

"Not a damn thing."

I started to back away. "Does that mean my services are no longer needed?"

She glanced over her shoulder and back into the house. "What would you do?"

I stopped and stood there, stuffing my hands into my pockets and staring at the sidewalk. "Talk to her."

She folded her arms again, at the same time scuffing the sole of a slipper on the surface of the concrete. "Oh, we're way past that."

"We're never past that, that's our job."

"Police?"

"Parents."

"I'm not her mother."

"Like it or not, you've got the job, or at least part of it." I started to turn to go but then stopped and looked back. "She's scared, maybe for the first time in her life. She has this God-given talent, and she's been pursuing a life with the conviction that that talent was enough and now she's coming to the stark conclusion that it's not."

She hugged herself again. "You might be right."

"She's on a cliff, and she's going to have to go in and apologize not only to the coach but to the entire team."

"Think that'll get her back on?"

"I don't really care if she gets back on that team, I just want to give her a semblance of normalcy—and I think that's what you're shooting for too." I started to go again but then stopped again. "On a grimmer note, I had a meeting with Artie Small Song."

That got her off the porch. "Where?"

"Believe it or not, on the roof of the Lodge Grass high school with an accompanying shotgun."

"At the high school with a shotgun?" She shook her head. "What did he have to say?"

"That he has nothing to do with any of this."

"And you believe him?"

I shrugged. "For now."

She glanced east, where a slight breeze had picked up. "I understand you found an armory over at the old fire lookout that Gordo Hanson confiscated."

"Along with some interesting interior design motifs, yep."

"I heard. So, where does one get that many human teeth?"

"As I recall, his girlfriend was a dental hygienist . . ."

"She moved to Albuquerque; besides, I doubt that was it." Shaking her head, she clutched the collar of the robe, pulling it up to guard against the raw air. "Maybe I'll move to Albuquerque."

"I hear Hatch is nice this time of year."

I started to turn, but she stepped closer. "Um, I think I owe you an apology."

"For?"

"Laying into you about that Willow Canyon thing."

I shrugged. "I haven't really figured out what that was all about yet either."

"You don't remember anything for more than thirty hours?"

"I remember a lot of things, it's just that they don't make any sense." I pulled the thin volume from inside my jacket and handed it to her. "I got this over at Paper Talk, that bookstore in Hardin."

"Lesa Hopkin's place." She took it and studied the cover, opening it and leafing through a few pages and then stopping and turning back to the title page. "Fort Pratt?"

"You know where that is?"

"Yeah, it's up near . . . No, it's where the . . ." She leafed through some more pages and then glanced up at me. "You know, I don't know where it is."

"It might be gone. Henry thinks it might've been one of those Indian Industrial Boarding Schools from the turn of the century."

She nodded. "Anything else I need to know from this century?"

I thought about a way of presenting the information that wouldn't send her inside looking for her sidearm. "The Wainwright family may still be in play."

She waved a hand. "That's her personal life . . ."

"Might be more than that."

She stared at me. "Really?"

"Possibly, but then possibly not—I'm doing some digging and I'll let you know."

She nodded. "You want me to arrest Pete Schiller and his bunch?"

"You can get them?"

"Me, or my friends over in Big Horn County, Yellowstone County, Hardin PD, Billings PD or the Highway Patrol—everybody's itching to stomp into those intellectually recessive gene puddles."

I started off. "I thought they were the superior race?"

"Compared to what, prairie dogs?"

I called back to her as I climbed into my truck. "I think you're being overly hard on prairie dogs."

I heard her murmur as she turned and started back into her house, and toward another battle. "You're probably right."

13

Rather than face cold cereal again, Henry offered to buy us blueberry pancakes at Maggie's so that I could talk to Father Kim at St. Labre about the Fort Pratt Indian Boarding School.

"Father Kim?"

"He is part Crow, part Korean. He was Captain Kim before—came here after a career as a US Air Force chaplain."

I shook my head, finished off the last of my pancakes, and folded up a side of bacon in a paper napkin for my sidekick out in the truck. "So, he's joining us after breakfast?"

"He has a previous engagement."

"Nuns?"

"Mass."

"Ah." I slipped the wrapped bacon into the breast pocket of my jacket. "So, the Lady Stars are in the National Native American Tournament?"

"For better or worse."

"And where's the first game tomorrow night?"

"In Billings, against the first-seed Navajo."

"The Lady Morning Stars don't stand a chance, do they?"

He sighed, looking out the window at the empty Main Street of off-season Ashland, Montana. "Not really."

"What if the team had Jaya?"

He sipped his coffee. "If there was a way to get her to play ball properly, they might have a chance, but I do not know of any way for that to happen."

"Do you think Coach Felton will let her back on the team?"

"No. The feeling I got on the bus last night was that they were all happy to be rid of her. I am afraid they will realize just how much they need her in the second half of the game tomorrow night."

"I could try to talk with her."

"You could try."

"You don't sound very hopeful."

"I am afraid it would take a movement of heaven and earth for it to happen."

"Well, maybe we can move the earth." I looked up at the sound of the door opening and a representative of the other realm, wearing a coyote-fur N-2B jacket in an iridescent blue, walked in. Standing, I proffered a hand. "Father Kim?"

He slipped off a fingerless wool glove. "Sheriff."

I pulled out a chair for him. "Thanks for meeting with us on such a busy morning."

He shook hands with Henry and slumped into the chair. "Not everybody has God, but everybody has religion on a Sunday."

The Cheyenne Nation smiled. "Not us, we have pancakes."

He opened his hands in a wide gesture. "And yet you asked for me?"

"Perhaps, but not quite for God—at least not yet."

He sloughed off his coat. "So, I am here as a lowly academic?"

"You know, you can always spot these Air Force guys."

He laughed. "It's like the Marines, but for smart people." The waitress came over and delivered a cup of what looked like hot tea in front of the priest as he winked at her and then lifted the mug, breathing in the smell of the contents. "I'm sorry I'm late, it's been a busy morning."

The Bear leaned in and smiled. "Did the St. Labre team make the tournament?"

"I'm afraid not after your Lady Stars got through with them."

"Maybe next year."

"Well, I'm assuming we're not here to talk about basketball." He sipped his tea. "Father Brayer said you had some boarding school questions?"

"You're kind of an expert."

He lowered the mug and laughed. "When I was in the seminary, I became interested in the subject, enough to have written a thesis on the matter. It got some interest from a university press and was published along with a number of photographs I unearthed in my travels back east."

"Sounds like grim material."

He raised a fist. "Kill the Indian to save the man. In the late 1870s they were only one part of the United States government's misguided attempts to assimilate the Native population into the mainstream culture." He smiled sadly. "*That*, let me make sure I get this correct, *by placing the savage-born infant into the surroundings of civilization that the Indian would grow to possess a civilized language and habit.*"

"Doesn't sound very forgiving."

"In many cases it wasn't, but there are stories of perseverance and triumph. Where there is life there is hope, but surely you gentlemen didn't ask me here to go over history that's easily discovered in the local library?"

Glancing at Henry, I pulled the booklet from the coat hanging on the back of my chair. I attempted to hand it to Father Kim and watched his smile fade. "Oh, my . . ."

Still holding it, I placed the booklet on the table between us. "Seen it before?"

"Once. A very long time ago."

"Where?"

He took a moment to respond. "I was at St. Mary's Seminary doing research on the Carlisle Indian School when one of the attendees discovered a copy of this book in a used bookstore in Brandywine, Pennsylvania."

"The Baldwin Book Barn?"

He sat back in his chair, looking at the thin volume but not touching it. "Yes, an old stone barn that has five stories of used and antiquary books. My . . . my friend's name was Paul Vanderhoven. He said that he was up on the top floor where they would store the books that were donated or purchased until they could be processed, and he looked up and saw this same volume on the top shelf. It was the only one there, and there were no ladders to reach that high. He said he saw a broom over in a corner, so he used it to knock the booklet off the shelf. He wasn't Native, but he recognized it as something unique, so he brought it back and showed it to me." He reached out to touch it with his fingertips but stopped short. "My translation skills weren't so good back then, but better than anyone else's at a seminary in Baltimore."

"And?"

"It scared me to death. It's an exorcism of chaos written in the first person. The small part that I was able to translate was terrifying . . ." He glanced at the book and then at Henry. "Have you read this?"

"I tried, but the language is archaic and difficult to understand."

He nodded. "As I recall, it's written in an old Cheyenne, very different from the current tongue."

"What happened to the copy you saw?"

"I don't know, the next weekend Paul disappeared."

"What do you mean, 'disappeared'?"

"A week after he found this book, he asked for it back, along with my translations and left school. He never returned. I remember asking a member of the diocese what had happened to him, and this person said he had taken a leave of absence and traveled west. A week later Paul's parents were there, and I was called in to tell them what I knew, which was nothing." He glanced at the book. "Short of the booklet he'd discovered."

"Did they ever find him?"

"No."

I let that one settle awhile. "Have you ever heard of Fort Pratt?" I nudged the book with my fingertips. "The title page says it was printed in a place called Fort Pratt, Montana. Ever heard of it?"

He stared at me for a moment more and then stood abruptly. "I'm afraid I have to go."

"Excuse me?"

He started to back away, knocking his chair over. "I'm . . . I can't help you."

I picked up the booklet and stood, holding it out, and from his reaction I might as well have been handing him a timber rattler. "Father, there's a postcard in here that looks to be a photograph of the school at Fort Pratt . . . ?"

Continuing to back toward the door, his hand fumbled for the handle. "I just can't . . . I'm sorry."

He disappeared through the door. I glanced at Henry and then started after the man. The Bear reached out and took ahold of my arm and I did something I'd never done in my life: I pulled away from him and made my way out anyway.

The wind blew down the desolate street, tiny, biting flakes

sweeping into my face as I spotted the priest unlocking his car door.

Dodging between the diagonally parked cars, I stepped off the curb, grabbed the sill, and held the door open as he stared at me. "Let go."

"Excuse my language, but what the hell is going on, Father?"

"I don't want any part of this."

I could feel the presence of the Cheyenne Nation pulling up behind me as I stared back at the priest. "Part of what?"

"I don't want anything to do with"—he glanced at the booklet in my hands—"with that."

I pulled the postcard from the book and attempted to show it to him. "But what about Fort Pratt?"

"Don't say the name of that place and don't try to find it." He started to close the door behind him but then stopped. "People don't come back from there."

The priest closed the door and started the car, backing it up and pulling out, taillights swerving away in the stark gray of daylight.

Stuffing the card back into the booklet, I turned to the Bear. "Was it something I said?"

He watched the car drive away. "I will call him later to see if I can find out what is troubling him."

We were on our way back in when Henry's cell phone rang. I held the door for him and then continued to the counter with our bill, paying the nice waitress and turning back to him. "Something up?"

"It is a text message from Chief Long, something about Coach Felton. A neighbor of hers had not heard from her this morning and went over to her house but cannot seem to get a response. Chief Long's on-duty officer is busy with a domestic situation, and she was hoping we could stop by, since it is near Ashland on Cheyenne Off-Reservation Trust Land."

"What's wrong with the Rosebud County Sheriff's Department?" He stared at me. "If I were Coach Felton, I'd be sleeping in." Walking out, I pulled the bacon from my pocket. "Tell her sure, we're always here to serve and protect the hinterlands."

Harriet Felton's house was a nondescript single story on Birney Road, and a Chevy Impala plastered with Lady Morning Star stickers was parked out front. There was a backboard with a chain-link net attached to the eaves of the garage. We walked up to the house only to be accosted by an elderly woman who must've lived next door. "I knocked, but she didn't answer," the woman said from the other side of a fence.

I stopped and spoke back to her. "Is she normally an early riser?"

The woman, in honest to goodness curlers and a plastic cap, nodded. "Yeah."

"Well, she had a rough night over in Lodge Grass."

"She needs to get a good man, is what she needs."

Henry stepped onto the porch and knocked. "Advice for the lovelorn?"

"Apparently." He knocked again as we waited. "That was an odd response from Father Kim."

"Yes, and the response to Fort Pratt was even more visceral. If he does not wish to speak with us again, I will contact Father Colton at the diocese to see what he has to say."

"Do you think it has something to do with the seminarian, the Paul Vanderhoven guy?"

"It does seem possible since he had a copy of the book, and he traveled west and subsequently disappeared." He knocked again.

We waited, but there was no response.

"I'm going to the back." Starting around, I noticed that the woman next door still loitered at the fence. "You can go back in; we'll check to make sure she's all right."

She didn't move. "There were some men here earlier."

I stopped. "Excuse me?"

"Early this morning, when I went out to get the paper, there was a white pickup truck in the driveway, with no back window."

"No back window?"

"Yeah."

I walked toward her. "Did it happen to have anything written on the doors?"

"Yeah—Mountain Painting or something."

I arrived at the fence. "Alpine Painters?"

She snapped a finger. "That's it."

"Two men?"

"Three."

As I started back, I called over my shoulder, "Do me a favor and call up the Rosebud County Sheriff's Department and tell them we need them here, right now."

Hustling around the corner, I approached the back stoop and could see the storm door hanging open, the inner door ajar. I unstrapped my Colt as I stepped inside and attempted to push the door farther open, but something was blocking it. Squeezing in, I could see it was Coach Felton in a nightgown and robe lying on the floor, curled into a fetal position, blood pooling on the linoleum.

I yelled out to Henry and then carefully checked her pulse and then her neck to make sure she could be moved. Most of the blood came from a wound at her hairline, but there were multiple contusions, scrapes, and bruises. Somebody, and I had a pretty good idea who, had roughed her up.

The Bear appeared in the door. "Is she all right?"

"I think so, but she's been beaten up pretty badly." I lifted her and carried her to the front of the house and rested her on the sofa. "We're going to need an ambulance."

"There is the health center here in Ashland. Otherwise, she will have to go to St. Vincent, and that is an hour away in Billings."

"The bleeding has slowed, but she needs to be x-rayed for any concussion . . ."

"No hospital, I'm fine . . ." The coach started to raise her head but then stopped and lowered it again.

"You're not fine, now just lie still. What happened?" She tried to touch her head, but I caught her hand, pulling it away as she saw the blood on her fingers. "Am I bleeding on my sofa?"

Glancing up at the Cheyenne Nation, I held on to the hand.

"Could you please go get a towel?" She called after him. "Not one of the nice ones."

Taking her other hand, I fought to keep her attention. "Would you please answer my question?"

"What?"

"What happened?"

She took a deep breath and looked away. "I guess I was attacked."

"By whom?"

"I don't know."

"Do you know a guy by the name of Pete Schiller?"

"No, should I?" Henry approached with a towel, and she gestured him away. "That's one of the nice ones."

The Bear started to turn when I snatched the thing from him and placed it under her head. "He's the one mixed up with Jaya's father, Lane, and he and some of his buddies stopped me on the road last night at gunpoint."

"What does that have to do with me?"

"The woman next door says she saw this Schiller guy's truck in your driveway early this morning."

"She's crazy."

"Maybe, but she described Schiller's truck to a T."

"That doesn't necessarily mean it was him that hit me."

I studied her. "Do you know him?"

"No."

I waited just a few seconds before asking. "You're sure?"

"Yes."

"Then what happened?"

"I went into the kitchen to make coffee this morning, and I must've fallen down."

"Then you must've gotten up again and fell down about seven times." I glanced up at Henry and then back to her. "Coach, I don't know much but I know a trouncing when I see one. You've been savagely beaten, and I know of an individual who is capable of such things, but you say you don't know him. All right, I don't buy it, but in the condition you're in I'm not going to press you. I've got an eyewitness who places his truck outside your house early this morning and that's good enough for me to put a warrant out for his arrest with or without you pressing charges."

"What makes you think he did it?"

I listened as a siren approached. "He has a pattern of violence."

Two cruisers pulled up outside as the Bear walked to the window and parted the curtain. "Let's pretend for a moment that that's the case and maybe you don't know him, but he knows you,

I can guarantee it. Supposedly, he and his buddies were hired by Lane to protect his daughter, and he's been very aware of where Jaya is, which means he knows who you are—I'm just trying to figure out why he would've done this to you, and without your cooperation the chances of that are inordinately slim."

Her eyes dropped. "I . . . I don't have anything to say."

"Well, you're going to the hospital."

Henry opened the door and stepped out to greet the constabulary and medical personnel. "My guess is you've got a concussion and that means you get it looked at and get x-rayed, which means Billings."

"I'm not . . ."

"You are, and there's not going to be any more argument." I stood as the technicians entered with a gurney. "You can lie to me all you want, but I'm going to find out what the story is here, and you're going to the hospital."

"So, you think she's lying?"

"I'm sure of it."

Gordo Hanson shrugged and leaned on the fender of his unit. He peeled off a few shriveled leaves from a pouch and stuffed them into his mouth. "Let's go pick him up."

"Where?"

He chewed awhile, getting the wad softened as he looked off into the distance like the Marlboro Man. "Oh, I know of a few places we can give a shot. I'm pretty sure his residence is in Billings, but that other peckerhead, Louie, lives over in Wood Place near the Amish settlement. If they're holing up over here, I'd bet that's where they'd be."

I shook my head. "You've got white supremacists on one side

of the county and militant Artie Small Song on the other—that's the makings of a civil war there."

"I'm not so sure it'd be so civil." We watched the ambulance pull away as Henry joined us with Dog, whom he had graciously allowed to water the lawn.

The Bear watched as Sheriff Hanson walked toward his unit. "We are going somewhere?"

"He says the Louie guy lives over in Wood Place, a town I've never heard of."

"Not so much a town, really, more of a place, with wood."

"Right. He says Schiller and his group might be over there, and I'd like to have a conversation with him."

At the truck, the Bear opened the rear door, allowing Dog to jump into the back and then climbed in the front himself. "Conversation, is that what we are calling it these days?"

I hit the ignition and pulled out, following the Rosebud County sheriff. "For now."

We'd gotten onto the main drag of 212. Before long, we took the cutoff toward North Tongue River Road, and he spoke again. "It is a head injury, so they are going to keep her overnight."

"Yep."

"And if it is a concussion, they will keep her longer."

I glanced at him. "What's your point?"

"She has a game to coach in Billings tomorrow night."

I stared out the windshield. "She doesn't have an assistant coach?"

"Have you seen one?"

"No." I thought about it. "What about Tiger Scalpcane, the athletic director?"

"He will be in Bozeman with the boys' team."

He stared back at me as the thought dawned. "No way."

"They like you."

"They like you too."

"In a different way—I scare them."

"Henry, I don't know anything about the game."

"We will get you some help."

"Besides Jaya isn't playing—my responsibility to the team is over."

"Those girls need leadership, and they talked about you when we were riding back last night—I think you are a settling presence in their lives, and they have very little to settle them."

I laughed. "Wait'll I start coaching them, then they'll get unsettled." I glanced at him again, noting his solemn expression. "You're not joking, are you?"

He turned and studied me. "These girls are having the chance of a lifetime stolen from them through no fault of their own. Last season they finished rock-bottom in their division, Jaya graduates this year, and the team will likely finish last in their division next year. They will never have an opportunity like this again."

"She's not on the team anymore."

"They will accept her if you say they should."

"I'm not so sure they should."

"It is her last chance too." Gordo made a left onto Greenleaf Road, and I followed, keeping a reasonable distance. "You never made bad choices when you were young?"

"You know I did, most of them were with you."

"Then give her a chance."

"Look, let's cross that burning bridge when we get to it. In the meantime, how 'bout we do cop things and go round up some bad guys?"

"You will consider it?"

"Sure."

"Really consider it?"

I nodded my head. "I will, honest."

Gordo took another left and pulled to a stop. Parking alongside him, I watched as he rolled his window down and leaned over. "Okay, it's not really a house, so don't be surprised."

"What is it?"

"Well, it started out as a house, but then Louie ran out of money after he got the basement poured, so it's more of a hole in the ground with a roof."

I glanced in the direction we were both parked. "It can't be as difficult to get into as Fort Artie east of here."

Gordo shrugged. "Maybe."

"You've been here before?"

"Serving civil papers."

"How did that go?"

"He shot at us."

"Louie?"

"He didn't hit anybody, but he about gave one of my deputies a shit hemorrhage—I think he's a lousy shot."

"Lucky for your deputy." I took off my seatbelt and opened up the door, stepping out and pushing Dog's head back inside. "So, how do you want to do this?"

Gordo met us at the front of the vehicles, and I noticed the Bear was carrying the 12-gauge he'd liberated from Artie Small Song. "Pretty straightforward. We'll just go up, and if he shoots at us again, I think we can feel free to return fire."

I pulled my Colt from the holster, figuring an ounce of prevention was worth a pound of buckshot. Henry stepped forward but then turned and looked at Gordo. "You first?"

He snorted. "I thought the Indian scout was always in the front."

"Your county."

Gordo shook his head. "God, I love this job."

He began walking up the road, and we fell in behind. "Funny, I didn't think of Louie as the violent type."

The Cheyenne Nation shrugged. "People change when they are behind a gun or in front of one for that matter."

We approached a ridge where the dirt road swept left and stopped at a plateau with a view from all sides. There, in the center, was what looked like someone had stolen a house but left the roof. It was cobbled together with asphalt shingles that had seen better days, and for the life of me I couldn't see any windows or doors. "Um, how do you get in?"

"There's one of those Bilco cellar doors on the other side."

I spotted the aged Dodge Power Wagon, the one I'd seen last night, parked beside a tree over the hill. "No windows?"

He pointed. "There are slits under the eaves."

Henry, always prepared, had taken the old Vietnam-era binoculars from inside my truck and lifted them to his eyes. "There is a rifle barrel stuck out from one of the slits."

"I take it back; what I said about this being better than Artie Small Song's fortress." I studied the structure and thought about what great targets we made standing out here. "Where's the gun?"

He lowered the glasses. "Right corner, but it is odd."

"What?"

"The barrel is pointed slightly up."

Henry handed me the binoculars. "Think he's expecting an air raid?"

"Or he is asleep." He gestured with a hand. "You two go that way, and I will work my way to the right and see if he moves."

"Why do you get to draw fire?"

"I am the Indian scout." He smiled at Gordo and then took the binoculars back and hung them around his neck. He studied his own weapon, nudging the button, and then quoting the old maxim of gun safety. "Red means dead . . . I am the one who shoved him in a locker, so he is most likely to shoot at me."

"Sound logic."

The Cheyenne Nation made his way to the right, Gordo and I starting off to our left. "Since when did the Bear start liking shotguns?"

"Since he liberated that one from Artie Small Song's armory—it was propped up in a chair, booby-trapped into shooting whoever opened the door. It's also like the one Artie had down in Lodge Grass and the one he used to blow out Schiller's truck window last night."

He made a face. "I miss a lot in the last twelve hours?"

I nodded. "It happens when you actually sleep."

We made the corner and looked down the length of the building—the gun barrel hadn't moved. Gordo continued, and I followed. He stood by a metal cellar door leading down into the foundation and whispered, "It's not locked, so he must be home."

"You want to announce our presence?"

He raised an eyebrow. "And give him another chance to shoot us?"

"He could shoot Henry instead."

He stooped, turned the handle, and began lifting. "Somehow, I doubt it."

"Stop." We both turned to see Henry standing a little way off.

The Bear moved in closer, stooping beside Gordo. "Something is not right here."

Gordo carefully eased the door handle back in place and stepped to the side. There were a few downed branches behind us, and I reached back to grab one. Stepping forward, I slipped the crooked end under the handle and moved to the side with the two of them and lifted.

The blast was deafening.

Most of the pellets ricocheted off the metal panel but a few embedded into its surface as we all crouched there, letting our ears work again. Gordo turned to Henry. "I owe you one, scout."

The Bear stood and took the stick from me to pull the door the rest of the way open. Keeping the muzzle of the tactical shotgun ahead of him, he paused for a moment and then started down the steps.

We followed as Henry paused at the bottom to remove the string setup connected to another slightly more conventional shotgun duct-taped to yet another chair propped against a fifty-five-gallon drum.

There were stud walls stapled with opaque plastic gently moving as a breeze blew in from the open doorway above. The rafters were naked; no insulation. I guess when Louie's money ran out, it really ran out.

"Doesn't he work at the mine?"

"Yeah, but he's also got three ex-wives and a half dozen ex-children."

"Ex-children?"

He moved past me toward a dangerously wired toggle switch. "That's what the civil visits were about." He flipped the switch and, unsurprisingly, nothing happened. "Looks like he couldn't pay his electric bill either."

Henry walked past us, staring down what, in a finished house, would be called a hallway.

Gordo pulled a Maglite from his belt and shone it around, the plastic reflecting the beam. "I guess we're the only ones here."

"Maybe." I followed Henry down the hall, smelling what I was sure he had smelled: a tang in the air, a metallic odor that in my experience could only be one thing.

There was an open doorway to the right where an army cot was pressed up against the wall, along with a heap of dirty clothes and a utility-size trash can overflowing with refuse. Tacked to the rafter was a large Nazi flag. All in all, it was hard to envision this as the den of a superior race.

Henry moved on, Gordo followed, and I brought up the rear, still smelling the familiar but unwelcome smell. We two stopped at the last doorway where the barrel of the rifle had been stuck through a coal chute, a furnace room in which piles of coal had been loaded—cheap fuel for a guy who worked at a mine. The shovel was still in his hand.

Louie Howard was there, at least a majority of him was.

Most people are fortunate enough to not see the cataclysmic effect of a shotgun blast on a body, but if you're in law enforcement you'll see it sooner or later. People often use them for suicide, I suppose to ensure that an unsteady hand will still get the job done.

But Louie hadn't committed suicide. Someone had gotten very close to him from behind and then shot him square in the back, and not too long ago. The chunk of meat and organs the double-aught buck had taken from the chest cavity was evident because someone had taken the time to roll the body over.

I wondered why there was a great deal of blood on his face. Reaching down, I used the barrel of my semiautomatic to pry his lips open, the rigor holding them in a postmortem sneer. "Somebody pulled out all of his teeth."

14

"We both know who the impromptu dentist was."

"Where did Gordo go?" I nodded as we sat there in the Stirrup Coffee Shop at the Dude Rancher Lodge in Billings, where I'd decided we would crash for the night after checking on Harriet. "That, and the welcome wagon reception." I sat my fork down beside the very little that was left of my trout dinner and stared out the window at the streetlights, just glimmering to life. "Why kill Louie?"

"He was in the van the night Jeanie went missing."

I glanced at him. "It's that simple?"

"Sometimes it is." Henry lowered his mug and grimaced. "He was there, he knew something, and someone wanted him dead."

"Artie wanted him dead."

He studied me. "It certainly would appear."

I rested my napkin over the remains of the noble trout. "So, what you're saying is unless someone was trying to make it look like Artie?"

"I did not say anything, but if they were, they certainly did a marvelous job."

I took a deep breath and slowly let it out. "Actually, if I were Artie, I'd be insulted."

He finished his steak and crossed his cutlery on the plate. "Any word from the Rosebud County sheriff?"

"No formal report, but he has the same concerns we do and if I were a betting man, which I'm not because it's just a tax against those who are bad at math, I'd bet the shotgun that was mounted at the door is the same Ithaca Deerslayer that killed Louie and the same one Lane was cleaning at his house when we first met him."

"It did seem vaguely familiar."

"You wanna go see Lane after we check on the coach?"

"Seems like a logical progression."

The waitress brought over the bill, but Henry grabbed it before I could. "C'mon, I'll put it on my expense account."

He fished his wallet from his jeans. "What expense account?"

"The one I'm going to start after I move to the beach and live in a trailer and buy a gold Firebird and an answering machine." I did my best James Garner voice, "This is Walt Longmire, at the sound of the tone leave your name and message and I'll get back to you."

"There are no beaches anywhere near Cheyenne, where you have a granddaughter."

"I completely forgot."

I followed him outside where sleet was trying to fill the air but failing instead, just making the surroundings wet and raw. I reached into my jacket, feeling the small book there. I couldn't convince myself that it was real. "I think I need to go up to Fort Pratt when this is all over."

"What if it does not still exist?"

"I'll look for the remains."

"Of a ghost town?"

"I guess."

"Certainly, a town with ghosts." He looked at me from across the hood as the lights shimmered off the freezing pellets. "Now, why would you want to do that?"

"You don't think something strange is going on here? I mean, more than we know?"

"There is always more than we know. Why is this different?"

I patted my chest. "This time there's evidence."

"Perhaps it is more my purview."

I pulled open the door and climbed in as my backup licked the side of my head. "Maybe I'm broadening my horizons." I glanced over as he climbed in and shook his head. "What?"

"You think it is dangerous, so you wish to do it yourself."

I fired up the engine and backed out, headed toward St. Vincent. "What could be dangerous about an old ghost town?"

"You are bullheaded and looking for a confrontation with something you do not understand."

I shrugged. "That's how most of my confrontations end up."

"I do not think you should do this."

I parked in front of the hospital. "Look, we've got other, more important things to contend with—I'm just talking about it."

"Talk leads to action." I started to get out, but he grabbed my arm like a grappling hook. "Promise me you will not pursue this without my guidance."

I stared at him, and this time I didn't pull away. "This Éveohtséheómėse has you rattled, huh?"

"I do not think it has you rattled enough."

I looked down at the hand and then back to him. "If I weren't taking it seriously enough, I am now." I smiled, just to let him know I appreciated his concern.

Harriet's room was on the corner and commanded a nice view of downtown Billings, where we could see the red neon of our motel only three blocks away. She pushed some hair that escaped from under the bandages out of her face and smiled at me from two black eyes. "After visiting hours."

"I've got this badge that makes people do what I tell them."

"I wish I had one, all I've got is a whistle."

"That's all right, I can't get anyone to run laps." She smiled, and I took off my hat, resting it on my knee. "How do you feel?"

"Surprisingly well."

"That's not what the doctor says."

The smile faded. "You talked to him?"

"Badge." I pointed at my chest. "He said you're heavily concussed, having continual headaches, ringing of the ears, blurred vision, nausea, and that they're keeping you for a few days under observation. I miss anything?"

"I've thrown up three times today."

I waited a moment before asking her, "So, are you ready to tell me about Schiller?"

She started to touch her head but then pulled her hand away, letting it drop. "Stupid, huh?"

I shook my head. "I've seen worse."

"I didn't know who or what he was." She sighed. "We got close and I confided in him about a period in my life when I'd made some mistakes—drugs and other stuff—and he made it clear that if I didn't do as he asked, he'd take the info to the state athletic association and get me canned. He finally got around to wanting access to Jaya, thinking I'd go along, and when I didn't . . ." She gestured to the hospital surroundings and then slumped back against her pillow. "You can't use that magic badge and get me out of here, can you?"

"Nope."

She looked toward the Bear as he stood at the window with his back to us. "I've been fighting to get these girls into the state tournament for seven years."

"Well, you did it."

"And now I can't coach them there."

"No, you can't. Isn't there anybody to take your place, an assistant coach or something?"

"No, I mean there are hangers-on that'll come in, now that the team has made it to the tournament; all the wrong kind of people. The girls won't respond to that, and they'll just fold." She glanced at Henry. "They're a very close-knit group, distrustful of outsiders, which works to their advantage in competition with other teams I suppose, but doesn't open them up to the idea of a new leader."

"What about Jaya?"

She stared at the sheets covering her legs. "What about her?"

"C'mon."

"They don't want her, Sheriff."

The Bear spoke to the plate glass, his voice ricocheting back at us. "The Navajo are a much stronger team; they may not want her, but they need her."

"They'd rather lose without her than lose with her."

He turned. "They do not have to lose at all."

"They don't have a coach."

He turned and approached the bed on the other side. "What about the man before you?"

"You're kidding, right?"

"I am serious."

"No offense, Mr. Standing Bear, but those girls are scared to death of you."

He smiled his paper-cut smile. "I am not talking about me."

She slowly turned to look at me.

I cleared my throat. "Not my idea."

She turned her head back to the Bear. "Does he know anything at all about basketball?"

"Not particularly, but I can assist him." Henry took a chair from beside the wall, pulled it out to the other side of the bed, and sat, taking a few seconds to compose himself. "These girls need a chance, and this is the only thing I can come up with, so unless you have another idea . . . ?"

She smiled but then stopped suddenly, placing her face into her hands.

I leaned forward. "Are you all right?"

She nodded briefly and then slumped back on her pillow.

"Do you have anyone else?" He waited, but she didn't respond. "I think they will accept him and at least that gives you breathing room until they release you."

She reached over and pulled a thick binder from the nightstand, dropping it into her lap. "They have three games in the next three nights and that's if they win every one of them."

He placed a hand on her hand, very different from the one he'd placed on mine. "Is that not what we are hoping for?"

After a few seconds, she lowered her hand onto the playbook and stared at him. "You're crazy."

"Yes."

She handed me the vinyl binder. "You're crazy too."

"Boy howdy." I sounded more certain of it than the Cheyenne Nation.

"I just want to be clear that this is a bad idea."

It was only about a mile to the south side of Billings, but it might as well have been another planet. While I drove, Henry ignored me and chatted with Gordo on his cell phone, nodding and grunting a lot but basically conveying nothing to me. "Uh huh."

Waiting for a train on Twenty-seventh Street, I carried on the monologue with myself. "Call my daughter and ask her about my abilities with teenage girls."

He nodded into the phone. "Uh huh."

"There were numerous times when Cady threatened to run away from home, and as a matter of fact she did run away to your place one time."

"Uh huh."

"Have you ever thought that maybe what those girls need is a little scaring?"

"Uh huh."

"This isn't funny."

"Uh huh."

I watched the cars speed by, wishing I was on one. "I mean it."

"What?"

When I turned, he'd hung up the phone and slipped it into the inside pocket of his leather jacket. "So, are we going to give Lane back his shotgun?"

The Bear peered through the fogged windshield and then reached over and flipped on the defroster. "If Gordo Hansen and the Rosebud County sheriff wish it to be so, but I doubt it."

The last of the trains pulled out, throttled up, and headed south. "Did you hear anything I said?"

"You have serious misgivings about your prospects as a high school basketball coach." He shrugged. "Gordo says it was indeed the same Ithaca shotgun, but because the only fingerprints on the weapon are mine, I have been moved up to suspect number one."

"You're kidding."

"I am, but you are obviously not in a joking mood."

I turned the corner, and we drifted into a run-down neighborhood. "No, I'm not."

"DCI and the FBI are on scene, but they haven't discovered anything out of the ordinary other than the somewhat extraordinary existence Louie Howard appeared to be living. They are also glad we are attending to Lane and may approach this as an official visit."

I pulled in and parked across from the tiny house. "Not our jurisdiction."

"According to the agent in charge and Gordo, we may proceed as if it were."

Dog whined, but I shook my head. "I'm not letting you out in this neighborhood, you're likely to catch something." I waited for Henry, and we started across the pavement, the ground fog making it feel like we were in a film noir.

"I have been meaning to tell you I had a dream about your wife last night."

This seemed to come out of nowhere, but I was curious. "Martha?"

"You have had another wife I do not know about?"

"Am I going to want to hear this?"

"She was dancing."

Stepping up onto the curb, I studied the house. "Really?"

"In a library."

"She was a really good dancer."

He nodded, perhaps with more enthusiasm than I saw fit. "Yes, she was."

"Okay, that's enough." I pointed toward the house, carefully unholstering my Colt. "The door is open."

As we approached, his head inclined, noting that the door to

Jimmy Lane's home was indeed ajar and that the light spilled out onto the gleaming concrete stoop. "Well, at least we know this one is not booby-trapped."

Coming at the door from an oblique angle, we could see a lamp lying on the floor not too far from the doorway. The slush on the stoop was disturbed where somebody had walked on it recently.

I looked into the living room but could see nothing other than the floor lamp, its shade torn and lying to the side. Nosing a little forward, I could see a gallon bottle of grain alcohol lying on the floor. I carefully pushed the door the rest of the way open and stepped over the stoop so as to not affect the prints there.

There had definitely been a struggle, and from the look of it, somebody had been dragged from the place.

He stood behind me. "Someone has taken Lane."

"I'd say that's a fair assumption." Just to be sure, I did a quick sweep of the house, then returned to the front room. "Nobody here."

"There was a struggle." He indicated the broken corner of the coffee table on which the man had rested his Deerslayer shotgun. "Blood and hair where his head must have struck." He pointed again. "A small amount of blood on the carpet, and I would say from the traces inside and on the stoop, he was taken from this place."

I holstered my .45. "Well, I'm not saying it's not Artie, but my money would be on Pete Schiller."

"As would mine, but why?"

"Like you said, too many loose ends."

"But why suddenly?"

"We're getting too close?"

"But he stopped you on the highway last night."

"I guess hoping to scare me off, but when that didn't work . . ."

"I suppose."

"You don't sound convinced."

He pulled the cell phone from his coat. "That is because I am not."

"Are you getting an address for Schiller from Gordo?"

"I am."

"Then I'll have a closer look around."

Continuing down a short hallway, I looked into the rooms as I went, ending at the bedroom, where I turned on the light and stepped in. The place was a disaster. The bed was a mattress lying on the floor, and the only other furnishings were two rubber containers and a clothes hamper. There were sheets thumbtacked over the windows, and another strangely placed on the wall above the bed.

I stepped forward and pulled the sheet back to reveal a symbol hastily spray-painted on the wall—the same one that had been at Artie's armory and in the thin book within my inside pocket.

I stood there looking at the symbol for the end of the world.

"Interesting." Henry stood in the doorway. "I find it hard to believe that Artie would put this here and then hide it."

"Agreed."

"So, does this mean that Lane is a member of this *cult*?"

"I do not know."

"I mean, he goes from neo-Nazis to the Cheyenne death cult?"

"He appears to be something of a joiner."

"Yep." I dropped the sheet. "You get an address for Schiller from Gordo?"

He nodded. "The Montana Department of Labor has his residence listed as the Baker Hotel, but there is no address or phone number."

I pointed at the phone. "You can look things up on that?"

He smirked. "Yes."

"Find Alpine Painters and get me an address, if you would be so kind."

It was in the industrial section of Billings, near the railroad tracks, with cyclone fencing all the way around and an unlocked gate, but the really worrisome deterrent was a Doberman pinscher who stood nearby, watching us as we watched him.

"What now?"

Opening up the door, I listened as the guard dog barked and leapt against the fence. "Luckily, I have a specialist." Pulling the back door open, I watched as Dog leapt onto the sidewalk and then stretched, looking at his potential adversary with a bored expression. "Go say hi."

He started toward the gate, his steps stiffening as his hackles rose. The Doberman looked a little less sure than he had a moment before but continued barking and leaping against the chain-link. Dog stood unmoving as the Bear and I approached, then turned to look at me as I reached up to undo the clasp. The guard dog finally left off and landed on the other side of the gate, growling and snapping, but no longer jumping against the fence.

When I started flipping the horseshoe-shaped latch up, Dog crowded the opening, intent on going through first. Throwing the latch, I pushed the gate open as the Doberman continued to growl but began backing up as Dog muscled his way in and approached him. As Dog continued to move forward, the guard dog backed away without a sound. The Doberman suddenly flopped onto his side, wagging his tail and looking up at the brute.

"Good boy."

"I believe it is a girl."

I looked closer. "Good girl."

We headed toward a massive, dented, and rusted warehouse where the Alpine Painters truck, missing its rear window, now sat parked. There was a light on inside, so I once again slipped the large-frame Colt out and moved to one side, with Dog and Henry staying behind me. It was a stealthy approach, until spoiled by the fact that the Doberman trotted through the doorway ahead of us.

Our cover blown, I poked my head inside and could see a few worktables and shelves of paint. A single bulb hung over the center table, swaying back and forth as if recently hit. I reached up to steady its motion and felt something wet on my fingers. Turning the bulb, I could see a dark liquid on one side. "Oh, boy . . ."

There were more fresh marks on the table, one in a strange circular pattern almost two feet across. Henry approached and swiped a finger across the thin line. "Blood." I spotted another stream of light coming from a doorway in the building behind some of the shelves that held stacks of the used paint cans, the remaining contents streaming down the sides.

I'd started moving that way when a sound came from that direction.

"Call Billings PD and tell them we've got a bit of a situation down here."

Henry pulled out his phone as I continued moving toward the direction of the noise. I had just turned the corner when I kicked something that shot forward on the concrete and scraped into the tin wall with a loud clang. Reaching down, I picked up what looked to be a metal hoop with a clasp, the kind you use to seal fifty-five-gallon drums, and I had a very bad feeling. Stepping sideways, I looked into the larger part of the building. It held what must have been close to a thousand metal drums. I looked around for a switch, but there didn't seem to be any lights other than the two strips of dim fluorescents. I turned to see Henry and the two dogs standing in the opening. "So, which one of these do you think Schiller stuffed Jimmy into?"

He whistled. "I think we leave that to the Billings police, who are on their way."

It was then that I detected a faint, unusual scent. "Hey, is it me or do you smell some sort of smoke?"

He stepped up beside me, sniffing for himself. "Yes, I do."

"Get the dogs out of here and tell the Billings PD to bring a fire truck." I moved forward, sniffing the air. There were no labels on the barrels, but there was a shipping document in a plastic envelope lying on the floor. I picked it up and pulled apart the enclosure. Inside was a manifest from Houston for 383 barrels of methanol. A simple aliphatic alcohol . . . Industrial, extremely flammable, and burns almost invisibly.

I hollered out into the next room. "Henry, can you hear me?!"

After a second, he appeared in the doorway. "Yes?"

"You're too close. As near as I can figure we've got over two thousand gallons of highly combustible solvent in here, and if it goes it's going to take this entire block with it." I tossed him my keys. "Throw the dogs in my truck and get the hell out of here."

"What are you going to do?"

"I'm just going to see if there really is a fire and if there's anything I can do about it."

"That is what firemen are for."

"I always wanted to be a fireman . . . Go."

He did as I asked, and I turned toward the back of the building where the smell seemed to be strongest. As I got to the corner, I could see some kind of flame reflecting on the metal surface of the corrugated steel wall. I looked behind the stacked barrels and could see another that was just getting going. It was open, with flames licking from the inside.

Real skilled arsonists are difficult to come by, and the amateurs are generally easy not only to detect but also to apprehend, if not by law enforcement then by nature. Most building materials these days are manufactured for fire suppression down to the drywall in most residential homes, where if you don't break through the walls to expose the wooden studwork underneath, a fire quickly dies. Most arsonists use a liquid fuel and pour it all over the carpet or furniture, but a metal building with concrete floors was a bit more of a challenge. Granted, with more than two thousand gallons of highly flammable liquid accelerant in the immediate vicinity, the odds increased. But the fire had to get to the accelerant.

Looking around in the decrepit building for an extinguisher proved futile, so withstanding the faint fumes I slipped on my gloves, reached out to take the barrel by the rim, and began dragging it around the multitude of others back toward the opening from where I'd come.

I'd just made it to the central walkway, and I looked into the drum where the makeshift arsonist must've stuffed some newspapers and shop rags, the remains of methanol doing the rest. As I looked at the floor, I saw something that shouldn't have been there. I kneeled and picked up the thin, cedar-seed, ghost-bead bracelet that Jimmy Lane had been fingering on his wrist when I first met him, when he'd told me about the fishing trip with his daughters. I looked up at all the barrels upon barrels and shook my head. "Oh, Jimmy, which one of these things are you in?"

I heard the grating noise of the corrugated door sliding shut in front of me.

Stooped there in the middle of the floor, I wasn't entirely sure what I'd heard, but the closed door itself substantiated my suspicions. Tucking the bracelet into my jacket pocket, I stood for a second, listening to what sounded like a chain being run through the handles on the other side and then secured. "You have got to be kidding me."

Figuring the flaming barrel was relatively harmless in the middle of the aisleway, I walked the rest of the way over and gave the door a yank—it did not move. I yanked again, but it still held as if it had been welded. I knocked. Loudly. "Look, Schiller, if that's you, do you want to open this door? I've got your burn barrel out here where it can't do any harm and the police are already on their way—not to mention that Henry and my dog are out there somewhere just waiting for the opportunity to sink their collective teeth into you."

Unsurprisingly, there was no response.

Turning back toward the incendiary barrel, I figured I'd look for another door.

"Oh, shit . . ." I had tracked back in the direction that I'd dragged the barrel, and there was a trail of tiny flames where the methanol must've leaked. My immediate thought was how much had leaked from the barrel as it had sat behind the others. When I looked that way, I saw much larger flames flickering from behind the wall of barrels on the corrugated tin. I ran back and could see that the methanol had crept across the concrete to pool in the low space behind the barrels and was now in full, pale-blue flame, licking up the walls in undulating waves.

As I stood there in disbelief, I could hear the barrels in the back row thumping as the chemical grandson of wood alcohol heated and expanded in an attempt to escape—and take me and a portion of the largest city in Montana with it. This was getting serious.

My attempts at finding another way of egress took on a bit more urgency. Quickly moving back toward the center, I scanned the walls but couldn't see another door. The walls looked too solid to try to kick a hole in them, and besides, I figured I didn't have time to find a loose panel.

I looked up to the roof where there was an elevated ridge vent that ran the length of the building. Some of the screens had come loose and hung from their frames. Glancing at the barrels stacked on either side of me, I was more than a little disappointed to find that the top of the one backed by the flames was the closest to the ridge. Hearing sirens approaching, I calculated my options, figuring the only chance I had was to start climbing, and that right soon—so I did. With the low boil-rate of the chemicals, there wouldn't be any small explosion with this stuff; it would just be a quick flash along with a loud *whoosh* and a hundred square feet would go up like a napalm strike.

I scrambled across a few barrels and pulled myself up to another layer of drums, now only about two levels from the top. The barrels were full, which provided a stable platform, but which also assured an impending dramatically explosive death.

After clambering onto the top barrel, I reached out for the edge of the elevated ridge but couldn't quite get to it without committing myself to leaning over the void. All I could hope was that the structure would hold and that my grip would last until I could get my legs through the opening.

I could see the flames still glowing behind the barrels along the walls and turned back to the weathered rafters in hope that they'd hold my weight; otherwise, I would come crashing down, a 250-pound catalyst.

I stepped off the barrels so that I could grab one of the exposed ridge beams. It seemed stable, so I lifted my legs and stuffed them through the opening, but unfortunately caught my jeans on some loose tin.

I hung there.

After a moment, I realized that I wasn't going to be able to force my way out like this. The only other thing I could think of doing was to pull back and flip my legs through the opening directly above me, effectively doing a summersault onto the roof.

To say that I'm not built for gymnastics would be the grossest of understatements, but I really had no choice—it was either try the summersault or let go and take my chances.

I pushed loose, swung back, and then, using the momentum to come forward, flipped my legs through the vent window above. Fortunately, I punched through onto the tin roof, the only problem being that I could feel the majority of my weight resting on the focal point at my hips. I was feeling a little less confident, especially when one of my hands slipped, almost sending me catapulting into the fuming void.

Grabbing the beam again, I slid onto the roof, not helped by the amount of water the fire department was shooting up on the metal surface but grateful the pitch wasn't too steep. I scrambled for the nearest edge only to find a drop-off. Growling in disgust, I carefully clamored back over the peak and started down the other side where the lights of the Billings PD and fire department streaked over every shining surface. There was a fire truck parked closer than the others, and I yelled out to a man, trying to be heard over the running engines and cross-radio chatter coming from all the vehicles.

"Hey!" He didn't hear me.

I spotted a pile of wooden truck skids stacked against the building, slipped to the edge, climbed down, and ran over to the fully suited fireman wearing a captain's insignia and a white helmet. "Hey, there's wholesale accelerant in that building, and it's going to blow."

The short, rotund man glanced at me. "Who the hell are you, and what are you doing over here?" He pointed behind him. "Clear the perimeter, we've got a man inside we're trying to rescue."

"I know. I'm that man. And I'm telling you that there's close to four hundred barrels of industrial methanol in there."

"You're the idiot who was in the building?"

"I was till I got out on the roof. Do you have anybody else in there?"

"No." He shook his head as he waved at a uniformed patrolman standing back by the gate. "Look, pal, there's no way anybody would store that many barrels of unsecure fuel in a building like that within city limits, so beat it."

"I saw the shipping manifest, and it said 383 barrels."

"The shipping manifest?" The fire chief turned to glance at the young patrolman who had just arrived. "This is the moron who was in the building."

He gripped my arm. "You were with the other individual with the dogs?"

I reached into my pocket, which caused him to suddenly go for his sidearm. I froze. "Hold up there, Wyatt Earp." Lifting my badge wallet from my pocket, I flipped it open. "Walt Longmire, Absaroka County sheriff—we're the ones who called you, and I'm telling you this building is about to go up like Tunguska, okay?"

He stared at me, still holding on to my arm.

Glancing around, I could see that the rest of the emergency crews were at a minimally safe distance, with only these two idiots and me in imminent danger. I figured every second we spent standing there made it more likely that we'd soon be wearing glowing coats of invisible flame or sizzling on the surface of the parking lot like hamburgers on a Weber grill.

I stuffed my wallet back into my pocket and did something I knew I was going to regret and punched the cop. I caught him when he bounced off the side of the fire truck and then reached out with my other hand and grabbed the fireman by the collar of his slicker.

The emergency crews watched as I approached the gate with the one man over my shoulder and the other who was struggling to get away, all the while screaming, "I want this man arrested!"

I got to the gate where there were a few individuals who were of a higher rank. "Hey guys, you might want to . . ."

That's when it went.

And I mean went.

One moment I was standing there, and the next I was lying against the chain-link fence, fortunately turned the other way. The heat was like being stuffed into a hibachi. I rolled over and looked up into the frigid night sky and watched the blue flames undulating, seeming to disappear, though I knew they were still there.

Luckily there was no wind, and the explosion had gone straight up; unfortunately, sheets of mangled tin and pieces of barrels were now raining down onto the parking lot as I listened to people running for cover.

Looking across the pavement, I could see the fire chief's vehicle flaming and smoldering, all the paint having been removed in an instant.

He turned to scream at me. "That was a brand-new truck!"

I thought about punching him too, just for good measure.

15

I lay on the bunk of the holding cell in the city hall with my hat over my face while Henry lectured me about professional ethics.

"It is not good to punch your coworkers."

"It was the only way I knew to shut them up and get moving. Where were you, by the way?"

"At a safe distance."

"I wonder where they put the dogs."

I glanced up to see the sheriff's detective, Chuck Shultz, investigator of cold case files and friend to the common man, standing outside the holding cell. He looked to his right and gestured toward the bars between us. "Tad, let these two out."

There was a mechanical sound as the lock whirred, and he pulled the gate open with a vintage groan. "Jeez, Shultz, thanks for putting us up in the Big House."

"Yeah, we only use this one for people we're going to release anyway. You should be impressed—it might be the only cell with actual bars left in the entire state of Montana."

"We've still got bars in our jail."

"Why does that not surprise me."

I shrugged on my jacket, and we stepped into the center walkway and partial freedom. "I blew a night's stay at the Dude Rancher."

He led us out to a young patrolman who yawned and then slid my Colt across the desk along with my badge wallet, regular wallet, the strange little book about the Wandering Without, and a clipboard, which I assumed I was meant to sign. Picking up the pen that was attached to it with a chain, I scribbled my name and rethreaded the pancake holster through my belt, stuffing away the rest of my things as Shultz reached over and picked up the book.

"What's this?"

"Oh, something I picked up at a bookstore in Hardin."

He thumbed through the pages and then flipped back to the cover, studying the image. "Hardin has a bookstore?"

"Well, she's trying."

The Cheyenne Nation followed suit, signing his name and collecting his wallet and antler-handled bowie knife.

"What's this mean, this design?"

The Bear tucked the short sword away and said, "End of the world."

The detective handed me the book. "Not a mystery then."

Henry smiled. "It is according to whom you are asking."

Returning it to its resting place in my jacket, I asked, "You from Montana, Shultz?"

"Born and raised. Great Falls, actually."

"Ever heard of a place called Fort Pratt?"

"Yeah."

"Where is it?"

"It's near . . ." He thought about it. "Up beside, um . . ." He still thought about it. "Near Browning, I think." He turned to Henry. "Right?"

"On the Blackfeet Reservation?"

I pulled the book back out and looked at it. "Not near Fort Shaw?"

"No, farther up than that. Hell, I think it's almost near Canada."

Henry made a face. "Babb, near Glacier?"

"I think." He considered. "I'd have to check a map."

"It's not on any of them. I've looked."

He glanced at the patrolman. "Where are you from?"

"Iowa."

"Well, you're no help." Schultz started up the stairs as we trailed along. "Maybe the Dude Rancher will hold your room for tonight—I hear you got a basketball tournament. My money is on the Navajo."

"Mine would be too, if I had any."

Henry shook his head. "That is no way for a head coach to talk."

"Head coach?" Shultz turned at the landing to look at me.

"Nobody else wanted the job."

He crossed through two sets of double doors and opened another, where we looked into the room to see Dog lying on a vintage green-velvet sofa next to a young woman who was stroking his massive head. I slapped my thigh, and though he looked a bit reluctant, he slid his girth off the sofa and trotted out to greet us, tail wagging. "What about the other dog, the Doberman?"

Shultz led us down a hallway and into a parking structure where my truck was waiting. "Belongs to the guy who owns the evaporated building and who is not very happy right now."

He tossed me my keys. "I can imagine."

"He says he leased the building to Alpine Painters but not the other side of the structure. Evidently Schiller was illegally subleasing it as a stopover storage for a couple of questionable trucking firms. There's no way you're legally allowed to store anything like that stuff inside the city limits."

I pulled the bracelet they'd neglected to confiscate from my pocket. "No traces of a body?"

He snorted and then readjusted his glasses. "You're kidding, right? They still haven't gotten the fire out."

I nodded and slipped the ghost bracelet onto my wrist. "Any word on Schiller?"

"You're sure it was him last night?"

"Somebody set the fire and then closed and locked that door—and Jimmy Lane is missing, and Louie Howard is dead." I turned to Henry. "There was also the third guy, the one who was at Jimmy's house. We never got his name."

The cop nodded and looked at his shoes. "We've got an address for Schiller, but he's no longer there."

"Any way to find the third man? He must work for Alpine. Anything there?"

"I can check the city database—there has to be taxes or something to track him down."

"You've got Henry's number?"

"I do."

We had started toward my truck when I turned back. "How's the patrolman I punched?"

"Wearing his black eye like a badge of honor; he got whacked by the great Walt Longmire."

"You'll tell him I'm sorry?"

"You saved his ass from getting quick-fried to a crackly crunch; I think that's enough." He waved and retreated into the building as I started the truck and sat there. "The third guy, Schiller introduced him the same time he did Louie Howard when he called him Lou-Dawg . . . It was something like Whispering Smith." I thought about it some more. "Silent A, that's what he called him."

Henry looked at me. "That is not much to go on."

"Message Shultz and tell him; at least it's something."

He thumbed the text into his phone. "I do not suppose the Brotherhood of the North has a clubhouse?"

I pulled out of the parking tower. "Probably not, and if they do the address isn't likely to be listed."

"All for the best in that you already have an appointment."

"Where?"

"Your first and most likely only practice is in twenty minutes." He grinned, thin as a hand-knapped spearhead. "Coach."

The MetraPark Arena had happily provided its facility for the National Native American Invitational. Pressed hard against the Rimrock cliffs, it was colossal in comparison with the gymnasium in Lame Deer. We walked through the pathway on the eastern side of the building, the air washing around us like a wind tunnel that had been known to lift small children from the ground.

The general manager, Bill Dutcher, adjusted his glasses and laughed, looking back at the girls. "The wind comes in from the northwest and channels along the cliff before getting trapped in here and blowing stuff up and onto the roof." He pointed at the top of the building, a hundred feet up. "Every week or so, we have to go up there and get the hats, jackets, and other stuff that get blown off people."

I couldn't help but ask. "What's the strangest thing you've ever found up there?"

"A wedding veil." He thought about it. "I bet somebody got in trouble for that."

Pushing the heavy back doors open where a Yellowstone County deputy stood, we followed him into the building and a mammoth loading dock, where he waved at the security guy in the glass booth to our right and then walked us down a short tunnel. "I can't tell you how excited we are to have you guys in the tournament. We haven't ever had Lame Deer up here, so we're kind of looking to you as the home team."

We walked out into the titanic twelve-thousand-seat arena. "It's a big home."

"Yeah, and you just got a new floor." He pointed to my boots, his voice echoing. "No hard shoes."

"Right."

He and Tiger Scalpcane continued walking along the side as Henry and I turned to the girls, who looked like they had just been informed that they were going to have to step from a spaceship without oxygen.

"Hey." The Bear turned and backed toward the court with his arms spread, palming a red, white, and blue ABA ball in one hand, his black duster splaying out like wings. "You have earned the right to be here." He cupped the ball in both hands, stepping just outside the inbounds line. "This arena is so fine that five years ago the gods decided to carry it back home with them, so they sent a tornado to fetch it—but it is still here." He glanced down at his chukka boots. "Look around you and if you count, you will see this is the largest indoor arena in the entire state and one of the greatest stages on which you will ever have the opportunity to play. But . . ." He stepped onto the court, dribbling the ball with determination. "This is inbounds, and where the magic happens, this is where you will hold court—and you will find that it is exactly like your home court back in Lame Deer, no longer, no wider, no taller . . . Exactly the same." He spun around, chucked the ball with all his strength, and we watched as it sailed across two thirds of the court, slamming into the glass backboard and clanging through the hoop.

We all stood there, utterly speechless.

Spinning, he gave out with a blood-freezing battle cry and then exhorted them to join him on the gleaming blond wood. "Máha'ósané énóváne!"

They rushed forward, slinging their coats and bags to the sideline, and began warming up. Standing there with Coach Felton's playbook, I tried to untangle how I happened to arrive at this strange juncture.

I turned to see Tiger. "So, what would he have done if he'd missed?"

"Make the rebound and dunk it." He sidled up to me and handed me a whistle. "Don't worry about it, people have been goofing this stuff up for years, why not you?"

I studied the chrome whistle. "How did I let you people talk me into this?"

"Just stay positive, and you'll be fine. I heard they played a heck of a game down in Lodge Grass."

"So they tell me; I wasn't there." Looking past him, I could see visitors approaching from up in the bleachers where advertisements festooned the walls—one was Lolo Long and the other, Jaya.

Tiger patted my shoulder. "Look, I've got to get the boys ready to go over to Bozeman, but I'll stop back in before we leave. Trust me, you'll be fine."

I watched him go and then turned to the chief and her charge. "Howdy."

Lolo watched the girls. "Need help?"

"Oh, just all I can get."

She gestured toward her niece. "First, Jaya has something she'd like to say to you."

The young woman stepped forward, clutching the red, white,

and blue ball to her stomach, her head lowered. "I wanted to say you were right, that um . . . I was only thinking of myself and that I'm sorry."

I stood there for a moment and then nodded, raising the whistle to my lips and blowing. The noise from the court stopped, and I waved the team over. As they approached, I turned to Jaya. "I think you need to be talking to the team."

She studied their faces, all of them. "I don't think they want to talk to me."

"Try. What have you got to lose?"

I put my hand on her shoulder and pivoted around to present her to the other young women. "Hey gang, Jaya would like a word."

She stood looking at her shoes and then slowly raised her head. "Hi."

They said nothing.

"Congratulations on the win—I know it wasn't easy, and I know I didn't help." Her voice resounded on the hard surfaces of the enormous room. "I don't know what to say . . ."

One of the girls coughed.

Jaya took a deep breath and started to speak, stopped, and then tried again. "You probably think I'm here to get you to let me get back on the team, but I don't think I have the right to ask that from you. I am so sorry for the way I behaved, and if you'll let me, I'd like to make it up to you." She stepped forward. "My sister, Jeanie, loved this team and this game, and when I think about how disrespectful I've been to her and the things that meant more to her than anything—it just makes me sick." She glanced around at the oversize arena. "The Navajos are good, really good . . ." She choked up a bit and translated it into a short bark of a laugh. "You know what they think of us, right? That we're just a bunch of misfits who don't have any right to be here. But you know those coyotes we hear in the time of frozen water out there on those hungry hills we call home? They want something, they want something so badly their bodies can't hold it, and they have to look up at the moon and let it out." She tossed the ball to Rosey Black Wolf. "You show them how hungry you are, how ravenous you can be, that you don't *want* to win this game—but that you *have* to." She struggled a smile. "I don't know what else to say, other than I really hope you win."

With that, she turned and began climbing the steps out of the arena, when a voice called out. "We can with you."

We all turned to see Misty Two Bears, who had taken a step forward. She took the ball from the center and pitched it to Jaya, who caught it in shock. "Shut up and suit up, Longbow."

Jaya was openly crying, wiping away tears as she came stumbling down the steps, and her entire team rushed over to her.

I felt like shedding a tear myself.

I felt a tap on my shoulder and turned to find my undersheriff, Victoria Moretti, dressed in basketball shoes, sweatpants, and a vintage Temple Owls T-shirt. "Hi."

"What are you doing here?"

She smiled, obviously pleased at my confoundment. "I hear you need an assistant coach."

"Desperately . . . But that doesn't answer my question."

She shrugged, looking over my shoulder. "Eh, I got a call."

I glanced behind me to see the Bear, now taking a few more shots on the court. "So, you have references?"

"Yeah, and I was the statistician for the Owls my sophomore year and point guard for the Philadelphia Police Athletic League, Twenty-sixth PAL, All-City Champions—besides, I know about a million times more about teenage girls than you ever will."

"You're hired." I threw a thumb toward the locker room. "Go introduce yourself to the Devil's Brigade."

She called back. "So, do you think they ever even heard of Hal Greer?"

"I thought you might be needing a little experienced help at this point." The Cheyenne Nation sauntered up, watching the Terror as she made the corner and disappeared.

"Probably a good call."

Chief Long joined us. "So, I heard the two of you tried to blow up this fair city last night? I saw the crater just off Twenty-seventh Street when I drove in this morning."

"Lolo, have you ever heard of a guy by the name of Silent A?"

She thought about it. "Silent A?"

"Runs with Schiller and that bunch." I held my wrist out to her. "I've got a feeling he might be circling the wagons. Louie Howard is dead. I think Jimmy Lane might've been in one of the barrels at the explosion, because I found his bracelet at the warehouse, so the only one that's left in Schiller's crew is him and this Silent A character."

"That's his name, Silent A?"

"That's what Lane called him when I first met him, here in Billings."

She reached into her pocket and pulled out a cell phone. "I know a guy on the payroll of the Bureau of Indian Affairs who keeps tabs on all the juvie gangs, and Silent A sounds like a gang name to me."

As she dialed, I asked, "You don't happen to have an address for Schiller, do you?"

"If I did, I'd call in an air strike." She listened on the phone. "And you're thinking that he has something to do with Jaya?"

"I'm thinking that he has something to do with Jeanie and

Jaya, or somebody close to him does so he's shutting everybody up . . . for good."

She held up a finger. "Adam, this is Lo, I'm looking for info on a guy by the name of Silent A? Call me." She turned back to us. "He's not there, but I left a message. Louie Howard is dead?"

I nodded. "Shotgun at his home, or kind of home."

"Why kill Louie? I mean, he was a goof but generally harmless."

"Somebody knew something, or a lot of people know something, and the only way two people keep a secret—"

Henry finished my thought. "Is if one of them is dead."

"Speaking of secrets, I hear Harriet Felton was having a relationship with Schiller, is that correct?"

My turn to shrug. "She's covering for him after he beat her, but that's as much as I know—if it was him that beat her."

"Who else?"

"I want to talk to this Silent A." I fingered the bracelet on my wrist, staring at the tiny cedar beads that were supposed to ward off spirits.

The MetraPark Arena was filling up.

Vic was putting the team through the paces as Lolo Long helped and Henry and I stood there like monuments to a bygone era. Jaya appeared a little rusty, but she was passing the ball off a lot more than before and the rest of the girls were looking good, moving the ball and making shots I hadn't seen them make.

Glancing over at the Navajo Eagles, though, I had a sinking feeling. They were taller than us, they were faster than us, they were smoother than us. "They're good."

"Really good." The Cheyenne Nation confided, "They have won this tournament for the last three years running."

My eyes returned to our team as Stacey Killsday lined up and shot from the side of the foul line, and I watched as the ball missed and bounced toward me. I picked it up and handed it to her as she squinted back. "Thanks."

Tiger reappeared on the sidelines with us. "They're looking pretty good."

"They got a lot better when the new coaching staff arrived."

"I'm glad to hear that." He sighed. "But as much as I regret it, I need to get over to Bozeman."

Stacey lined up again but once more missed the shot. Watching her chase after the ball toward us again, I reached over and drew the glasses from Tiger's breast pocket. "Do you mind?"

He looked at me questioningly as I scooped up the ball and handed it to Killsday but then stopped her by touching her shoulder. She looked up at me as I unfolded the glasses, guiding them onto her face. "Try these." She stared at me and then glanced around as if seeing the world anew. I looked back at Tiger. "Okay with you?"

He smiled. "I, and my son, would be honored."

We watched as she rejoined the team and sank her first shot and then turned to us with the broadest grin I'd ever seen on her face.

"I think you've got this situation under control."

"Not exactly, but maybe we can hold it together till the final buzzer."

"Thanks for doing this."

"You bet." He made his way out, and I watched the rapidly filling seats. I was about to turn back when I thought I saw something, or someone, in the stands who put a glacial freeze in my veins. I turned to the court but then turned back again, sure that

I'd seen who I thought I'd seen. My eyes stopped about halfway up the first section where Harley Wainwright and his mother, Connie, were waving at me. "Hey, coach."

"Hi." I stepped toward them. "You guys decided to come to the game?"

"I'm getting a divorce, so I can do what I want." She shrugged. "Someone dropped off an anonymous packet with me and the Rosebud County Sheriff's Department concerning my soon-to-be ex-husband's extracurricular activities." She studied me. "Any idea who that could've been?"

"I can't imagine."

Harley shook his head at her and then called out as he waved to me. "Good luck!"

I waved back and was certain it hadn't been them. Glancing around, I could see all the regulars I'd become associated with at the gym in Lame Deer, including Lonnie Little Bird and his new assistant, Willard, "Big" Betty One Moon and her husband, and even most of the people who had been in the van that night, including Edwin Black Kettle, Leanne Chelan, and George Three Fingers.

Even Lyndon Iron Bull and his wife, Ethel, were there.

"Something?"

"What?" I turned to see Henry, now looking into the crowd along with me. "I thought I saw . . . Somebody."

"Who?"

"Um . . . I'm not sure."

The dark eyes scanned the crowd, and I was positive he was seeing more than I had. "Who did you see?"

I shook my head, dissembling. "It was probably nothing."

With one last glance, I turned back to the players as the buzzer sounded and they made their way to the bench.

Vic, now dressed in slacks and a sweater, came over and stood by me. "Okay, here's the deal. I'm going to coach this game, and you're going to just keep coming over and pretending like you're coaching, okay?"

"Thank God."

As the visiting team, the Navajo Eagles were introduced first to resounding cheers. "When we huddle up, just stand there and look imposing. Throw a word or two in if you want but don't do anything fucking stupid like try to coach, got it?"

I nodded as the announcement for our players started. The cheers were strong, and I was beginning to feel excited for our girls, until they got to Jaya, who was booed. I turned to look up at the crowd, more than a little disappointed. There was some cheering, but it was drowned out by the locals. Watching Jaya, I saw her despondent look before she touched hands with the team and loped onto the court. Once out there, she turned and looked back at the bleachers and her face began to harden.

I was just beginning to lose hope when she did something miraculous.

She began to dance.

Swooping her arms low to the hardwood floor she started to twirl, stamping her feet and nodding her head to an imaginary rhythm. It was a shawl dance that I'd seen before, but this one was different: it was defiant and proud. She glared up at the crowd, twirling and flashing those dark eyes like chain lightning.

The boos began fading as more and more of the Cheyenne stood and chanted along with the dance, stamping on the flooring, which was echoing in the arena like thunder.

I was close and could see the tears on Jaya's face as she extended her hands to Rosey Black Wolf, leading her farther out onto the court. The tall girl paused, not knowing what to do, but the blood was there, and if she didn't know what to do, her ancestors did, and soon her feet began moving and her arms reached for her teammate, her fingers quivering like buckskin fringe.

They danced, the two of them, then reached their hands out to Stacey Killsday and Misty Two Bears who joined them, leaving only Wanona Sweetwater looking on. The young woman wanted to join, but her self-consciousness wouldn't allow it.

Jaya began singing in a silvery voice that cut through the rhythm of the pounding bleachers, a song in counterpoint to the defiance I'd seen before; this was a song of protection, acceptance, and healing. I didn't know the song, but *they* all did and soon they were all singing and began circling Wanona, pulling her along with music and movement. Slowly, her shoulders began to dip and weave, and soon she was dancing and singing with them as they circled the center court.

The Navajo players backed away, uncertain as to what was happening. This was something magical, something poetic, something you didn't interrupt.

And just like that, they stopped.

It was as if the whole thing had been choreographed to the smallest detail, but they just knew—it was time to play.

Thunder, plangent applause like I'd never heard as the entire place stood, stomped, and cheered. I suddenly found myself laughing as I turned around and admired the crowd on both sides of the court. I glanced over at the Cheyenne Nation, at the swelling of his chest and the thrust of his chin as he tried to keep the welling in his eyes from spilling over.

Vic's eyes were wide with amazement. "That is going to be a hard act to follow." The ref blew his whistle, and the players approached their positions as we started to sit, Vic grabbing my hand. "You stand, you stand, and pace like you know what you're doing."

"What are you going to do?"

"I sit, but don't worry. I'll call the times and argue with the referees—it's what I do best."

"Boy howdy."

Rosey stood silently in the tip-off with a strange little smile on her face. The ball launched straight into the air and we all watched as the very tall girl lifted a hand high above her opponent, tacitly flipping it to Jaya, who drove between two Eagle players, hell-bent for composite leather for the hoop.

There was a mass exodus as both teams gave pursuit, but Misty Two Bears was just too fast and there was no way anyone was going to catch her. She got the ball, although as usual didn't seem to know what to do with it. Fortunately, Jaya was the closest in the rundown, and Misty passed it to her, relieved to be rid of it. Jaya bound down the lane at an angle and halfway from the foul line she began to levitate, not jump, but simply climb from the earth like a meteor with her arm rising—and then something stunning happened.

She passed the ball away.

As the entire Navajo team converged on her, she slipped the ball behind her back and into Stacey Killsday's hands. Acting as if someone had handed her a grenade, the newly bespectacled girl shot without thinking, probably the best thing that could've happened. Just a quick bubble shot that whisked through the net—first points of the game.

Tangled with one of the Eagle players, Jaya tumbled into the padded wall but was the first to stand. She took a deep breath and then stuck out her hand to assist the other girl, who slapped it away. Jaya held her hand out again. The Navajo player started to stand but slipped and Jaya grabbed her hand, pulling the girl from the floor. They bumped chests and then just stood there looking at each other.

It was going to be a long night for somebody.

The Lady Morning Stars backed up the court, keeping an eye on the Navajo Eagles players as if circling a herd. The short-haired girl who had collided with Jaya took the ball as it was passed inbounds and began moving it up court, slipping to the left where Jaya stood with her hands extended, flexing her fingers in anticipation.

I walked toward the scorer's table but then stopped, the color red catching my eye in the stands again.

She was there.

High in the stands, near the aisle.

My eyes strained, but even at this distance I could see it was her. I glanced back at Henry, who was watching the side of my face and stood to look back along with me.

She had a large red scarf over her head and clutched one side to her face in an attempt to stay hidden in plain sight, but the action had driven her to cheer along with the crowd and I could now see her features.

Henry did too, and stood, striding over to me. "Jeanie."

"Yep."

"Got it." Like a hawk, the Cheyenne Nation swooped to the steps and began ascending as the girl spotted us and quickly turned, scurrying up the two steps behind her and disappearing into the lobby above.

I'd never seen a man move that fast, and all I could think was that I was glad that Henry Standing Bear wasn't after me.

With all the effort I could muster, I turned back to the game in time to see number 7, the same Navajo player as before, roll in a pivot and slip by Jaya for a pass off to her teammate and then dart toward the basket as she took the return pass, kissing the ball off the glass with a deft finger roll resulting in a quick score.

I tried to breathe, but the urge to run up the steps was almost more than I could stand. I looked up expecting to see the Bear with the girl in trusteeship, but it didn't happen. The Lady Morning Stars brought the ball in as the Navajo Eagles fanned out, guarding their opposites but still keeping their eyes on Jaya as she dribbled up court, pausing a moment before popping the ball to Sweetwater, who tried to heave it to Rosey who stood in the paint. Black Wolf reached for the ball, but the Eagle center tipped it into the hands of one of her forwards instead, who charged out with it, headed for the other end of the court in a dead run.

Jaya had been caught flat-footed but turned after the girl as if shot from a gun. The forward glanced from the out-of-bounds line for someone to pass off to, but she was so far ahead, there was no one, so she angled toward the basket just as Jaya intersected with her, reaching behind and tipping the ball away, then sliding on the gleaming floor as if stealing second.

The ball bounced between them, but the Eagle player had to reverse, which slowed her down as Jaya rolled and leapt up, slapping the ball in the other direction as the crowd of players closed in. She hit the ball again and then followed at Mach speed, knifing her shoulders between them without touching and then retrieving the ball.

Now only the guard who had tackled her before stood between Jaya and the basket. Without hesitation, Jaya charged forward and slipped past her opponent at a sharper angle for an easy layup—or what would've been an easy layup if the Eagle player had not charged underneath her, causing Jaya to fall sideways and slam a shoulder into the wooden floor.

Unable to help myself, I stepped forward as Jaya lay there in a heap.

I felt a hand in mine as Vic grabbed ahold of me, not letting me move.

Slowly, an arm snaked out and Jaya pushed herself off the surface, stretched her neck, and pulled at her shoulder. The nearest ref blew his whistle and signaled for two foul shots.

I sighed and then looked into the stands for Henry. Nothing.

"I have to go."

Vic looked at me wide-eyed. "What?"

"I saw Jeanie in the stands, and Henry went after her, but he hasn't come back."

"Are you kidding me?"

"No. I've got to go find him—and her."

She glanced at the court where Jaya was lining up to shoot the first of the foul shots. "We have to call a time-out, but let her shoot first, please?"

I nodded as Jaya twirled the ball in her hands. She lifted the ball and shot it as if it had wings of its own, and it nested in the basket with a *swish*. A portion of the crowd cheered as she lined up for another one, which ended with the same result.

Vic raised her hands at the head referee, and he blew his whistle, converging with us at the scorer's table. The balding man looked at us questioningly as I started to speak. "Um, I've got . . ."

Vic didn't look at me. "He's having a heart attack."

The chief scorer and referee looked at her and then in alarm at me.

"Uh, yep."

The ref started to turn toward the court and call the game, but Vic grabbed his arm. "It's okay, he's had them before."

The scorer interrupted. "We need to get you medical attention."

"I can do it myself, it's okay."

"We have to get you to a hospital."

"I can drive myself."

"What?"

"I've done it before." I started edging toward the steps and pointed toward Vic. "She can take over for me, honest."

The ref and scorer looked at each other again and then back at me. "Where are you going?"

"I, um . . . I'm parked this way." Not waiting any longer, I started up the steps amid the strange looks from the crowd. Finally, at the top, I stopped at the entryway that led out of the inner recesses of the arena into the lobby, making sure this was the way I'd seen both Henry and the girl go and then made my way down the short hallway into the outer lobby.

Because the game had started, there weren't that many people loitering about, but there were a few at the concession stands and a few more standing around talking in small clusters. I chose the nearest man to question. "Hey, you didn't happen to see a girl in a red scarf run by here and then a big guy with long hair?"

"Indian fellow, yeah." He nodded. "Didn't see any girl, but the guy looked pretty serious."

"Which way?"

He pointed down a hallway to the right and said something else, but I was already out of earshot. There was a row of bathrooms to the right, but I ignored them, figuring half of them I couldn't go in and the other half Henry had probably checked. There was another double door straight ahead and I pushed it open to find a string of other doors that looked like a row of administrative offices.

"Can I help you?"

I turned to find a young woman in business attire. "I'm sorry to bother you, but I'm looking for a young woman in a red scarf and a large man, Native, with long hair?"

She was dismissive. "There's no one like that who's come through here."

"You're sure?"

"Well, since I came out of my office."

I pulled out my badge wallet and flipped it open. "If I were to come through these doors, is there any other way out of this suite?"

She glanced up from my badge. "There's a stairwell at the end of the hall."

Flipping the wallet closed, I tucked it away and headed in the direction she'd indicated. "Where does it go?"

"To the catwalk and roof going up, and then downward toward the ground floor and storage areas."

"If you see said large Native man, please tell him which way I went."

"And if I see the girl?"

"Lock her in a broom closet," I called back and hustled down the hallway to where there was a solid-looking metal door.

I peered through the small window into the stairwell that led both up and down, then pushed the door open, and stepped onto the concrete surface. If I were trying to escape, I'd have gone to ground level, but Henry would've made that same assumption. I looked up. Why would you go to the roof? The thought was dumb, so I started down but then stopped.

I looked up the stairwell at the flights I would have to climb just to get to the door on the roof.

Why in the world would she go that way?

I started down, but then, again, stopped.

Shaking my head at myself I turned around and started up, clomping the stairs as I went, figuring if Henry had gone in the other direction at least he'd know where to find me.

After eight flights, I was starting to regret my choice when I came to another security door that led onto a catwalk above the basketball court, which I assumed led to the roof. There was nowhere else to go, so I pushed the door open and found myself in the uppermost corner of the arena overlooking the highest seating section. I paused as the Navajo Eagles made a fast break with quick passes that zoomed by the Lady Morning Stars before laying it up in a reverse.

The catwalk was caged with walkways that strung out in all directions, including to where the scoreboard was suspended. The catwalk I was on ran along the end of the building and then reversed in a stairwell that led up to the roof. If anybody had come this way that was where the person had to go. Swallowing, I looked up and began climbing again, and after a few more minutes, I was standing at another door, striped yellow and black, that read THIS DOOR LOCKS FROM THE OUTSIDE WHEN CLOSED.

Pushing the door open, I looked onto the snow-covered roof. There was a brick lying just inside. I reached down and slipped it in the tread. Stepping out, I glanced around, my breath fogging my view as hard, sleetlike flakes descended at a ready angle from the pervasive wind.

The Rimrocks were relatively close to the eastern side of the building. Moving past the large HVAC unit that was humming away at my left, I turned the corner of the access structure and looked around the vast roof, easily the size of two football fields.

There were more HVAC units scattered in equal increments, but no other door openings—only one way up and one way down.

I took a few more steps before deciding I'd made a mistake and, shivering in my shirtsleeves, started to turn to go back down when I saw something—something red.

She was there, to the right, standing at the railing about a hundred yards away, the scarf in her hand. She stood at the edge of the railing buttress to the east, overlooking the alleyway where we had come in the building. She was leaning out, looking southwest at the Beartooth Mountains. I kept my eyes on her profile as I moved toward her, her dark hair swirling in the vortex of wind that arena GM Bill Dutcher had mentioned. She looked exactly as she had in the poster. It was only as I got closer that I saw her lips moving. She was singing just the way Lyndon Iron Bull had described, and it *was* the saddest song I had ever heard.

The silvery sounds mimicked the song her sister had sung on the basketball court less than thirty minutes ago, and if I hadn't believed my eyes, I would've sworn it was Jaya singing now. "Neh-Ehvah sii Eh-jest, Na-Hoe-eh sidun . . ."

I stopped about twenty feet away, unsure of what to do. I wanted to speak out to her but was afraid I might startle her.

"Bring me back, I don't belong here, and I want to go home . . ."

She raised her leg, placing a knee on top of the edge of the railing.

"Jeanie."

She froze.

"Jeanie, I need you to get away from that railing."

She stayed like that for a long moment, her hair still gyrating around her head from the updraft of the northeast wind that whirlpooled between the building and the Rimrock cliffs that were only seventy-five feet away. Then she turned her head toward me for a moment before maneuvering her body the rest of the way onto the rail, where she sat facing me.

I took a step toward her. "Jeanie."

Gracefully, she perched there, looking at me, her face partially hidden so that I could no longer see her lips moving when she spoke. *"Bring me back."*

"I . . . I'm trying." I took another step. "You need to give me your hand."

"I don't belong here."

"I know that, and there are a lot of people worried about you." I took another step and was now only about ten feet away from her.

Her hand came up, and she gently parted the hair so that I could now see the ebony eyes, so dark they almost seemed black, the high cheekbones. She and Jaya could've been twins. *"I want to go home . . ."*

A blast of cold air hid her face again as she flew backward, disappearing over the edge as I dove for her hand, the scarf she'd been holding blowing through the air on the updraft, slapping me in the face as I stumbled forward, clutching the railing.

Pulling the scarf off my eyes, I looked over the edge to the entrance of the building below.

There was nothing.

I stared at the concrete walkway ninety feet down—no sign of her body. Turning to look at the snow-covered roof, I saw only one set of footprints leading to where I stood. My own.

16

In the stairwell, I studied the scarf, thinking about what Bill Dutcher had said about articles of clothing being blown onto the roof of the place. I also thought about the bits of red prayer flag I'd found tied to the juniper tree at the Rosebud and how they seemed to match perfectly. It was a rough kind of silk, well worn with tied threads on the ends forming a kind of fringe.

No label, no name, and no Jeanie One Moon.

I reflected back to my experiences in the mountains with Virgil White Buffalo a couple of years back when I thought I might be losing my mind. To settle my agitation, I put my hand to my collarbone and could still feel, through the fabric of my shirt, the silver ring with the circling turquoise and coral wolves, hanging on a chain.

Pushing the door back open, I returned to the roof, turned the corner, and looked at my path to the railing across the snow-covered expanse where there were only my footprints leading there and back. It was about then that I decided I wasn't telling anybody about what had happened here.

With a sigh, I draped the scarf around my neck, kicked the brick from the doorway, and then started down the steps. Wondering where the heck my Indian scout had gotten off to, I moved down the metal stairwell, peered from the catwalk through the steel rafters, and could see that there were cheerleaders and a band playing on the court. Halftime.

I reached the office level and met the young woman I'd seen in the suite. She was still carrying the laptop but now had it bundled up for the trip home. "Find your culprits?"

"Um, no. I guess that means you haven't seen them either?"

"I'm afraid not." She started off down the steps and then turned to look back up at me. "Nice scarf."

Well, at least I wasn't the only one who could see it.

"Thanks." I stood there for a moment more and then followed after her, watching through the glass as she continued toward the parking lot. I hadn't seen Henry on the sidelines when I'd looked down at the court, and I didn't think the Bear was out in the parking lot, so that left only the next flight down.

Why would he have gone that way and, more important, why would he have stayed? Had he had an experience similar to mine, and even if he had, where was he now?

At the bottom of the stairs was another heavy door, which I pushed open to reveal the lower concourse flanked by storage areas. One of the doors hung slightly ajar, so I pushed it and watched the motion sensor lights flicker.

Chairs.

Thousands and thousands of chairs, a labyrinth of empty chairs that must've been when the facility was being used as a concert space. The theater-style seats were maroon and black and stacked six high, and there was a constant thrumming sound that made it difficult to hear or be heard from more than fifty feet away. I must have been close to the inner workings of the building.

There was a short concrete walkway to my left and then a really long one to my right. If I committed to the long one, I wasn't sure how far I'd have to go before taking another direction or doubling back, so I took the short one. It was a tactic that worked for about ten yards before it jogged to the right and went straight ahead, leading to another labyrinth of stacked seating like the one I'd just seen.

I was about to turn back when I could've sworn I heard something. Automatically, I reached to the small of my back, when I remembered that I'd locked my sidearm away in the center console of my truck, because I figured the administrative staff of the Metra probably wasn't open to having their coaches prowling the sidelines armed.

I turned a corner and started down an incredibly long aisle. The lights here were on sensors as well, and they flickered on as I approached. When the nearest one sputtered, I noticed something on the floor and kneeled down to dab a finger in what was certainly blood. Pulling my hand up to my face, I smelled it to be sure and then saw that there was more of the stuff spattered on one of the large air-circulation tubes near the floor. If I was to make an educated guess, I would say that someone had been shot, and because I knew Henry was not carrying a sidearm, it was most likely that it was he who had gotten tagged.

There was a break in the stacked chairs with just enough room to crawl through to the other side, and there lay my friend. Crouching down, I pulled myself through the cramped space and gripped his leg.

"That is where I am shot."

"Sorry. Why didn't you say something?"

"Because I thought you might be the person who shot me."

"This is interesting, I'm the one who usually catches a bullet." I studied his leg, his jeans blood soaked and torn near his calf. "How bad?"

"I do not think I can walk on it, but the bullet passed through without striking the bone."

"Let's get you up."

"No."

"What do you mean, no?"

"I am fine and comfortable—you need to go find the shooter."

"Who was it?"

"I do not know, but I am assuming it is Schiller. There was a noise in the stairwell, and I followed it down here, heard someone in this storage area, and gave pursuit. I was running down that row when I heard the shot and felt it hit my leg. I fell, and by the time I looked over there, there was no one."

"I'm not leaving you here."

He made a disgusted sound. "There is someone here, armed. You have responsibilities." He sat up a bit, and I helped him prop himself against one of the folded seats. "If it is Schiller, he may attempt to get Jaya and you must stop him."

I pulled the bandanna from my jeans and tied it around the wound as he grimaced. "Have you got your phone?"

"I do, do you want it?"

"Nope, but if I get shot, I want you to be able to call 911 and get help."

He nodded and pulled the phone from his jacket pocket and punched a button. "Go find Schiller."

I stood, and once again thought seriously about getting my large-frame Colt from my truck. Instead, I made my way down the aisle as more lights flickered on.

"Hey?"

I turned back to look at the Cheyenne Nation.

He pointed at my neck. "The scarf, you found her?"

"Um, kind of . . ."

As I moved back through the storage level, I cursed the movement-activated lights that were making me a marvelous target, and I looked for something handy, like a steel bar, baseball bat, or machete that might've been left lying around. Nothing—the maintenance staff of the Metra were far too conscientious. At the far end of the building, I found a freight elevator and, beside it, another doorway. I stood there for a moment wondering what the heck to do: either keep prowling this level for a would-be assassin, or head toward the main arena where the most likely target was playing in a championship basketball game.

I headed through the doorway and found myself in an electrical area with humming breaker boxes, junction boxes, and conduits I didn't want to go near, and finally at another set of doors that led to a loading dock at the rear of the building where we'd first entered. There were forklifts, mobile cranes, and other heavy equipment, and an office with windows facing into the loading area. The same young man was watching monitors on the wall. When he saw me, he stood and slid the window open. "Hey, you can't be in here."

"Yep, I can." Pulling out my badge, I said, "Sheriff Walt Longmire. I've got a wounded man down in the seating storage area—he's been shot."

The kid stared at me.

"Which part did you not get—sheriff, wounded man, seating storage area, or shot?"

"I better call somebody."

"If you would do that and make it the Yellowstone County Sheriff's Department please." I glanced around as he picked up the phone from the desk. "In the meantime, you didn't see anybody come by here, did you?"

"No." He was interrupted by someone on the line. "Hello, yes. I've got a guy here who says somebody's been shot in the seating storage area." He paused for a second. "No, shot, like with a gun."

"His name is Henry Standing Bear."

"Wait." He looked at me. "There's a bear in the storage area?"

I started down the hallway to the left and the stairs that led to the upper concourse, figuring it might give me a better perspective in my search for Schiller. "No, the guy who got shot with a gun. His name is Henry Standing Bear, and he's going to need medical attention."

He hollered after me, "Hey, you're going to have to stay here."

When I got to the next set of doors at the top of the stairs, there was an opening to the lobby. The only person there was Theresa One Moon, who sat at a vacant table and was doctoring a large soda with a pint of Old Crow. She looked up at me and smiled. "Hey, Marshal."

"Sheriff."

"Whatever." She took a sip and gestured toward the tunnels leading to the arena. "Hell of a game."

"Boy howdy. Theresa, have you seen anybody come through here?"

"My mother won't let me sit with them. My own mother, can you believe that?" She gestured toward the arena with her cup hand, spilling a little high-octane onto the floor. "I been looking for Jimmy, but I guess he decided to sit this one out."

"Um, yep."

"Say, aren't you supposed to be coaching?"

I started to move toward the tunnel. "Something came up."

"You want a drink?"

"No, no, I better get inside." I started to turn but then paused for just a second. "Theresa, promise me you won't cause a scene? I mean, don't go out on the court for any reason, do you understand me?"

She shook her head and took another sip. "Not you too."

"I'm serious." I turned to go but then came back and expressed my desires with a little more emphasis. "And no folding chairs, you hear?"

She stared up at me, noncommittal, and then took another slug from the soda cup.

Sighing, I turned away from her table and moved through the tunnel to the main arena where a great deal of cheering was going on—even the concessioners were standing near the opening to watch the game. There was 1:32 on the clock, and the two teams were tied. Everyone in the place was standing and screaming. The Lady Morning Stars were on defense as the Navajo Eagles brought its offense up the court, careful to not give our girls a shot at taking the ball.

The same short-haired girl who had been handling the ball when I had left was dribbling toward Jaya, who spread her arms like a bird of prey, fingers thrumming like pinfeathers. I looked out over the crowd of close to ten thousand rabid fans in search of a Nazi needle in a haystack. I moved to the railing trying to get an idea of what the maniac was thinking. *Kill her here, on the court, as some kind of statement? With a handgun? No way to get away. And why?* It didn't make any sense, and if he was the one who had shot Henry, why hadn't he stayed there and finished the job before coming up?

I continued to scan the crowd as number 7 on the Navajo team pivoted to Jaya's right before rolling off to the left and driving for the basket. Jaya had evidently seen this action before and tipped the ball away from behind. They both scrambled after it, but an Eagle forward scooped it up and fired it to the center, who tipped it into the net, the Navajo team taking the lead with only a little over a minute on the clock.

Moving along the inner walkway, I circled the arena, scanning the crowd, suddenly aware that someone was looking at me. It was my assistant coach by way of Philadelphia standing at the sidelines with her hands on her hips, looking up at me, mouthing the words, *What in the galloping fuck are you doing?*

I held up a finger, hoping this would give me a few more minutes.

The crowd was going ballistic. I concentrated on the area across the court behind our bench. If I were going to try something, that's where I'd be.

And that's when I saw him.

Two rows down in the lower level at the far left with no one sitting on either side of him.

There were a few armed Yellowstone County deputies at ground level, but there was no way I could get to them without raising his suspicion.

I started moving around on the walkway, figuring the best approach would be from behind as the Lady Morning Stars brought the ball into play. As the athletes moved up the court, Jaya passed the ball to Wanona Sweetwater, who paused as usual but then, in an unprecedented move, began bringing the ball past the half-court line. Her opposite number stopped double-teaming Jaya, matched Wanona up, and tried to swat at the ball. But Wanona passed it off to Jaya, who quickly passed it to Rosey, who was blocked, forcing her to pass it out to Misty Two Bears.

Two Bears had an open shot but paused just an instant too long, so she passed it back to Jaya, who was immediately fouled for a one-and-one.

While they grouped up, I got to the walkway and slowly moved with all the stealth I could muster. But it didn't matter, the man turned and studied me, then turned back to the game as if I weren't really there. I excused myself, stepping in front of people before finally standing beside him.

"Jimmy Lane, I presume."

Jaya's father ignored me and continued watching.

"I believe I have something of yours." I peeled the bracelet from my wrist and held it out to him. At first, he didn't move, but finally he reached up and took the bracelet, his other hand staying underneath his jacket. "Have you got that .38 on me?" He nodded, and then we both turned our attention toward the game where Jaya was lining up for the first foul shot. "Promise me you'll do nothing until the game is over; she's worked too hard and sacrificed too much to be here."

He swallowed and then responded. "What I'm going to do can wait."

Jaya twirled the ball, the way she always did when preparing to shoot, and the arena grew silent. The ball flew from her hands as the other players crowded the lane, but she didn't move, instead looking off to the side in a disinterested manner as the ball whisked through the net with a sound like torn fabric that I could hear all the way from the other side of the arena.

The whole place erupted, and I watched as two of the uniformed Yellowstone County deputies were pulled from the sidelines at the opposite end of the court to disappear down the tunnel leading toward the loading dock, the storage area, and my wounded friend. "Why did you shoot Henry?"

Jimmy glanced down. "I didn't mean to. I didn't know it was him, I just knew someone was chasing me and thought it might be one of the Brotherhood of the North."

"So, Schiller was the one who got killed last night and stuffed in a barrel?"

"Yes." He looked uncomfortable for a moment. "I'm sorry about locking you in there, I . . . I guess I panicked."

"And you're the one who started the fire?"

He nodded.

"What about Louie?"

He nodded again.

"And Silent A?"

He stood there, watching the game, and for a moment I thought he hadn't heard me, but then he shook his head in a sad way. "You don't get it, do you?" He glanced at me. "That's okay, I didn't understand at first either."

"So, explain it to me."

His attention returned to the game. "It doesn't matter, man. Nothing matters, and it's all coming to an end anyway."

Jaya prepared for the second shot, reproducing the exact performance from before, the ball twirling, but this time she stopped and looked up at the time.

:42

She shot, and once again, it was nothing but net.

The noise of the crowd was deafening. Jimmy waited till the clamor had died down at least a bit before continuing. "Jeanie started getting those notes, but none of us paid any attention, figuring it was just the usual shit—but then she went missing. She went missing, but people started seeing her all over the place. There's this Crow rancher near where the van broke down . . ."

"Lyndon Iron Bull."

"Yeah, him and plenty of others . . . Including me."

The Eagles set up and brought the ball in, moving it down the court but protecting it, determined that if a shot got off, it would be theirs.

:39

"I was at my house after work, having a few beers, and I heard somebody outside singing. I don't know why, but it irritated the shit out of me, so I picked up this .38 and yanked open the door . . . Nobody." He glanced at me. "Pouring rain, and there was nobody there. So, I started to go back in when I saw this girl standing under the streetlight on the corner, the rain just coming down in sheets. She was wearing a hoodie, so I couldn't see her face, but the way she stood, I knew . . . I mean, part of me knew it was her. There was some part of me that wasn't sure, though, you know? So, I yell at her, what are you doing in this neighborhood this time of night, and she sings—"

"Bring me back."

He turned, staring at me. "How'd you know that?"

"Go on."

"So, I yell at her as I start across the street and tell her I don't know what she's talking about, and she starts singing again—"

"I don't belong here."

"Shut up, man." He choked a sob, roughly wiping his eyes. "Have I told you this story?"

"Go on."

He wasn't sure how to continue at this point but stammered, "Yeah, well, I started yelling at her there in the pouring-down rain in the middle of the street, sayin' yeah, you don't belong here in this neighborhood and you need to get the hell out of here. I'm getting closer to her and that part of me knows who she is, and I just stop. It was like my legs were trying to give way, my knees just started letting go, and I was embarrassed that I was carrying the gun, so I stuck it into the waistband of my jeans. I stood there looking at her and started reaching my arms out to her and she said—"

"I want to go home."

He turned to me. "What the fuck."

I still couldn't look at him. "How are Schiller and his bunch involved in all of this?"

"I knew Schiller from inside and from work, and he said he and his boys could provide some protection if it was needed, so I hired them when Jaya started getting those same notes."

Number 7 took the pass just past half-court, dribbling determinedly as Jaya backed away, making sure the opposing player couldn't slip by, but giving her an opening to shoot from distance if she had the nerve.

:28

"I asked a friend of mine who figured out that it was them that had started writing the notes to Jeanie, killed her, and then started again with Jaya—just the same protection shit they'd done up in Deer Lodge."

:22

Jaya's head dropped as she stood there like a bulwark at the side of the key, and you could see the Navajo girl thinking about it. During the entire time I'd seen number 7 play, which had been limited, she hadn't taken any outside shots. Had Jaya sensed it too? Would the girl take a chance on what could be the last shot of the game?

"So, they killed Jeanie that night the van broke down?"

:19

Number 7 hesitated and almost brought the ball up for the shot, but instead drove. Her timing was off because of Jaya, but she seemed determined as she approached the defender, looking as though she was prepared to power right through her.

"Schiller swore it wasn't him, but I knew better, so I killed both of them."

"That doesn't make sense, Jimmy. Why would they kill Jeanie? She's wasn't any use to them dead."

:17

Jaya prepared for the collision, but at the last instant the Navajo player bounced the ball to the center at the baseline. Jaya's hand shot out, but not quickly enough, and it looked like the game was about to be over.

"She found out it was them that was writing the notes." He let out a sob. "She was so smart, she was so smart, man—and brave. Jeanie knew it was them, and she confronted Schiller." He swallowed and continued. "Besides, I had an inside man."

:15

Only one problem—it was the wrong center who grabbed the pass. Rosey Black Wolf stepped from the crowd in the paint, almost from nowhere, and simply caught the ball at her knees. Knowing she couldn't get free and that it was unlikely she would outrun anyone, she did what she did best and reared back in order to chuck the ball down court like a shot-putter.

"This Silent A?"

"Yeah."

"Artie Small Song."

:12

Jaya had the advantage of being the farthest up court and happened to be facing the right direction when the ball soared over her head, and the race was on with the Navajo number 7 right on top of her. The ball bounced once near center court, and Jaya was on it, palming it forward and running with every ounce of force she could muster.

"You're going to have to find that one out on your own, Lawman—if you live long enough."

:08

Jaya was just ahead of her closest pursuer as she angled for the basket, passing the foul line, once again levitating from the polished wooden floor. The Navajo girl reached out as she leapt too, and try as I might, I couldn't see any way that Jaya could get the ball by her.

"What are you going to do, Jimmy?"

:05

If you had asked me what would happen next, I might have given you a hundred scenarios, none of which were what actually took place.

Jaya passed it off.

Knowing that the only other person on the court who could've given the two athletes a run for their money was Misty Two Bears—Jaya dished it off to the right where Two Bears had caught up to them.

"What do I have to do—to end all this shit."

:02

Jaya and the Navajo girl both flew under the backboard. Misty looked at the ball in her hands and allowed her momentum to carry her toward the basket. She dribbled once and then palmed the ball up, where it slid between the rim and the glass backboard with a squeak before rolling on the rim nearly all the way around and then teetering before falling in.

Buzzer.

Game.

The arena erupted into utter chaos as the fans flooded the court, a sea of people that swept in like an avalanche as the Lady Morning Stars jumped up and down, screaming and hugging one another. I looked for Jaya but couldn't see her as a group of players hoisted Misty up onto their shoulders where she hid her face with both hands.

Jimmy Lane stood there beside me as more people streamed around us. We stood there like boulders in a river, inevitable and unmoving.

"What now?"

"We're going to stay here until things start clearing out."

I finally spotted Jaya leaning against the padded support of the basket, her arms wrapped around herself as she smiled up at the lights in the ceiling high above—or maybe it was something else.

"I don't think you're going to have that luxury, Jimmy."

Down below, there were three uniformed deputies working against the tide as they made their way toward us, having to leap-frog the bleachers because the walkways were so full. Jimmy saw them and backed up, stepping over a bench and allowing his hand with the .38 to slip out, aimed at me, the ghost bracelet dangling from his wrist.

I could hear a deputy shouting from behind me and was sure they'd drawn their weapons as I stepped between them and the armed man. "Give it up, Jimmy."

He shook his head as his eyes teared. "What would you have done?"

There was more screaming from behind me as I raised my hands. "Put the gun down."

He glanced around, his eyes becoming more fervent as he backed up another row. "They killed my baby girl; they killed her and then hid her where we can't find her."

"We'll find her."

He continued stumbling back. "Maybe you will, but for me it ends here and now."

"Jimmy, don't make these guys shoot you."

"It doesn't matter, don't you get it—it's all coming to an end." He glanced around in a panic. "That thing is out there, and it takes our people and never lets them go, and it's got my daughter or at least a part of her."

"Jimmy."

His eyes came back to me, and his mouth quivered as he studied me. "Where did you get that scarf?"

I said nothing.

He screamed at me. "Where did you get that scarf?!"

The deputies continued yelling, some of them having moved up beside me as I continued to hold my hands above my shoulders. "I got it from your daughter, Jimmy."

The gun dropped slowly, and he looked gut-punched. "You saw her?"

"I did."

"She's alive?"

"I don't think so, but she's out there, somewhere, and she wants to come home."

"Where?"

"I honestly don't know, Jimmy, but I saw her."

He cried out, "Where?"

I tried to think of what to say to the man but was coming up empty. "I don't know how to describe it, but I saw her in the last hour." I flicked my eyes around us. "She was here."

Slowly, the .38 came back up and the screaming of the officers around me became deafening. "You're going to tell me where my daughter is . . ."

"I wish I knew, Jimmy, but she's out there, and I'm going to need your help to find her and that means you can't force these men to shoot you."

He slowly shook his head as he looked at the revolver. "It's over . . ."

"Jimmy, don't."

"I hope you find her, but I made a deal with the Éveohtsé-heómėse and now I have to pay up. Who knows, if it has my daughter, maybe I'll find her before you."

"Jimmy."

The deputies continued yelling as I stepped up on the next bench seat and held my hand out to him. I was trying to look him directly in the eyes but his darted around looking for some way of changing the course of things. "Jimmy, this isn't what Jeanie would've wanted."

"Dad!"

From the corner of my eye, I could see Jaya being held back by one of the deputies.

"Dad, what are you doing?"

"I love you, baby—don't you ever think I didn't." Jimmy's hand shook as he took aim at my chest, and I could almost hear the deputies squeezing their collective triggers.

The impact pushed him forward as he fell, flopping onto the aluminum bench in front of me, the .38 skittering down the walk-way and then falling through the bleachers, disappearing with a clatter.

Theresa One Moon stood over her ex-husband, still holding the folding chair. She pushed her hair back out of her face and then dropped her weapon of choice to the side before raising her hands. "I didn't figure you'd mind if I used that chair one last time."

EPILOGUE

"Play me."

Back at the outdoor court at Lame Deer high school on a darkening Monday afternoon, the shadows stretched as the phenom planted another turnaround jumper from thirty feet out. Catching the ball, I bounced it back to her, then blew into my hands in an attempt to warm them. "I told you, not my game."

She dribbled toward the baseline and shot an extended one-hander that whispered through the same ragged red, white, and blue net. I glanced around at the snow-covered parking lot and then at the wet court that she'd shoveled off herself.

"Hey, what do you say we go inside where it's warm?"

"I like it out here." She glanced around, smiling. "This is my home court—not the fancy one inside."

I caught the ball and tossed it back to her. "You guys pretty much made mincemeat out of those other two teams in the tournament."

She thought about it. "Yeah, Little Wound Lakota were rough and the Seminole Tribal Club team were good, but I think if the White Mountain Apache had made it farther, it would've been more trouble but, yeah, the Navajos were the toughest."

"So, who are the front-runners in the Jaya Long Moon lottery?"

She smiled at the ground, her breath creating a halo around her anointed head. "Who told you my new name?"

"Your aunt."

"She knows everything." She made the statement without malice. "I figured I'd hyphenate the two, including my ancestors, but starting my own tradition."

"Long Moon, I like it."

She nodded, then took aim from the top of the key and watched as it dribbled in from the back of the rim. "Stanford and Duke, right now." Catching the ball, I threw it back as she smiled. "What do you think I should do?"

"Study." I smiled back at her. "Hard."

"Mom hasn't had a drink since Friday."

"That's something." I smiled. "But has she picked up any chairs?"

She laughed. "My grandfather is letting her stay in the room out in his shop, and she's been there every night." The phenom dribbled out on the perimeter, then stopped and held the ball. "Dad going back to prison?"

"I'm afraid so."

She held the ball, studying the pebbled surface. "Life?"

"A couple of them, I'd imagine."

She took a deep breath and then let it out slowly. "He killed Schiller and Louie?"

"Not much question about it."

"He was trying to protect me."

"I guess so."

She looked up. "And Jeanie?"

I swallowed. "Unfortunately, no one is here to answer for that. Your father said it was Schiller who killed her and buried her in the creek bed near the Iron Bull place."

She dribbled the ball once and then walked toward me. "You don't seem so sure." She sidled up and cupped the ball at her hips with both hands, the child of her not-too-distant future. "Where's your dog?"

"Henry's recuperating at his house in front of the fireplace and Dog-sitting for me."

"And that assistant coach?"

"Vic? She headed home. Somebody's got to run the county."

"You're all alone?"

"I guess."

"Come on over to Big Betty's, we're having a celebratory dinner."

"I can't . . . I don't think I can take both Big Betty and your mother in one visit again."

"Then what are you going to do?"

"What do you mean?"

She extended an index finger and poked me with each word. "What. Are. You. Going. To. Do?" She walked toward the chain-link fence, threading the fingers of her free hand through it, and looked north. "Friday night, the night of the first game—I saw her too, you know."

I said nothing.

She turned and walked back toward me, reaching up and running her fingers through the fringe at the ends of the red scarf I still wore. "There's no way she would've ever missed that no matter where she is or who or what has her." She looked up at me, the magnetite eyes impenetrable.

Pulling the scarf off, I wrapped it around her neck. "You're too smart for your own good."

"That's what they keep telling me." She sighed, running her fingers over the material. "I felt her there before I saw her. I know it sounds crazy, but then I looked up, and there she was."

I said nothing.

She stepped away. "This case is kind of getting out of your jurisdiction, isn't it?"

"Maybe."

"Then why?"

I stuffed my hands into my jacket pockets and looked at the shallow puddle at my feet and my own reflection. "Because some part of her is still out there, somewhere."

She turned and looked at me, and I could see the extraordinary woman she would become. She remained still for a moment and then came over, resting the ball between her feet, running her hands over the material of the scarf again before taking it off. She reached up to drape it around my neck. She pulled it tight like a bulletproof vest, tucking it under the lapels of my jacket and then patting it for safekeeping. "Something tells me you're going to be needing this more than I am."

Jaya picked up the ball, turned, and dribbled in a lackadaisical manner as she sauntered toward the rusted '64 Wildcat with the 2REZ4U license plates. She tossed the ball into the passenger seat as a copilot and then turned to look at me. "I think I owe you an apology."

"For what?"

She climbed in, slamming the door after her, and looked at me through the open window, her arm hanging out, the ghost bracelet on her wrist. "For thinking you were just another old white guy."

I laughed. "I am just another old white guy."

"No, you're a lot more than that." She stared at me with the side-eye of that lodestar pupil and then hit the starter on the Buick.

And then hit it again.

And again.

She shook her head and then slumped in the seat. "So much for my dramatic exit."

I walked over. "Pop the hood."

She did as I asked, and I lifted it and stared at the engine, the way old white guys do. Amazingly enough, I saw where the choke cable had jammed the carburetor linkage. I reached in, flipped it loose, and untangled them.

"Try it now." She did, and the Wildcat caught, sputtered, hissed, backfired, and then settled into an uneven quasi-purr. I closed the hood and walked around to the driver's side door. "Are you sure this heap isn't related to Rezdawg?"

She ignored my question. "I graduate in May, and I'd like you to be there."

I dropped my head, unable to look her in the eye. "I'll see what I can do."

"I'm giving you another reason to come back."

"Am I going somewhere?"

She stared at me again for a very long time, the way women do when they know you're telling an untruth. "This is the part where my war pony and I ride off into the sunset."

And they did.

Watching the rattletrap motor down to the school's exit, I was overwhelmed by a sense of loneliness and a palpable feeling that I would never see her again. Taking a deep breath, I pulled the scarf a little closer around my neck and thought nothing but good thoughts for the phenom, that she would light up the sky, just like the piercing stars that were just beginning to puncture the winter night.

Standing there in the empty parking lot, I looked back at the basket, the rim, and the horse tail net casually moving with the breeze, and I could feel the frozen tendrils of the high-plains winter reaching in and squeezing at the blood attempting to circulate in my veins.

At least that's what I hoped it was.

Driving west, I watched as the sun disappeared over the Beartooth Range. I took the Pryor Creek exit, or the Cottonwood Creek one, or maybe it was Indian Creek—so that I could park near the broken-down van that had given up one of its occupants that cold night.

I parked and got out, walking toward whatever damn creek it was, and looked up at the makeshift poster still stapled to the power pole. The snow was falling steadily, very much like the night Jeanie One Moon had gone missing, almost as if the fates were toying with me, laughing in my face. I reached up and tore the now brittle plastic from the tree, having been fastened there for over a year, and studied the photo of the missing girl with half her face faded away, as if she were lying in a snowdrift somewhere, waiting to be discovered.

Carefully folding the notice, I slipped it into the inside pocket of my jacket just as a pair of headlights appeared in the distance from the south, roiling the snow in their wake. I watched, fully expecting it to continue on I-90 up to Billings, but instead it slowed, turned in, and pulled up behind my truck. The big, full-ton turbo diesel dually engine rattled to a stop and the lights shut off. A large man extricated himself from the driver's seat and lumbered toward me.

"How did you know I would be here?"

Lyndon Iron Bull stomped through the couple of inches of snow and pulled up the collar on his blanket-lined coat, his glasses steaming with his breath. "This is my land; the land of my people, and I felt a presence within it."

"Really?"

He grunted. "Yeah—that, and I saw your headlights when you pulled up." He gestured with an old Stanley thermos, not so much different than my own, along with a mug—the pink one with the "BOSS-LADY" spiraling cursive. "And before you ask the next question, who else would be out here in this kind of weather?" He gestured to where a number of work lights and equipment were set up by the creek. "Except those yahoos from the Division of Criminal Investigation."

"They exhumed Jeanie's body?"

"And about half of the creek bed." He stood there for a long while watching the work lights to the south before loosening the chrome cap on the thermos. Then he undid the stopper and poured me a cup without being beckoned. "Me and Ethel, we went to all three games."

I took the pink mug. "How is the Boss?"

"She's good. Asleep, so that she can get up in two hours and go to the bathroom."

"How long have you been married?"

"Fifty-two years." He filled the chrome cap. "You?"

"Widower."

He grunted. "I figured."

"How?"

"You're wounded; bleeding all over the place, and you can't even tell." He raised the cup. "To the women."

We touched containers and took a sip.

I stared at his big, weathered face and decided to break a promise I'd made to myself. "I saw her."

"I figured you eventually would, if you kept looking for her." He took a few steps back and then leaned on the grille guard of my truck. "That where you got the scarf?"

"I think so."

"You still looking for her?"

"Yep." I walked over, taking a sip of my own coffee, figuring I better tank up since I had some driving to do. Pulling the postcard from my pocket, I handed it to him, along with the Maglite so he could see what I'd given him.

He clicked on the flashlight and stared at the old, sepia-toned postcard with scalloped borders; the photograph on the one side, weathered but still readable, picturing the archway over a white picket fence—FORT PRATT and INDUSTRIAL INDIAN BOARDING SCHOOL. Thirty young boys of different ages in the front yard of the large, two-story building that was in the background, shrouded by trees, the Native boys in uniforms and matching caps as they all stood at the gate at attention. The one smaller boy was front and center, looking back in perfect focus, the others slightly blurred, as if at the instant of tintype capture, they had all moved.

He flipped it over, looking at the number handwritten on the back. "Thirty-one, mean anything to you?"

"No, you?"

"No." He turned it in his hand, studying the image. "Who gave you this?"

"Jimmy Lane."

"The one going to prison."

"Yep."

"Where did he get it?"

"He didn't say."

He handed it back to me. "Still got that strange little book from the bookstore?"

I slipped the booklet from the inside pocket of my jacket and attempted to hand it to him. "Would you like it?"

"No, I would not." He sipped his coffee and then turned his

head south, back toward his ranch, the pasture, the mist, and the creek. "Good God, man . . . Don't do it."

"I have to."

"No, you don't." He turned back and looked at me. "I don't know what it is that you'll find up there, and more important, I'm not so sure what'll find you—but whatever it is, it's been waiting a long time."

I placed the postcard back into the booklet and then slipped it into my jacket pocket along with the weathered reward poster. "Then it would be impolite for me to keep this . . . Éveohtsé-heómėse waiting."

He sighed but said nothing.

"I guess I've got a good seven hours of driving ahead of me." I pulled my keys from my pocket. "If I get going, I should be there sometime around daybreak." I handed him his wife's mug and then watched as he stared at me for a moment more before trudging back toward his truck.

He lowered the passenger window with an electric *whir* and continued to study me as I pulled open my own door. "Just one question before you go, Sheriff?"

"Sure."

"How do you know it was really her?"

He stared at me for a few minutes more as if trying to memorize me for posterity, and then pulled out, the headlights leading the way through the falling snow toward a cozy home, a warm bed, a loving wife, and a haunted pasture.